THRO
VENGEANCE

RINA KENT

It doesn't matter if you start late.
It matters that you start.

AUTHOR NOTE

Hello reader friend,

If you haven't read my books before, you might not know this, but I write darker stories that can be upsetting and disturbing. My books and main characters aren't for the faint of heart.

Throne of Vengeance is the second book of a duet and is not standalone.

Throne Duet:
#1 *Throne of Power*
#2 *Throne of Vengeance*

Don't forget to Sign up to Rina Kent's Newsletter for news about future releases and an exclusive gift.

When vengeance strikes...

You don't know me, but I know you.

I'm the shadow that creeps behind you without notice.

The moment you see me, you're dead.

An assassin. A killer. A nobody.

Until I became somebody.

I'll make everyone who reduced me to a shadow pay.

To do that, I'm willing to risk everything.

Everything except for my reluctant wife.

Rai Sokolov can show me her worst, but this will only end
when death does us part.

The road to the throne is paved with loss, betrayal, and blood
baths.

To win, we go all in.

Our lives included.

PLAYLIST

Let Down—Palisades
Killing Me—The New Low
Despicable—grandson
I Don't Care—Apocalyptica & Adam Gontier
The Beginning of the End—Klergy & Valerie Broussard
Why You Gotta Kick Me When I'm Down—Bring Me The
Horizon
Sweet Disaster—DREAMERS
Bad for Me—FNKHOUSER
The War We Made—Red
Lucid Dreams—Flight Paths & Divisions
Golden Dandelions—Barns Courtney
Rusted From the Rain—Billy Talent
For My Eyes Only—New City
I'm Trouble—WAR*HALL
Eyes That Kill—CooBee Coo
Cold Blood—Dave Not Dave
Secrets—OneRepublic

You can find the complete playlist on Spotify.

ONE

Kyle

Age five

TENDER HANDS STROKE MY SHOULDER, AND THE scent of milk and honey infiltrates my nostrils.

It's nice. Like summer and playing by the pool.

My eyes slowly open, and for a moment, I think I'm seeing an angel with its white halo and soft touch.

It's not any angel, though. It's *my* angel, specially made for me so the other kids can't see her.

My mam.

My lips pull up in a smile, but for the first time since she became my angel, she doesn't return it. Her brows are drawn over darkened eyes and her pale lips are thinned in a line.

"We need to go, sweetheart."

"But it's night. Ye said bad kids go out at night, Ma."

"Aye, but not this time." She strokes my long hair behind my ear. "Follow me."

I don't. I just stare at her. Her clothes are wrong 'cause she's not wearing one of her beautiful floral dresses. This time, she's in black trousers and a jacket. It doesn't look good, even though she is the prettiest ever. She has soft skin like a baby and cotton candy. Her hair is like the sun on a hot summer's day. Sometimes, I think my mammy came from the sun just to be with me.

No one can escape the burning sun, aye? But Mammy did just so she could be with me every day.

It's not fun here 'cause I was born in a palace. Naw, it's not like the palaces from the wee stories Mammy tells me every night. It's a real one, pure huge one with many men dressed in black and holding heavy metal things.

They keep watching me and Ma 'cause Da wants it. He a big man, my daddy. He a leader, too, and no one raises their voice when he's there.

Mammy doesn't play with me either when he's around. The men in black say I have a duty and can't play 'cause playing is for losers. I mean, what is duty? It's not food, 'cause our chef doesn't cook it for us. Is it like the place we went to in Ireland? People were so mean to Mammy there. I don't like them.

I only like Mammy 'cause she plays with me in secret and has even built a wee tent where she can teach me and tell me stories about wizards and magical ogres. I love 'em, ogres—they're massive and no one can beat 'em.

When I grow up, I'm gonna be an ogre to protect my mammy from them daft men in black suits.

"Come on, Kyle. Be a good boy." Her voice and lips shake. The veins are visible under her skin even in the small light from my side table's lamp. When I asked her if she has transparent skin, she laughed.

Mammy has the best laugh ever, like them wee sounds from Daddy's music CDs. It's Mammy's laugh that I think of when he's yelling at me because I'm being a brat. He doesn't like that I don't stay with the teachers he brings me. They're daft and scowl like the guards.

Mammy is smarter, anyway. I like spending time with her and eating all the delicious food she makes me—especially tarts and pancakes.

"Where are we going?"

"Ye don't need to know." She shoves some of my clothes in a bag that she brought with her. "Hop on."

"Mammy…?" I ask, my voice spooked like the little elves from last night's book. She sounds like 'em men in black suits.

She snatches my coat from behind my room's door and makes me wear it, then grabs and holds me.

It's the first time she's not soft and welcoming. It's like she's becoming just like Daddy.

"M-Mammy…I'm scared."

"Don't be, sweetheart. It's going to be okay."

"Really?"

"Really. We're just going for a wee ride, won't ye like it?"

"But I'm sleepy."

"You can sleep in the car."

"Are we gonna come back in the morning?"

"No."

"Why not?"

"Sweetheart, would ye like it if we lived far away from here and all those bad men in black suits?"

"Yup!"

"Mammy is gonna make it happen. We'll live far away in a new home."

My eyes nearly pop out. "A new home?"

"Aye. Wouldn't ye like that?"

"But what about Daddy?"

Her gaze trails to the door, then back to me. "Don't worry about him. It's going to be ye and me."

"Because ye're a wizard and I'm an ogre?"

"Exactly." She ruffles my hair. "Now, I need ye to be silent, sweetheart."

"Why?"

"Because we don't want them to stop us."

"Are the men in black gonna tell Daddy and he's gonna get mad and punish us?"

"Aye. You're such a smart boy, Kyle. I knew my baby boy would be this bright."

"Don't worry, Mammy. I'll protect ye and punch anyone who comes near ye. Look, I'm gonna have ogre hands." I raise my fists in the air and she laughs, the sound happy.

After she places my feet in warm shoes, Mammy puts the backpack on and holds me, telling me to wrap my legs around her waist.

"Don't ever let me go, Kyle. Okay?"

"Okay."

She steps out of my room, placing a hand on my head. Our house is proper massive. It's on a hill and has so much water surrounding it that the waves hit the rocks all the time.

I told Daddy it looks like a fight, but he said it's a war and if I want to win it, I need to follow his steps.

We walk for a long time through hallways I've never been down before, 'cause I'm still a kid and Daddy doesn't like it when I go to his office.

Mammy only has the backpack on her back. I think we're not gonna stay long in the new home 'cause Daddy will be mad and then Mammy will be sad.

I rest my head on her shoulder and breathe in the smell of milk and honey. It's my favorite scent ever 'cause it means everything will be okay. Then I pat her back 'cause she's shaking. I wanna ask her if she's cold, but she said to be silent.

So I pull back and smile at her. Her face is pale and her eyes have red lines in 'em, but she smiles back like the angels from the painting in Daddy's office.

When I asked her what angels do, Mammy said they're pure, bring light, and help children like me grow up. That's why Mammy was made for me. She's the angel who will help me grow up, and then I'm gonna be the ogre who protects her 'cause ogres are stronger than angels, even if they smell sometimes.

Mammy stops near a door, peeks outside, then holds me tighter as she walks slowly, her back to the wall until we reach our garden. It's massive as well with long fences and wires. They appear like the devil's horns from the creepy show Uncle was watching while I spied from afar.

She stops beside a wire and pulls out her phone from her trousers, then puts it to her ear. Her foot taps rapidly on the ground as she listens through the phone.

Tap. Tap. Tap.

Her hold around me tightens the more she focuses on the phone, then she puts her thumb in her mouth, chewing on her nails. Daddy doesn't like it when she does that.

"Pick up…pick up…" she murmurs. "Bleeding hell."

"Mammy, isn't that a bad word?"

"Shh, Kyle."

"But ye said it was bad."

"I'm sorry, baby boy, I shouldn't have said that." She smiles. "Mammy is just a little excited. Forgive me, okay?"

"Okay. I won't repeat it in front of Daddy."

"Good boy."

"What are we doing in the garden, Mammy?"

"I'm waiting for a friend to come to pick us up."

"You have a friend?"

"Aye." Something weird passes in her eyes. "He's an old friend. I think ye'll like him."

"Why haven't I seen him before?"

"Because I knew him before ye were born, baby boy."

"Am I going to meet him now?"

"Hopefully."

"Is he going to play wizards and ogres with us?"

"We'll try to invite him."

A soft sound comes from behind us. It's as quiet as a bird landing on a dead leaf, but Mammy freezes and places a finger on my mouth.

I stay silent. I don't mind staying here, but if Mammy is leaving, I want to go with her too.

"All clear," a man says in a rough, harsh way. I think it's Luke, Daddy's best man in black. He came all the way from Ireland.

Daddy is the big boss man from Ireland, too. I had fun when we went there months ago, but I don't think Mammy did.

She told me she's from Northern Ireland and Daddy is from Dublin. Apparently, Northern Ireland and Ireland are different countries, but they speak similarly. Not too similar, though, because Daddy hates it when I speak like Mammy. But I like how Mammy talks; it's how angels speak. Daddy knows nothing.

Luke and his voice disappear, but she continues holding my mouth for a long time before she releases a breath.

She then puts the phone to her ear again. "Come on…come on." Her eyes light up even in the dark. "Oh, thank God. Where are you? Yes, I'm at the back gate. I already disconnected the cameras, and it won't be long before someone finds out. I have mere minutes. Kyle is with me."

She listens for a little, then she trembles like a child in the cold. I stroke her cheek with my tiny fingers to make her feel warmer like she does to me.

Mammy is too focused on the phone as she whispers, "He *knows*. It won't be long before he kills us."

Her lips pale as she listens a wee more. I hate the one she's speaking to because he's making Mammy unhappy. I'm gonna punch him.

"What do you mean you're attacking? That's not what you

promised. You said ye'll help me get out of here. I need to leave. Ireland and the States aren't safe for us anymore, and..."

She trails off when loud bangs erupt in the house.

Pop. Pop. Pop.

I flinch in her arms and Mammy holds me close, tears streaming down her cheeks as she speaks to the bad man on the phone. "I trusted ye, a Russian, over my own countrymen—how can ye do this to me?"

She doesn't wait for a response as she shoves the phone in her pocket and runs. The pops are getting closer, like in the stories she told me while doing the sound effects.

Even though she's trembling, she doesn't stop until she reaches a small wall with no wires on top. She grabs my hands and winds them around her neck. "Hold on tight and don't let go, Kyle."

"Okay."

She pushes my hair out of my face and smiles, but it's filled with tears. "Ye're such a good boy, sweetheart. Ye shouldn't have been born into this world. I shouldn't have brought ye into this chaos. Mammy is so sorry, but I'll make it better."

Mammy starts to climb the wall while I'm wrapped around her.

"Where do ye think ye're going, Amy?"

Mammy gasps.

My head slowly follows the voice to stare at Daddy. His dark eyes shine in the night and blood trails down his knuckles 'cause he likes to punch people.

He looks like one of the angry men in that painting with angels.

Mammy hops down and holds me hard as she faces him. "Just let us go, Niall."

"Let ya go where?"

I try to look at him, but she wraps a hand around my head to stop me, pushing my nose and mouth against her shoulder.

"Ye already know."

"Already know what?"

"I just want to leave. We're not safe!"

"Not safe? I gave ye everything. *Everything*. Ye were a no-body and I made something out of ye, and this is how ye repay me? Guess no one can change a whore, can they?"

"Don't say those words in front of Kyle," she whispers. "At least respect me in front of him."

"Did ye respect me? Did ye fucking think of me?" he roars. "Take him, Luke."

"Nooo," Mammy shrieks as Luke snatches me from her.

I try to hold on to her with all my might, but Luke wrenches me with steel-like arms. Her hits and shrieks fall on deaf ears. I try to bite him, but he doesn't even wince in pain.

"Mammy!" Tears fall down my cheeks and I wipe them with the back of my hand 'cause Daddy doesn't like it when I cry.

She stares at me for a second, not bothering to wipe her face, then turns to Daddy. "Don't hurt him. *Please*."

"Ye are the one who hurt him when ye betrayed me, Amy. Once wasn't enough, so ye stabbed me in the back two times. Now, ye will have to pay." He stares at his other man in black, Patrick. "Take her away."

"Please...please, Niall. I promise I'll be good. I p-promise."

"Ye made that same promise the other time as well, but did ye keep it? Did ye honor me like I honored ye? I should've listened when they said a whore will always be a whore." He motions at Patrick with his head. "Lock her up."

The man in black grabs her by the arm so hard that she winces.

My lips tremble and I twist against Luke's hold. "Mammy! Mammy, don't leave! Ye said ye'll always be with me!"

"Shut it, Kyle," Dad scolds.

Usually, I would listen, but I can't tonight. Tonight, I want Mammy to hold me and put me back to sleep, even if it's not in our new home. We can just stay with Daddy so he doesn't get mad.

"Sweetheart." She smiles at me through the tears. "It's going to be okay."

"Really?"

"Really." She faces Daddy again. "I will tell ye."

"Ye will tell me what?"

"All I know about the Russians' attack. Also, ye should know there's a traitor by yer side."

He narrows his eyes. "Why should I believe ye?"

"Because I wouldn't have wanted to leave if he weren't a threat."

"Ye will truly tell me everything?"

"Aye, but ye have to let me be with Kyle."

"Ye will never escape again?" He doesn't seem mad anymore, just...sad. But why? Daddy is never sad.

Mammy shakes her head once. "I won't."

"How do I know ye're not bluffing?"

"I would never put Kyle in danger. Ye know that."

"Right. Go on."

She opens her mouth to speak, but it remains suspended with no sound coming out as a loud *pop* echoes in the air.

I hold my breath and my tears, not sure what just happened. A liquid pours out from the center of her chest, soaking the black jacket as she staggers and falls in Patrick's arms.

"M-Mammy...?" My voice is small, hesitant. She's not moving.

"Amy!" Daddy bellows, falling to his knees in front of her. "Get the fucker who did this!"

Patrick drops Mammy and runs in the opposite direction, but I don't focus on him. The only thing I can see is Mammy on the ground, not able to move. Why can't she? Is it because of the patch of liquid on her chest, which Daddy is squeezing?

"Mammy..." I call her again 'cause she always replies.

She doesn't now.

Her head is lolling to the side and she's coughing blood. That can't be good. Mammy said blood gets out of people when they're hurt.

"Amy...fuck..." Daddy holds her cheek tighter. "Stay with me...I'll forgive anything if ye just...*stay*."

"K-Kyle..." she mumbles.

Daddy motions at Luke, and he puts me on my feet beside her. Her eyes are half-closed as if she wants to go to sleep, but she smiles up at me. "S-so sorry, sweetheart. Mammy is *so sorry*."

"Why?"

"B-because I couldn't protect ye."

"I will." Daddy places an arm around my shoulder. "So don't go. Kyle is the reason ye went through all of this, so it's useless if ye die now."

"Ye're a good man, Niall. Ye truly are, but ye're influenced by bad apples who clouded yer reason." She places her hand on top of his. "I've never regretted making the decision to be with ye. Ye kept us safe as ye promised and...I-I'll forever be grateful."

"Amy...ye're not allowed to leave."

"I-if ye ever loved me, t-take care of Kyle...please..."

"Mammy..." I place my small hand on her mouth, wiping away the blood. "Are ye hurt?"

"I-I think so, sweetheart."

"I'm gonna remove the blood so ye're not." I wipe at it with the sleeve of my coat, but it keeps coming out over and over again, streaming down her chin.

"Th-that's my good boy." She smiles a little. "Ye were born for great things, sweetheart. Make Mammy proud, okay?"

Daddy's lips thin. "Stop talking like that, Amy."

"Will ye take care of him, Niall?"

"Ye'll wake up and do it yourself."

"Promise ye'll raise him properly. P-promise."

"I will."

Her lips remain frozen in a smile as a tear slides down her cheek. "Thank ye…"

She blinks once, then stops altogether, her eyes open wide but not looking at me.

"Mammy!" I scream. "Mammy!"

"Fuck," Daddy murmurs under his breath, still grabbing her by the chest. "Fucking fuck!"

"Why isn't Mammy moving?" I shriek. "Help her! She's hurt."

He squeezes my shoulder, and it's like he's about to crush my bones. "I'm sorry, lad. So sorry."

"I don't want ye sorry. I want Mammy to move."

"Take him to his room, Luke."

"Not so fast." The familiar voice comes from behind us.

Daddy turns around, but it's already too late. A *pop* echoes in the air and a patch of red explodes on Daddy's white shirt. His hand falls from my shoulder as he staggers and his face hits the grass.

"D-Daddy…?"

I stare at how he's sprawled on top of Mammy, but they're not moving. It's like they're asleep, but they shouldn't be asleep with their eyes open and blood all over them, right?

The blood has to be gone.

All of it.

I turn around to tell Luke to help them, but someone hits me across the face. My body swings back and I fall on the ground with a thud.

My vision moves between my parents, unable to take my eyes off them. If I sleep, they'll be there in the morning, right?

"What should we do with the lad, boss? Kill him?" one of the men in black asks.

"Aye, of course. He's a liability that we need to take care of," another replies.

"No." The one who shot Daddy interrupts them, his eyes glinting in the dark night. "I have better plans for him."

TWO

Kyle

Present

Iclose my eyes for the briefest of seconds to chase away the assault of memories.

That night, my fate was decided.

I wasn't only deprived of my parents, I also lost the only two people who protected me from the world. The disaster was brutal and happened without a warning.

But that was the mere beginning of my life, the starting point of how I turned into this shadow.

It's not the end.

Life might be a bitch, but I didn't just die. I was given a second chance in the form of becoming a shadow, a chance to cut their throats one by each one.

I'm close.

After nearly thirty years, I'm so fucking close to making my mother proud. I've become worse than an ogre. I'm a monster with nothing to lose, and those who were behind her death will pay in the same blood that left her body and Dad's.

It's not only my own, the Irish, but it's also the Russians. The one Mum trusted and gave information in exchange for getting us out—he betrayed her and was one of the main reasons behind her death.

It's as unforgivable as the Irish fucker who killed my father in cold blood and seized his power. He tossed me aside as if I were an insect so I didn't get in the way of his grand plans.

He's now anxious about what will happen to him, but that's only the beginning of it.

The Irish and the Russians will clash and eventually destroy one another. I'll stand there and watch every second of it.

So yes, it was never about the power, the brotherhood, or whoever gets to reign. I don't give two fucks about that or what everyone keeps plotting behind everyone else's back.

This is about vengeance. *Justice.*

Life for life and blood for blood is the only philosophy I believe in. I might have stayed alive, but a huge part of me was shot dead with my parents that night, my childhood and my whole fucking life.

After I finish my call with Flame, I put on my jacket and stand in front of the mirror. Usually, Rai would slip in front of me and fix my jacket or the collar of my shirt, because nothing is perfect enough for her.

Despite the composed image she shows the world, Rai is meticulous and doesn't like to be caught off guard.

She'll probably fight me tooth and nail once everything comes to light, but I'm ready for that. I've been ready since the beginning.

I take extra care to make myself presentable because today will be one of the last meetings I'll have with the Russians before I leave them.

But I won't leave *her*. My wife.

It doesn't matter that this marriage started in the most unconventional way possible. It's still true and she agreed to it, sealing it with her 'I do.' Those words mean a lot more than she'll ever know.

It also doesn't matter that I plan to go back to my old ways—the days of killing and roaming around like a lone wolf. The only difference this time is that Rai will be by my side.

I have no doubt she'll resist me every step of the way. As much as I hate the brotherhood and plan to destroy it until no one is left, Rai considers it home.

She had the chance to switch back with her twin or disappear, but she didn't. She chose the rotten place where half disrespect her and the other half are plotting to ruin her.

The loyalty in that woman is no joke, and getting her to abandon Nikolai Sokolov's legacy won't be easy, but I'll find a way.

After deeming myself presentable, I head to the exit. As soon as I open the door, a potent premonition hits me in the face.

Something doesn't feel right. I don't know what it is or why it's coming now, of all times, but I know it's there.

It's impossible to ignore my instinct when it's kept me alive all this time. The moment killers start brushing over their instinct, they die. It's as simple as that.

Did the Russians perhaps figure something out?

They can't possibly suspect me after I used my body to save Sergei. That gesture, although not intentional and only the result of needing to protect Rai, means something in their loyalty ledger.

My legs come to a slow halt at the top of the stairs. Initially, I don't believe what I'm seeing, even though it's right in front of me.

This feeling is like being trapped in one of those surreal

nightmares, and the only way out is another nightmare. Perhaps the flashback I had earlier about the darkest night of my life is coming back to haunt me and haul me to another black hole filled with blood.

I blink once, twice, but the scene in front of me doesn't disappear.

Why the fuck am I not waking up?

I close my eyes for a second, then open them, and the view hits me as if it's the first time. As if I'm that five-year-old boy who could only stop and stare as his life was stripped away from him.

Rai lies at the bottom of the stairs, her head lolled to the side and her limbs sprawled at unnatural angles as if they're broken, but that's not what robs me of breath. It's the fact that she's not moving.

"Rai…" I whisper, but that does nothing. "Rai!"

I rush down the stairs and nearly fall from the force of my movements. I kneel by her motionless body and slowly place a hand on her shoulder.

Her chest is rising and falling, but barely.

Bloody fucking hell.

She must've fallen down the stairs, but how come I didn't hear it? That doesn't matter now—she does.

I carry her in my arms, trying my hardest not to move her too much in case she's badly injured.

Her face is pale, lips parted, and there's blood on her palms as if she scratched herself.

"What happened?" Ruslan runs toward me, followed by Katia, their attention on Rai in my arms.

"Get the car," I bark. It would be better to wait for an ambulance, but we don't have time for that.

"Yes, sir." He storms out of the house. Katia and I follow and she opens the door for me.

"What happened?" she asks.

"I should be the one to ask you that. Why weren't you with her?"

"She sent me on an errand, and Ruslan was getting the car ready."

Fuck.

I get in the back seat, and Katia helps in positioning Rai's head on my lap before she slides into the front seat.

"Get us to the hospital," I tell Ruslan. "*Now.*"

His nod in the rear-view mirror is my only response as the car leaves the house with a loud screech of tires.

I run my forefinger under Rai's nose. She's breathing, slowly, but it's there. However, she's not showing any signs of consciousness.

"God damn it, Rai."

I try to keep her steady as Ruslan flies through the traffic, cutting in front of cars as if he's on a chase.

Katia keeps staring back at us as if to make sure Rai is still alive. I'm the same. I check her pulse every chance possible.

In that moment, before I feel her breath, my heart hammers so loud like it hasn't worked for a long time and is now resurrecting back to life.

It's a painful sensation. To have your heart rise from the ashes, but the person behind that change not be present to witness it.

"Come on, Rai. We didn't even start yet and now you're bailing out? You're not a coward, are you?"

I stroke the ruffled hairs away from her face. She always ties it up outside of our bedroom, but now, the clip is loose, probably because of the fall.

I hold her hand in mine, and her pulse keeps weakening by the second. This is bad.

"Faster, Ruslan."

"Yes, sir." He hits the gas, and I hold Rai tight so she doesn't fall.

My forehead meets hers and I close my eyes, inhaling her in. Her scent is a mixture of roses, citrus, and something exotic just like her. Her scent used to give me calm, but it's now filling me with terrifying dread.

Tentacles of fear tighten around my throat, stealing my breath and sanity. The thought that I won't be able to smell her again makes my entire body fucking cold.

The car comes to a screeching halt in front of the emergency room and Katia rushes out to open the door. I carry Rai in my arms and barge inside.

"She fell down the stairs," I tell the nurses who rush to us. "I don't care what you have to do. Give her back to me."

One of the nurses stares at me, then at Ruslan's bulky frame and Katia's unwelcoming expression. She must realize what type of people we are because she gives a curt nod.

I begrudgingly put her on the rolling bed and let them wheel her into one of the exam rooms to which we're not allowed entrance. I could storm in there, but that would distract them from Rai, and I need all their attention on her.

I remain in the waiting area with Ruslan and Katia. It's white and smells of antiseptic and death. Unlike what people think, death isn't rotten; it can be as clean as a hospital smell.

Over time, Katia and Ruslan take seats on the bland green chairs. I don't. The adrenaline wave that's been gripping me since the moment I saw Rai lying at the bottom of the stairs still beats under my skin.

It's different from the residual burn in my chest from the gunshot wound.

The wait takes forever. It's probably half an hour but feels like fucking years. I travel the length of the area back and forth like a trapped bloody animal.

The fact that I can't do anything messes with my fucking brain. It's so similar to that time when I watched my parents die and waited for them to move to no avail.

No. The verdict won't be the same this time.

"How did she fall?" I catch Ruslan whispering to Katia.

"How would I know?" she murmurs back. "I was out, remember?"

"It doesn't make sense for the miss to fall down the stairs. It's just not her."

"I know. Unless…"

He faces her fully. "What?"

"Do you think…do you think someone pushed her?"

"What the fuck is that supposed to mean?" I snap, glaring at them.

They stare at me right back. Ruslan and Katia have never hidden the fact that they don't like me, probably because of the stories Rai fed them about me or because they think I'm controlling her a bit too much. Or maybe it's because I've been occupying most of her time lately, and she can't sit down and play with them anymore, or whatever the fuck it is they do when they're together.

But they're forced to respect me due to the brotherhood hierarchy, so they don't glare or ignore me.

Ruslan remains silent. He's always been blank since we were both Rai's guards nine years ago.

"It's just that I find it odd for Miss to fall down the stairs," Katia says matter-of-factly.

"Why would that give you the idea that she was pushed?" I stop my long walk and face her.

"Because it feels like it."

"*It feels like it?*"

"It's an instinct."

An instinct. *Fuck.* It's the same instinct I had when I came out of the room earlier.

If this was indeed caused by someone, I'll find out, and when I do, they should start counting their fucking days.

The door to the exam room slides open and I rush to the

doctor, meeting him in front of it. He removes his mask, revealing greasy skin and droplets of sweat on his thin upper lip.

"How is she?" I ask.

"She sprained her neck and bumped her head, and although it was mild, it's probably the cause of her fainting."

"And? Is she fine?"

"Well, yes, we believe so."

"What the fuck do you mean by *we believe so?*"

"You're her husband, right?"

"Yes."

"It would be better for you to come in and see for yourself, but please don't distress her."

"She's awake?"

"Yes. She's just opened her eyes."

The sense of relief hits me like an overwhelming wave, and I take a moment to soak it into my burning lungs.

I push past the doctor and jog inside, uncaring about the strain I'm causing to my wound.

Rai is lying on the bed. The color has somewhat returned to her cheeks, but she's still pale. Her eyes appear lifeless and without light as she stares at the ceiling.

"Rai! Are you okay?" I ignore the chair beside her bed and sit on the mattress. I hold her pale as fuck frail hand and pretend we're not in a place that reeks of death.

I'm getting her out of here as soon as possible.

Her head turns in my direction and she stares at me for a second too long. Unblinking but unfocused.

Her blue eyes were once bright and expressive, but they're now emotionless like a wax doll.

The fuck?

"Hey, Princess. Are you okay? Talk to me."

Her pale lips twist and she murmurs the words that cut me in half, "Who are you?"

THREE

Kyle

I'M STUNNED INTO SILENCE.

A long, excruciating silence.

Did Rai just ask me who I am, or have I somehow lost my mind?

I gently touch her shoulder, trying not to inflict pressure, even though all I want to do is hold her close and make us both forget this morning ever happened.

She flinches, and for the first time, I see the current of uncertainty in her eyes. I've never witnessed such emotions in them before, like they're fire in the ocean. No matter how much it whirls and embraces the wind, it'll eventually be drowned.

"Why are you touching me? Who are you?"

"My name is Kyle. I'm your husband."

She shakes her head the slightest bit. It seems like she wants to do it more, but the soft neck brace stops her. "I don't know you, and you certainly aren't my husband."

I tighten my hold on her shoulder to feel her warmth as I smooth my voice. "It's me, Rai."

I maintain eye contact because I need the connection I've always had with Rai right now. She may change and gather her hair up to be the woman the world demands of her, but when I stare deep in her eyes, I see the burn for more, the flames that rise with the need of passion.

Not today.

Today, the connection is off, as if the fire and the flames were drowned by the sea. Her pupils are dilated and she's stiff as a board in my arms.

It's like she doesn't know me at all. As if she's being touched by a complete stranger.

"Let me go." There's a note of fear in her voice.

My fingers dig into her shoulder, perhaps not too gently because of the current of emotions traveling through me right now, but I try to speak as calmly as possible. "Rai, you might be confused, but I'm really your husband."

"Let me go!" she screams. "Help! He wants to hurt me. Someone help me!"

The fuck? "I would never hurt you."

The doctor and the nurse barge inside, but remain close to the door when I glare them both down. Ruslan and Katia join, too, their eyes studying Rai intently.

"Help me." She tries to wiggle free, but I don't allow her room to move.

"Stop asking for others to help you from me," I snap, my temper getting the better of me. "It's supposed to be the other way around."

She flinches, but her lips thin in a line.

"You can't talk to a patient like that," the doctor scolds.

"Fuck off. You don't get to tell me how I speak to my wife."

"H-help me," Rai whispers, tears streaming down her cheeks. "Please help me, please."

This is not the Rai I know. She would never plead with others, let alone allow them to see her cry.

"Do you need anything, miss?" Ruslan's unsure gaze slides to me, then back to her.

"Who are all these people?" She stares between the three of us, and then back to her guard as if he is her only reprieve. "Ruslan?"

"Yes, miss?"

She sucks in a deep breath like a child about to throw a tantrum, then exhales again. Her voice turns hysterical. "Get them out of here! Get them all out!"

"Miss." The doctor approaches her slowly. "You need to calm down."

He tries to touch her, but I grab his wrist and twist it backward, making him wince in pain.

That causes Rai to scream louder. "Get out! Get out!"

"Sir." The doctor strains, but he's smart enough not to fight me, so I let him go. If he tries something funny, I'll break his fucking wrist. "It's better if you leave."

"No."

"If you don't, she might have a panic attack."

"Fuck that. She's my wife and I'm not leaving her side."

"Sir, it's not in her best interest for you to keep staying here."

"Out...out..." Her shaking has worsened and her lips are too pale. She's not the type who has these strong visceral reactions, and yet she appears on the verge of a breakdown. I can't be the reason behind that.

Even though there's nothing I want to do more than hold on to her, I need to let her go. Just for a while.

It takes all my power to release her, stand up, and step back.

She continues watching me even when I'm far away from her bed, and I motion at Ruslan and Katia to leave with me.

"Ruslan…" she calls. "S-stay."

"Yes, miss."

Why the fuck is she calling for him but not me? Even Katia appears taken aback, but she steps outside with me.

The doctor and the nurse remain beside Rai, talking to her in soothing tones. Judging from the slowing rise and fall of her chest, that seems to have managed to somewhat calm her down.

I keep watching from the doorway, unable to look away. She appears so soft, fragile, and all I want to do is to hold her hand and protect her.

The nurse keeps talking to her while the doctor steps outside. I grab him by the collar and slam him against the wall. "What the fuck is wrong with her?"

"Sir, if you don't release me, I can't speak."

I push him away with a shove. "Talk."

He massages the back of his neck and fixes his collar. "Mrs. Sokolov seems to be suffering from selective amnesia."

"Because she fell?"

"Yes, we believe the fall has caused some swelling in her brain and that's why she has amnesia."

"You said selective—does that mean she'll regain her memories soon?"

"No, selective means she lost part of her memories."

"What part?"

"From the initial questions we asked, she seems to have forgotten everything that happened for the past ten years."

"What?"

"Mrs. Sokolov believes she's eighteen years old. As a result, she doesn't remember the events that happened in the past ten years. That applies to people she met in that period, too."

I didn't know her ten years ago. No wonder she thought I was a stranger.

"How can she get her memories back?"

"Unfortunately, there's no cure for amnesia. Fortunately, it's not completely irrevocable. If she's surrounded by *supportive* family and friends, she might be able to recall things." I don't miss the way he stressed the part about being supportive. This fucker is exactly two seconds away from being throttled to death.

"How long will it take for her to remember?"

"There's no definite answer to that. It can be a few days or a few decades. Most likely, she will never recoup those lost memories."

Fuck!

"One more thing," he says.

"What?"

"She needs patience and care during this period so she can get back to the outside world. Everything has changed for her, and ten years is a significant gap for a woman her age."

I nod sharply. "But is she physically okay?"

"Aside from the neck sprain that should heal in a few days, she has no serious injuries."

At least she's safe. I'll find a way to deal with her brain.

Ignoring the doctor, I step past him toward Rai's room.

"Sir?"

"What?" I stop but don't turn around.

"It would be better if you didn't go inside. She had a strong reaction toward you, and if she has a panic attack while she is very confused, it might lead to serious health complications. Please limit your contact with her—for now, at least."

My fists clench on either side of me, but I don't step inside. The doctor leaves after I flop down in a chair in front of her room.

There's no way in hell I will stay away from her, but at the same time, I could never put her health in danger.

I keep watching from the window. Ruslan stands beside her bed, both hands in front of him. The reason she's not rejecting him like she did me and Katia is obviously because he's been by her side for more than ten years.

He and Vladimir were always there, like fucking shadows.

"Katia," I call out without ripping my gaze from Rai. "Go get her clothes and anything she'll need for her stay in the hospital."

She doesn't make a move to leave.

"What are you waiting for? An invitation?"

"Do you want to go home to rest? Your injury must hurt," she offers. "I'll stand guard here."

"I'm fine." I throw up a dismissive hand. "Go home and bring the little rascal, Peter. Ask Sergei to send more guards here until her discharge, but don't disclose anything about her condition to any of the Vory's members. Rai wouldn't want them to witness her in this weak state."

She nods and storms out of the hospital.

I don't care if Rai won't see me now. I'm not leaving this place until she does.

Ever since I saw her lying at the bottom of the stairs, the thing beating in my chest has been burning and roaring like a volcano on the brink of eruption.

And the only way to extinguish that fire is through her.

My wife.

My Rai.

⁂

We spend three days in the hospital.

Three days of CT scans, analyses, and whatever the fuck the doctors come up with. None of them seem to provide the solution to making her remember.

Whenever I go near her, she screams at me to get out. When I don't, she starts to hyperventilate and cry.

Every time I do that—insist on being by her side while

she chases me out—Ruslan and Katia glare at me as if they are ready to cut me up limb by limb. Fuck them and fuck the doctors. No one keeps me away from my wife.

She's slowly accepting Katia as her second guard, but Ruslan is the one she looks at the most, probably since she clearly remembers him.

After waking up, she asked about her grandfather. When Ruslan told her he's dead, she spent the entire night crying.

Even though I was sitting by the door, I could hear her sniffles and deep intakes of air that came after a long time of crying.

I listened to her all night in silence, and when she fell asleep, I quietly stepped inside and watched her sleeping form in the darkness. I wanted to hold her and wipe the tears on her cheeks, but she has become a light sleeper and would've started a riot if she found me touching her.

So I spent most of the night watching silently like a fucking creep.

The fact that she recalls and accepts most people except for me has been slowly but surely eating away at me like acid.

She was friendly with the fucker Damien when he showed up to visit her. Even though Katia kept quiet, the elite group learned about her being in the hospital, and eventually found out about her amnesia. Sergei and Vlad came, too, obviously. Her only remark to them was that they've gotten old.

Sergei asked me about the baby, and I told him everything is fine. He naturally didn't want to talk to her about it because it would freak her out in this situation. Since she's not pregnant, the doctor didn't mention anything about that, so she's still clueless in that regard, and it's best it remains this way until she hopefully gets her memories back.

Rai's accident shuffled Sergei's cards, and I could see the doubt about the future in his wrinkled eyes. Rai holds V Corp upright, and if she doesn't remember the last ten years of her life or the education and experience that came with it, there's no way she will be able to finance the brotherhood's war with the Irish.

It's a legitimate concern, but I don't give a fuck about any of that.

Kirill is now inside with his closest guard, Aleksander. Damien came again, too, even though I told him to stop showing up. He just gave me the middle finger while strolling inside.

Kirill is here to confirm that his greatest foe is indeed out of it and won't hurt him in the long run. Damien, on the other hand, is being a fucking leech who's enjoying the fact that she doesn't remember me a bit too much. Needless to say, I stand at the entrance to eavesdrop on their conversations.

The two leaders are sitting casually on either side of her while Ruslan, Katia, Aleksander, and Damien's guard stand by the walls.

"What are you doing here, Kirill?" Rai slowly peels the skin off her apple with a small knife. She's sitting, the hospital table in front of her. Thankfully, she appears healthier despite the brace around her neck. "I didn't know we were close enough for you to pay me a visit."

He readjusts his glasses with his middle finger. "We're not. But you're not close with Damien either."

"Hey, motherfucker." Damien snaps his fingers at him. "Shut the fuck up and fuck the fuck off."

"He's tolerable." She points her thumb at Damien, then directs her attention to Kirill. "You're not."

"Wise. Very wise, indeed." Damien retrieves a cigarette and places it in his mouth.

"No smoking in the hospital." She scolds then frowns. "When did you get a haircut?"

"Last week. You like it?" He lights the cigarette anyway.

"It makes you look like an old man."

"If I'm an old man, you're an old woman, Rai, and Kirill is…ancient."

She snickers at that before she glances at Kirill. "Are you going to tell me the reason for your visit?"

"I just wanted to make sure you're fine. Can't I do that?"

"Did you expect me to fall for that?"

"I can be a good sport, Sokolov."

"Maybe in a parallel world, and even then, I won't believe it."

"Ouch." Damien laughs. "Give him more, Rai. I'm interested to see how much his poker face can take on."

Kirill ignores him and his body angles in Rai's direction. "I heard you don't remember."

"I don't. Not the past ten years, at least," she says quietly before she chews on a small piece of apple.

"Does that mean you don't recall the time you came into my club, drank until you nearly passed out, and then danced alone like a lunatic?"

"I would never do that!" She stares at Ruslan, who bows his head.

Wait…she did that?

My fist clenches at the thought that someone other than me saw Rai drunk. She becomes so loose and fucking adorable when drunk.

"Yes, you did." Kirill tilts his head to the side. "You didn't leave either and insisted on staying the night. You passed out in one of the rooms upstairs."

"Yeah? So what?"

He narrows his eyes but soon goes back to his normal expression, which is blank, but in a welcoming kind of way instead of mean like Damien's. "So do you remember coming on to me?"

She did that? I'm ready to punch Kirill in the nose when she laughs. "In your dreams. You're far away from my type."

"How would you know when you think you're just eighteen?"

"I know I despise your guts and your face and your foxy nature and everything you do to get power. I would cut your dick off before letting you come near me."

Damien bursts out in laughter, and I can't help the smile that grazes my lips. *That's my woman.*

"So you remember nothing of what happened that night?" Kirill probes.

"No, but that doesn't mean I would ever come on to a psycho like you."

Kirill smirks. "Isn't your husband similar to me?"

She purses her lips. "I have no husband."

"But we all attended your wedding."

"I don't remember it, so it didn't happen," she snaps.

Damien takes her hand in his. "That's the spirit, Rai. Truth is, you and I were always meant to be together."

My blood boils and I'm a second away from barging in there and throwing him to the floor.

"Really?" she asks slowly.

"Really. I'm the love of your life. It started when you saw me kill for the first time. You said it was hot." He grins. "Then we had a lot of kinky sex."

That's it.

"You'll have a kinky death if you don't get the fuck out." I barge inside, my fists clenched on either side of me.

Rai stiffens and tightens her hold on the knife. Kirill stands up and offers her a fake smile. "I hope you never get better, you little devil."

Rai flips him off, and he smirks as he leaves with Aleksander following after him.

"What are you waiting for?" I motion at Damien. "Piss off."

He takes a long drag of his cigarette and blows a cloud of smoke. "Isn't it the husband whom she doesn't remember?"

Fucker.

"Hey, Rai." He grins at her. "The only reason you married

this tool is due to being forced. Now, you can divorce him and come back to me. I don't believe in the whole virgin kink so it's a win for both of us. What do you think?"

I swing my fist at him, but her voice cuts me off. "Get out. Both of you."

My eyes slowly close at her tone. Rai and I always had our problems, but the way she keeps on rejecting me ever so brutally is taking its toll on me.

"I'll be back." Damien staggers to his feet and smirks at me before he and his guard leave. I keep glaring at his back as he strides down the hall. Why does she remember this fucker but not me?

"Out." She points at the door with her knife.

"You can't chase me away for the rest of your life. I'm your husband."

"Then I can just divorce you."

I grit my teeth, then release them to not sound agitated. That's the last thing she needs. "You can't just *divorce me*. You have duties toward the brotherhood, remember?"

"Ruslan, get him out!" Her pitch rises, fingers trembling around the knife.

"I'll come back," I tell her matter-of-factly and step out of the hospital room.

I'm sitting on one of the plain chairs when a large shadow falls on me. I stare up to find Vladimir's boring bloody face.

First Kirill and Damien, and now Vladimir. Fucking perfect.

"You should go home, Kyle."

"I'm fine," I spit out.

"You have dark circles and you stink."

Of course I do. I haven't changed clothes since the day I brought her here, and I've been washing up in the hospital bathroom. I also sleep sitting up in the seat because I can't let my guard down.

"Do you want her to see you this way?" Vladimir asks, but it's clearly rhetorical since he continues. "Go shower, change clothes, and then come back. She's not going nowhere."

I don't like the way he speaks to me. It's that fucking Russian condescension that runs in all their blood.

"I'll stand guard in front of her room until your return. She's asleep anyway."

I throw a glance at her. She's lying on her back, eyes closed, and her hand is splayed above her head on the pillow. It was one of her most adorable habits that she eventually got rid of.

If she's really going to be the Rai from ten years ago, that means she might never accept me as her husband again.

I try to pretend that doesn't slice me open in a hundred different painful ways.

Staggering to my feet, I motion at Peter to stay in front of her room. I lean in to whisper, "Tell me if anything happens."

"Yes, sir," he murmurs back.

He's a useless kid in battle, but he's good when it comes to spying, at least.

As I leave the hospital, I vow one thing.

I'll make sure Rai remembers me, even if it's the last thing I do.

FOUR

Rai

I LIE STILL IN BED.

My gaze is set on the ceiling, and it's not because of its plain white color. I keep wondering when on earth my life went wrong.

It's not only because of the accident or the situation I find myself in. I think it started the day I chose to be in Reina's shoes and become the Bratva's next princess.

At that time, all I thought about was my twin sister's safety, but...I was also attracted to this life, to the danger, to the bursts of excitement that didn't exist in my calm life with Dad.

One thing led to another and I started running after danger so I could grab it by the horns.

What I didn't know is that during that race, I lost pieces of myself, of the little girl who loved her family and was ready to do anything for them.

The sense of protection *Dedushka* implemented in me

has grown to become a monster whose shadow follows me everywhere.

The only way to get rid of it is to completely give up, to blow away my goals and everything I've worked for thus far.

During my life in the Bratva, I've seen grown men tremble in fear because of what they've done. I've been surrounded by men who go to unimaginable lengths for power, money, and everything the brotherhood offers.

I never wanted to be one of those men. And unlike what they think, I never wanted to rule over them or snatch the throne with ruthless hands as they do.

The only thing I ever wanted was to be recognized for what I have to offer, regardless of whether or not I have a penis between my legs.

I never once had any misconceptions about what I am or what I can do. I knew my limits and my strengths, and did everything to remain on top of things.

So how come in a fraction of a second, I find myself in the middle of nowhere? How come I've stooped as low as thinking about giving up?

You might not be a man, but you're a Sokolov, Rai. And do you know what Sokolovs do? We snatch the throne even if the price is high. Don't be afraid to shed blood, even if it's your own.

Dedushka's words slam into me like an earthquake, rattling me from the inside out. Who am I to give up? My life isn't the only one at stake. There's also my twin sister, Sergei, and Ana—whom my granduncle forbade from visiting me for security reasons. There's no way in hell I'd give up on them even if I give up on myself.

The door opens then closes before Vlad strides inside with his usual broody silence.

Sometimes, he looks just like the ceiling I was staring at: strong, hard, and impenetrable. And I need that strength right now.

It's not bad to admit I'm weak. It's just another form of strength.

"Do you feel better?"

"Is he outside?" I murmur.

"No. I convinced him to go change his clothes."

"Finally."

He lowers himself into the chair opposite me, his frame dwarfing it. "Why were you so insistent on having him leave?"

"I haven't lost my memories."

"*What?*" He stares at me for a second, as if I've completely lost my mind.

I slide to a sitting position and yank the IV needle from my arm, then throw it away.

"Are you going to explain what's going on? Was the fall also false?"

"That part was real, though I don't remember how I ended up there. I believe someone pushed me."

"Who?"

"I don't know. They had no accent and sounded male."

"That doesn't help. There are a hundred men in the mansion, but they wouldn't dare to touch you."

I know exactly who dared to do that, but I don't say his name aloud. If I do, Vlad will go straight to action and kill Kyle.

He can't die. Not yet.

Not only did he cut me open and stab me countless times, he also used me to ruin my whole damn family.

If he dies now, I won't be able to know how deep his plan goes and how far ahead he planted his destructive seeds.

When I was grabbed by that shadow, I thought my life ended, and foolishly, the last taste on my tongue was that of bitter betrayal. A tear escaped my lid, too, because the man I'd slowly been giving my trust to had been plotting my fall.

And in that moment, all I wanted to ask him was why. Why would he do that to me?

Those idiotic thoughts disappeared as soon as I woke up in the hospital. I have another chance, and I won't use it to ask why. I'll use it to make him pay.

Finishing Kyle isn't that hard. The moment I tell anyone in the brotherhood about what I heard, he'll be dead. I could tell Damien since he's been eyeing him unfavorably for some time, or even Vlad, but that isn't the best way to hurt him.

Since his sole purpose has been to ruin us and the Irish, the perfect method to ruin him is to abort his plan. Only then can he die. Only then can he pay for his sin.

"Rai?" Vlad calls my name.

I consider my words before I speak. "I'll find out. They will eventually try to get me again."

"That's dangerous as fuck."

"No accomplishments have ever been made without taking risks, my dear Vlad."

He grunts. "It's not Vlad."

"It'll always be Vlad for me, so you might as well save your breath."

"Back to the topic at hand—why did you do that?"

"Do what?"

"Make everyone believe you lost your memories. Do you realize the amount of stress you have caused the boss?"

"I need the perpetrator fooled, and for that, everyone had to stay in the dark. Only the doctor, Ruslan, and Katia know."

"How did you come up with this plan in the first place?"

"My twin sister, Reina, had amnesia once, and I just copied what she told me had happened to her."

"And now what?" he grumbles, running his hand over his beard. I can sense him losing his patience.

"I think I know an in with the Irish."

"I already have a spy."

"No. This one is more in a leading position."

"Yes?"

I nod.

"And you have to act like you lost your memories for that?"

I pick my words carefully to not mention Kyle's name. Vlad can't know about that yet. "Yes, because the one I got this information from thinks I heard him. If he believes I lost my memories, his guard will be down and he'll feel like he got away with it."

He narrows his eyes. "Who is he?"

"I'll tell you when it's time."

"Or you can tell me now."

"That's not the point, Vlad."

"And what is?"

"That I need him to think I have amnesia."

"But he will keep his eyes on you, and when he figures out you're lying, he'll come back for you."

"By then, I will have finished my mission."

"You'll still be gambling."

"If a gamble is what it takes, then I'm all in."

He grunts. "That's dangerous."

"Danger is only an obstacle. I vowed to give back to the brotherhood as much as I took, and I'll not allow anyone to take that away. I just need you to have my back, Vlad. You and my guards are the only people who know my condition."

He gives a grumbling yes before he asks, "How did you convince the doctor to lie on your behalf? Did you bribe him?"

"Sort of. His wife works for V Corp, and I promised him shares." I smile. "And Ruslan threatened to knock his teeth out if he as much as gets out word about it."

That's so Ruslan. If I didn't have him, Katia, and Vlad in these circumstances, I don't know how I would react.

Vlad watches me peculiarly for a second too long, as if he's trying to solve one of his puzzles. He has a lot of those—huge puzzles he spends weeks solving. It's a weird quirk of his, but it speaks of his personality. While Vlad's appearance and general attitude peg him as a muscle man like Damien, he's not. Vlad would never barge in like a crazy bull. He calculates first, and then when he attacks, he can be as violent as Damien, if not more.

"What?" I ask when he doesn't say anything.

"I'm thinking."

"About what?"

"About why Kyle isn't part of this."

My chest squeezes at the mention of his name, but all it finds is emptiness. I don't want to hear his name, because that will force me to remember what he said on the phone. The cruel, final words that destroyed the bridge we were slowly building as if it'd been made from sand.

Rai is nothing. I'll just leave her behind.

He smashed everything we could've ever had together.

I might have considered forgiving him, but that's also shattered into little unredeemable pieces. He didn't only betray me, he also betrayed everything I stand for.

My family.

My duty.

My honor.

He crushed me and left me no choice but to crush him in return.

"He doesn't need to know," I tell Vlad in a voice void of emotions. "He's not part of the Bratva."

"But he's your husband."

"That doesn't automatically give him the right to know everything about my life."

Vlad narrows his eyes as if he feels I'm bluffing him. "Back then, when he said the bond between husband and wife is more important than anything else, you didn't seem to disagree."

He did say that. The hypocrite.

"That doesn't matter. Let's just keep it from him."

"Why?"

"Because. Why are you so insistent on bringing him in?"

"Why don't you tell me why you want him out? Unless…"

"What?"

"Are you suspecting him? Because if you are, I'll torture that fucker to death."

Shit. Shit. This is exactly why Vlad shouldn't know.

I keep my expression the same, because he's watching me so closely he'd feel the change.

"No. Of course not. I just don't trust that he's completely into the brotherhood."

"You trusted him enough to fall pregnant with him."

"I'm not pregnant, Vlad." He should at least know that truth.

"You're not?"

"It was a false positive and I didn't want to disappoint Sergei."

"Huh."

"Is that a relieved tone or a disappointed reaction?"

"Neither. Just piecing things together. So? What's next in your grand plan?"

I inhale deeply and release it through my teeth. This is it. My turn to play.

"Come closer, Vlad. Here's how it's going to go."

FIVE

Rai

Later that day, I tell the doctor I want to go home. Or more like, I inform him, since I didn't stay around to treat any sicknesses, anyway.

I'm about to change my clothes when Kyle steps inside, remaining at the door.

In these past few days, I tried everything to separate myself from him. Not only did I strategically plot my amnesia so he's in the part of my life I don't remember, I also pushed him away every chance I could.

Honestly, I should get acting awards for the ways I feigned panic attacks. But that first day? The one in which I cried? Yeah, those tears weren't entirely acting. The betrayal was so tangible and raw and I had to express it somehow.

I glare at him, but soon cut off eye contact because I'm not supposed to be glaring at someone I don't remember.

Kyle is perceptive to a fault, and what makes it more

dangerous is that it's not obvious on the outside. He gives off a nonchalant vibe when he actually observes everything in his environment. Part of it is because he's a killer, and the other part is because he's naturally distrustful.

If I let my guard down even for a second, he'll pounce on me. And because of that, I need to be careful while pushing him away.

"The doctor said you're free to go home. If you're not feeling well, you can stay longer."

"I'm fine." I motion at my dress on the bed that I was planning to wear before he came in. "Can you get out? I need to change my clothes."

He reaches me in two steps. "I will help."

"No. Just leave me alone."

I try to ignore how close he is and how his frame is nearly perching over mine with the height difference. His hair is damp and falls to his strong forehead. He must've taken a shower, changed clothes, and come right back in.

He can pretend to be worried about me and my wellbeing all he likes, but I'm not an idiot who will fall for it after he's been using me all along.

Kyle doesn't even attempt to leave. On the contrary, he barges into my space until his clean, distinctive scent robs my air, and just like that, I'm caged by his presence.

There's something about being trapped by him. Oxygen ceases to exist, and the world turns blurry except for the place where he stands. That's not blurry at all. If anything, it's lighter, shinier, and crystal clear. But not everything visible is beautiful. After all, the devil looks his best when luring in his victims.

"Didn't you hear what I said?" My voice doesn't lose the edge, but I try not to come off too strong so it doesn't raise red flags.

"I did hear what you said, Princess. But I'm not leaving."

"Why the hell wouldn't you?"

"Because I said I will help."

"I don't need your help."

"Yes, you do. Look at how you're barely standing." He reaches his hand out to grab my arm, but I pull away.

"Katia will help me."

"Why Katia?"

"Because she's my guard."

"And I'm your husband."

The confident way he says those words almost makes me believe they're real, that I somehow hold a special place in his black, cold heart.

Wishful thinking. Just like everything about him.

"You're not my husband. I don't know you."

"Then you will get to know me." He turns me around and undoes the flimsy thing that holds my hospital robe in place.

The thin material falls to my knees, then pools around my feet on the floor.

I force my body to go numb and frigid like what he did to me. It doesn't matter how much he touches me or how much his hands used to bring me unimaginable amounts of pleasure, because my body isn't an entity on its own. It's connected to my brain, and my brain recognizes that he betrayed me first.

He broke the rules *first*.

Kyle's fingers wrap around my nape, studying the skin after the doctor removed the soft brace. His hands are gentle, almost as if he doesn't want to hurt me.

The injury stings, but I hold the reaction in, refusing to let him see any pain.

It's strange how he's touching me like this. No, it's not that he's touching me like this, but more that he's not doing it in a sexual way as usual.

He runs his fingers over my skin as if he's relearning my body. Maybe he's recalling something. Maybe he was the one who choked me.

I wouldn't be surprised if he was, but he couldn't have been considering he was talking inside the room.

"Who put their hands on you?" His voice is laced with a threatening energy.

"Didn't you hear the doctor? I don't remember."

"Whether you remember or not, I promise to find whoever touched you and crush them before your eyes."

"I don't need you to crush people for me. I can take care of myself." I pause, unsure if that will give me away.

But I hear the smile in his voice when he speaks. "Some things never change."

Phew.

"But as your husband, I will avenge you."

"I don't need vengeance."

His voice drops. "But vengeance is my specialty, Princess."

My heart thumps at the way he calls me that. *Princess.* At first, it was a term of degradation because I'm the boss's grand-daughter, but ever since he came back, it holds more meaning than it ever should.

"I'm not your princess."

He grabs my bra and slides it up my arms, still soft and caring. "Yes, you are. You're also my wife."

"I don't remember marrying you."

"I can show you the registration papers or the video taken during the marriage when you said 'I do', although there was a very unfortunate event at the end of the wedding. I doubt you would want to see it."

He straps my bra in place and loops an arm around me to run his fingers along the soft flesh of my breast. At first, the touch is experimental, innocent almost. But I should know better; there's *nothing* innocent about Kyle.

His fingers linger more, becoming explorative as he feigns keeping my bra's strap in place. He wraps his hand around my shoulder then trails it to my back, then returns to the front again.

It takes everything in me to remain still. It's not me; it's a chemical reaction and stupid hormones. It's not because of Kyle, right? I would have the same reaction even if someone else were doing this.

My legs tremble as I step into the dress and he slides it up my arms, wrapping his hand around my waist in the process.

The pads of his fingers dig into my hipbone, stroking back and forth. My body's memory kicks in from the times he used to do that while making me wear that toy.

No.

"Stop touching me that way," I snap.

His eyes gleam as he slides the dress up. "What way?"

"Like you're molesting me."

He chuckles, the sound amused. "That's impossible since you're my wife."

"Well, I feel molested."

"How so? I'm only helping you get dressed ever so casually."

"You're not helping me get dressed. You're feeling me up."

"That's because I missed you, Princess." His voice drops as his lips touch my ear. The shiver that breaks across my skin is too violent to ignore.

I push away from him, but in my haste, I trip. Kyle catches me by the arm, an infuriating smirk tugging on his lips.

"This is what happens when you don't accept help offered to you."

"I said I don't need your help."

"Are we back into the first stage of our relationship? Should I try to woo you all over again?"

"You can try—though I doubt you ever wooed me."

"Oh, I did. After all, you screamed my name every night."

"Won't happen again."

"We'll see."

"I can assure you that you won't succeed."

Kyle steps behind me and lifts the zipper of my dress agonizingly slowly, as if he's enjoying the act. Goosebumps multiply on my skin as his fingers glide up the middle of my back.

I bite my lower lip to not let out any reaction. There is no way in hell I'm giving him the satisfaction of seeing me react to him.

"You underestimate me, Princess." His voice gains a low, dark edge. "You *really* underestimate me."

"It doesn't matter what you do. I would never fall for your charms."

"You did the first time."

"I doubt it."

"Why would you?"

I flip my hair back, and even though I'm so tempted to pull it into a bun, I don't. I only started that habit after my grandfather's death.

Facing him, I stare him right in the eye. "Simple: you're not my type."

He smirks, but there is no humor behind it. "I'm everyone's type."

"Not mine, arrogant jerk, so you might as well divorce me."

Kyle loops his arms around my waist, pulling me against the hard ridges of his body. I gasp as an unmistakable bulge presses against the bottom of my stomach. "That won't be happening. Do you know why?"

"No, and I'm not interested in finding out."

"I'm interested in telling you. I might not be your type, but you're mine."

Of course he won't make this easy. I think of that and not the fact that he just said I'm his type.

Lies.

Everything out of his mouth is a lie.

I try to wiggle free, but his fingers dig into my hip, keeping me in place and guiding me out of the hospital and toward his car. Katia and Ruslan follow after us, asking me silently if they should interfere, but I discreetly shake my head.

Sure, I can fight, act out, or feign another panic attack, but all of those are temporary solutions.

To make sure my plan works, I need to play his games.

The irony. It seems games are the only things Kyle and I will ever agree on.

He was always a step ahead, but this time, the ball is in my court.

This time, it's his world that will be flipped upside down.

SIX

Rai

WHEN WE ARRIVE HOME, KYLE HAS HIS HAND around my back, his fingers digging into my skin as if he wants to make sure I'm indeed there.

Every step I take is a fight to not get caught in his touch or the way he sometimes strokes my skin as if he's a doting lover.

Years ago when Kyle left and never looked back, I thought, with time, my life would return to normal, but months and years went by and I couldn't go back in time to erase him. I already took a turn onto a one-way road and there's no exit.

I guess a part of me will never be completely over the change he brought to my life. I can—have to—admit that so I'm able to move on with the rest of my life.

I might not have been able to make him disappear, but I can—and will—get past him.

Sergei calls us into the dining room as soon as we arrive.

Kyle leads me inside with a grumble. "You should be resting, not attending to Sergei's power demands."

"He's your boss."

He pauses at the threshold, his expression blank. "No one is my boss, Princess."

It's odd how he used to say things like that in the past, but I seldom focused on them, on the truth and his real self behind them. I was in too deep to see the truth he offered subconsciously.

"I thought you were loyal to the brotherhood." I feign nonchalance.

"Nah. I'm only loyal to you."

Liar. Fraud.

I pull away from him and step inside the dining room. Sergei is sitting at the head of the table with Anastasia by his side. My grandcousin's eyes are red and puffy as if she spent the night crying. Upon seeing me, she jerks upright and runs toward me. Then, she stops at the last second and stands in front of me. Which is much better than if she were to hug me. If she did, I wouldn't have been able to play the role.

"Anastasia? Wow. You're all grown up."

She blinks. "So it's true. You really don't remember?"

"I'm sorry." And I really am, because I have to make her believe I've forgotten about the last ten years of her life.

Anastasia shakes her head violently. "You don't have to be. I understand."

During the conversation, Kyle has joined me, standing by my side like a soldier. I don't miss the way he's watching my every movement. I don't think he actually suspects me, but the way he looks at me with knitted brows and the twinkling in his cobalt blue eyes gives me the eerie feeling of being thrust under a microscope.

I continue talking with Anastasia after we sit down for a family dinner. Usually, Vlad or one of the others would join, but it seems Sergei gave instructions so it's only the four of us. It's on purpose, and Sergei has something up his sleeve.

He coughs, but it doesn't turn into a fit. After taking a sip of water, he clears his throat and speaks in accented English. "It's very unfortunate that you lost your memories, Rai."

I pause sipping from the soup. "Yes."

"However, it won't end well if it goes on like this."

"I agree." Kyle peels a piece of lobster then places it on my plate like some doting husband. He's excellent at playing the protective role and being there every step of the way.

It would've been so much easier if he were cold and treated me as he said on the phone. Like I'm nothing. Like he'll leave me behind.

Because no matter how much I try to ignore it, this act has been throwing me off since the hospital.

"What do you mean it can't go on, Papa?" Anastasia asks in a small voice.

"If the shareholders know Rai has lost her memory, they will actively try to dismiss her from her position. Her memory loss will remain between us."

"Damien and Kirill found out," I say.

"Vladimir, too." Kyle's voice is calm, but it's deceptive, lethal.

"I've spoken to them and they will keep this a secret."

"Damien and Kirill?" I scoff. "Damien might not care, but Kirill wouldn't let this slide just because you told him to."

"He's smart enough to know changing V Corp's management would be detrimental for the brotherhood, especially at times like these." Sergei sips from his water, clearing his throat and huffing out deep breaths. I know it's taking everything in him to rein in the cough.

If it were anyone else, they would've given up and spent their days in a peaceful private clinic. But like me, Granduncle knows sacrifices should be made. As *Dedushka* once told me, nothing great is easily accomplished, because if that were the case, anyone could be great.

"Rai," he calls.

"Yes?"

"You'll act as you usually do. Fortunately, there's not much difference personality-wise, but ten years ago, you didn't have your degree and were dependent on Nikolai."

"Ruslan and Katia will help."

"I need someone closer to watch over you." He grabs a fork and points it at the man sitting beside me. "Kyle."

No. This isn't how the plan is supposed to go. I can't have Kyle with me at all times. That will definitely expose my plan.

Said jerk places his hand on top of mine and squeezes gently. "Of course. Anything to help her."

"I can figure it out on my own." I try arguing with my granduncle. "I have Ruslan and Katia. Vlad, too."

"I'm not taking any risks. We have a lot at stake right now, and if V Corp's profits are in jeopardy, the brotherhood won't have anything to fall back on."

I get Sergei's angle, I really do, I just don't like where this is going. I've spent so long growing V Corp, and now Kyle will get his filthy hands into one of the legacies I've been fighting tooth and nail for.

I don't like that I have to keep up with Kyle even in company matters. I grew that company, it was *me*, so why does he get to stick his nose in it?

"Kyle and Anastasia will help you in the company so you don't slip in front of the employees."

"Anything to help Rayenka." She beams, and I smile back even though I want to tell Granduncle there's no way I'd slip. I can't, because that would blow the cover I've spent too long perfecting.

After dinner, we retreat to our room.

I remain near the entrance, arms crossed, as I concentrate on the situation and my options.

Kyle is already inside, removing his jacket and laying it casually on a chair—the same chair he fucked me over the other night while I screamed his name. I close my eyes to chase away the assault of the memories. That's the last thing I need in this situation.

Focus, Rai.

Facing him, I speak in my sternest tone. "I want separate rooms."

He doesn't even lift his head, and I'm not sure whether or not he heard me, so I repeat, "I said, I want separate rooms."

This time, he stares at me as he unbuttons his shirt, his fingers gliding on the buttons unhurriedly, almost like in some strip show. "And I want you to remember. Sadly, we don't always get what we want, Princess."

"If you expect me to share a room with you, you're crazy."

"What's so crazy about a married couple sharing a room?" He stalks toward me, his shirt half-unbuttoned, revealing the snake tattoo that's rippling against his chest muscles. "Have you forgotten that we're married?"

"I don't remember that so you're simply a stranger, and I can't share a bed with a stranger."

He halts in front of me, somehow caging me between his frame and the door. Kyle pauses at his fourth button, hinting at his chiseled chest, but not exactly showing it. And now I'm staring at his chest. *Jesus.*

I snap my head up, but if I thought his face would be easier to stare at, I'm proven utterly wrong. Maintaining eye contact with Kyle is like swimming against a violent current. I know I'll probably drown or hit my head on a rock, but I still carry on anyway.

"Perhaps I should refresh your memories, Princess."

"What?"

He grabs me by the arm and spins me around. I gasp as he gently pushes me backward and I end up crashing on the bed.

The mattress is soft at my behind, but the impact feels like that current from earlier throwing me down a crushing waterfall.

Kyle hovers over me, his thighs on either side of mine as he grabs my wrists and imprisons them atop my head. I attempt to fight, but he's caging me so tightly I cannot even begin to escape his brutal clutches.

I try to lift my knee and hit him in the balls, but he smirks as if figuring out my intentions and keeps my thighs pressed down with his legs. "Easy, tigress."

Huffing, I turn my head away. I need a break from being caught in his gaze. Besides, this position and the familiar bed only remind me of the ludicrous things he did to my body night in and night out.

"Do you remember the first time we met?" Kyle asks in a low, slightly husky voice.

"No."

"Right. You lost your memories." He gently clutches my chin and forces me to face him. After he makes sure I'm staring at him, he slides his thumb beneath my bottom lip. "The first time I saw you was about nine years ago. You attended this *Swan Lake* performance by some European ballet with Nikolai, because he was infuriatingly Russian and liked to show it even in ballet performances. Adrian was there, too, because he's interested in that for some reason or another. You had your arm in Nikolai's and you wore gloves, white, like your dress. It was long and bright in the light, which reminded me of a distant image I thought I had long forgotten. Angels. Not real ones, but those from my father's favorite painting. You were speaking animatedly to Nikolai and Adrian, discussing the performance. Your grandfather had laugh lines around his eyes as he listened to you. Do you know what I thought back then?"

My lips have been parted the entire time he's been speaking, trapped in the calm way he retells our first meeting. I remember that day, because even though I thought he was another one of *Dedushka's* 'killers', I was somehow caught in the gleam in his eyes, the way they darkened as if he were empty and trying to drag everyone else into that emptiness.

"No." Instead of snapping, my voice is as calm as his. "And I don't want to know."

"I thought you looked like a typical mafia princess," he continues, as if I haven't said anything. "But I was soon proven wrong when I heard you talk to Nikolai. You weren't spoiled or acting like a brat with privileges. You were straightforward, knew what you wanted, and went to it."

"Telling me about the past won't make a difference."

"Yes, it will. How else are we going to get familiar with each other again?"

"Why should we?"

"Because you're my wife and I'm no fucking stranger you'll sleep separately from. If familiarity is what you need, then I'll give it to you."

"What if I need space?"

"I don't believe in space. That's a word invented by losers who couldn't figure out their own minds."

"And you have?"

"I have." There's so much conviction in his tone, it takes even me by surprise.

"So what now? Are you going to keep holding me like this?"

"I'm also telling you about the past."

"The one I said I don't want to hear about?"

"The one you want to forget about, but we'll rectify that. Where was I? Right, the first time I met you, after the ballet. You don't go to those anymore, because they remind you of Nikolai. The one time you went to one after his death, you hid in a corner and reemerged with your eyes red. Since they weaken you and you're in no position to allow weakness, you stopped going altogether."

He…he shouldn't know that. I made sure no one saw me that way —not even Ruslan and Katia.

"So that's the thing, Princess. I didn't only see your strength, I also witnessed your weakness. It was bound to happen after Nikolai asked me to keep an eye on you when I wasn't on a sniping mission. You were a proud thing and didn't want to admit when you needed help, but you were a fast learner. You obviously enjoyed my company since you wouldn't leave me alone, and that's when you fell head over heels for me."

Lying asshole.

I didn't fall in love with him. The most frustrating part is that I can't contradict him because that would mean I do remember.

"But then again, I'm the very loveable type, Princess."

You've got to be kidding me.

"Every morning," he goes on in his serene voice, "we woke up early and jogged together, then I taught you how to shoot for long distances because, as you said, Vladimir sucks as a teacher."

He's the one who said that, not me. *Jesus.* He tells a story so convincingly, mixing lies with truths. If I didn't know my own memories, I wouldn't suspect it.

"Needless to say, you fell in love with me more with every passing day. Especially after I kind of saved your sister."

"I don't believe any of that."

"I'm the one with the memories, remember?" He brushes his lips against mine and I taste something different than any of the other times he's kissed me, but I can't quite put my finger on it.

Kyle has always had a distinctive taste and smell, but right now it feels like a mixture of longing, despair, and something else.

"That doesn't mean whatever you said happened."

"It did."

"In your dreams, maybe."

"In my dreams, I'm thrusting into your wet cunt and feel it strangle my dick as you scream my name. Do you want me to show you?"

Blood rushes to my cheeks. How can he remain so calm while saying shit like that? I'm on the verge of combusting. "Let me go."

"You're a fan of that sentence, but you should know by now that it doesn't work on me. I need to continue touching you so you can familiarize yourself with me again. You usually get aroused the moment I touch you."

"That's not true!"

Challenge twinkles in his eyes. "Do you want me to prove it?"

"No!"

"I'm in the mood to check." His fingers leave my face and bunch the material of my dress.

Shit.

He can't get that close this early. He just can't. Because if he goes any further, I have no clue how I'm going to react to him.

"Are you going to force yourself on me?"

He pauses, the dark blues of his eyes zeroing in on me. "What the fuck did you just say?"

"I don't want this, so if you go any further, you're taking me against my will."

"Against your will," he repeats, as if he's getting a taste of the words.

"Well, aren't you?"

"If I want to fuck you, I will." The darkness in his voice penetrates me to the bones. "I can and will use your body against you until you beg me for more. You're my wife, Rai. You took vows, you said your 'I do', and guess what? I believe in till death do us fucking part."

My heartbeat explodes like a thousand bombs thrown all

at once. I try to regulate it, to think of the current situation, but the way his eyes hold me hostage keeps me pinned in place.

He's going to act on his threat, and I have no will or strength to escape.

His mouth hovers an inch over mine and I slam my eyes shut, not wanting to look at him. Maybe if I don't, this whole thing will end and—

Kyle's lips brush against my forehead and he releases me. I blink, but before I can form a proper reaction, he lies on his back and pulls me atop him so my head is nuzzled in his chest.

"You're tired, so sleep for now, Princess. I'll deal with you when your strength is back."

SEVEN

Rai

KYLE HASN'T LEFT MY SIDE.
He stays with me every step of the way, refusing to budge. When I wake up in the morning, he's there to join me for a walk. When I sit down for meals, he pays extra attention to placing food on my plate. When I ask either Ruslan or Katia to help me with something, he dismisses them and takes over the task.

It doesn't matter that I keep shooing him away; he bounces right back like he's rubber. He's impossible to deal with—or rather, get rid of. So I come up with the simple solution of pretending he doesn't exist.

The keyword being, pretend. Because there's no way in hell his presence can become invisible.

It's been a week since I was discharged from the hospital, and as per Sergei's orders, Kyle has been accompanying me to V Corp. In order to work without hassle, I had the doctor tell

Kyle that even though I lost my memories from the past ten years, I can still access the part of my brain that stores my cognitive skills, and therefore I do remember how to do business.

While Kyle has been doting on me, he's not an idiot. If I somehow give off vibes that I do remember and I've been lying to him all along, things will take a turn for the worse.

During the past week, I've been purposefully pretending to be asleep so I can listen to his phone calls. He hadn't made one, but he often texts on his phone or uses his laptop. I tried snooping around in those, but as expected, they are password protected.

I still haven't figured out his plan, but I will soon. If he's going to remain secretive, I'll have no choice but to take this to the next step.

Sergei appointed Kyle as a director, but his position doesn't require him to be present on an everyday basis. Even so, he still shows up by my side as if he's my senior bodyguard or something, and that makes it hard to concentrate on work and meetings, like right now. The more I ignore him, the darker his shadow perches on my life.

"That's it for today," I tell one of the directors. "Email me the proposal and your suggestions."

He nods. Rustling of papers fill the conference room before the rest of the board members take their leave as well.

I stand up and grab my bag. On my way to the exit, a strong arm wraps around my stomach and pulls me back against his the ridges of his strong body.

"What are you doing?" I search the room, and thankfully, everyone else has left. Not that Kyle cares either way. He somehow always has his hand on me, whether at the small of my back, on my nape, my thigh, my hand—everywhere, basically. It's like he can't stop touching me or something,

"I'm taking you out for lunch."

"I don't want lunch. I have paperwork to finish."

"You can finish it after lunch."

"Or I can finish it now."

"Or you can go with me and eat. You didn't have a proper breakfast this morning."

I hate that he notices the little things. He shouldn't. That's not how this is supposed to be.

"Whether I eat or not is none of your concern."

"Of course it is. I can't have my wife faint due to malnutrition."

"My answer is still no."

"You can go willingly or I can just kidnap you. I don't have to tell you which option I would prefer, do I?" He winks, and I'm tempted to claw his eyes out.

It's useless to fight him when he decides to be his awfully protective self. It's a side of Kyle I haven't witnessed a lot before, but it doesn't affect me as much as I thought it would. Maybe because now I know what he truly is, *who* he truly is, so I don't see it as protectiveness but as another way to manipulate me. After all, the reason he approached me was to get information and destroy those I love through me.

Shooing those thoughts away, I pull away from him and head to the parking lot. This is my chance to take this further. We don't have time to waste—we never did—but I guess during the time I've been pretending I've lost my memories, I was hoping to unravel something from him and not have to do this.

Desperate times call for desperate measures.

I get in the car first and fasten my seatbelt, then type a text to Vlad.

Rai: Are you free?

Vladimir: Depends on the reason.

Rai: What if I told you I can get you the one who knows about the Irish's plans?

Vladimir: Then I can carve out time.

Rai: You might have to torture the answers out of him.

Vladimir: You say that as if it's a chore.

I know full well it isn't. Vlad specializes in torturing, and it's one of the reasons why he has a scary reputation. He's the type who doesn't stop until he gets answers. Maybe this is why I didn't want the situation to reach this level.

Kyle climbs into the driver's seat, and I hide my phone. My fingers brush against the small bottle I've been keeping on me since I got out of the hospital. I knew I would have to do this sooner or later.

The vehicle doesn't move and silence is the only other occupant in the car. I sneak a peek at him and pause at the overly concentrated expression. He's watching too intently, as if it's the first time he's seeing my face.

"What?"

"Just watching how beautiful you are."

Even though I try hard not to be affected, I can feel the burning in my cheeks. I clear my throat. "Didn't you say we were going for lunch?"

"We will after I get my fill of you."

"I don't know what you're doing, but it's not going to work."

He raises a brow. "Do you want to bet?"

"I don't need to, because I'm one hundred percent sure I never cared about you."

"You're so certain for someone who doesn't remember."

"I don't have to remember to be sure of it, I just feel it."

"Hmm." He pauses, tilting his head to the side as if he wants to get a better look at me. "Do you know what you used to tell me in the past?"

"I don't want to know." Every memory I have with him is filled with anguish and sadness.

"But I want to tell you." He takes my hand in his. My skin crawls at how he's touching me with the same hands he's been planning to kill my family with. "You used to say I'm closed off and I never show you my true self."

"Oh, really?" I try to keep the sarcasm out of my voice.

"I guess I didn't want you to learn about my lowly beginnings. When I first came to the brotherhood, I was rejected by my godfather. I talked about him once—he was the man who raised me after my parents died. So in a way, he was the only person I considered family. What I didn't tell you is that in my screwed-up attempt to keep that family close, I've done something that can't be forgotten or forgiven. I'm actually still surprised he didn't kill me, considering he has no tolerance for traitors. In a way, he didn't really forgive me, just sent me on my way, which was a worse punishment than death to the younger me. I roamed around for a few years, then found myself here, at Nikolai's. He was an old acquaintance of Godfather and me since we used to kill for him a long time ago, before you came along,"

"Is your godfather's name Ghost?" I murmur.

A rare grin I've never seen on Kyle's face loosens his expression, making him appear younger, less guarded. "You know him."

"Everyone in the Bratva does. *Dedushka* used to mention his name among the inner circle. He's the hitman my grandfather worked with the most. He used to say Ghost kills without leaving a trace behind and is the best at what he does."

"He is. We are."

"So you belong to the same organization as him?"

"I do."

I want to probe him some more, but I could slip with what I already know about his organization. So I remain silent, hoping he will be the one to continue talking.

The way he spoke about his godfather—Ghost—is so different from anything he's spoken about before. It's clear that he shares a connection with the man to the point that he calls him family. But he mentioned doing something unforgivable, so maybe that's the reason he's barely talked about Ghost before.

This is one of the few times Kyle has opened up about the past without me having to poke and prod. He's closed off to a fault and always dodged any of my questions with his charming humor. What an irony that he's talking this freely after he thinks I lost my memories.

He strokes the back of my hand, leisurely, as if we're an old couple satisfied with being in each other's company. "After I was separated from Godfather, I had no purpose. I was so used to being his right-hand that I didn't know what to do with my life after. So I decided to go back to my roots, and that wasn't that much of a fun idea. But then, something happened."

"What?" I ask, despite myself.

"You did, Princess."

"Me?"

"After I met you, I saw one of Godfather's traits in you."

"Which traits?"

"You're special in your own way, but one day, you might end up like him."

I get the meaning behind his words without him having to spell it out. One day, he will do something unforgivable and then our paths will never cross again.

Once he knows what I'm plotting for him, that's probably what will happen.

Not releasing my hand, he kicks the car into gear. The entire drive is spent in doomed silence. I bring out my phone and focus on replying to mundane emails. However, my mind keeps skipping back to what Kyle told me. My mind goes into overdrive analyzing the bits about his godfather and the organization he spent his entire childhood in.

He must have suffered when he was younger. He must've been robbed of basic human rights. Here I thought my childhood was screwed up, but it doesn't compare to his. However, does that give him the right to screw other lives over? Mine included?

The car comes to a halt in front of a fancy Italian restaurant, cutting off my train of thought. I step out but ignore his elbow when he offers it to me.

When the hostess asks us if we have a reservation, Kyle offers her his charming smile. "Nicolo's friends, love. Tell him Kyle sends his regards."

Her eyes nearly bug out and she appears flustered as she calls for one of the waiters. "Of course, sir. Welcome."

So this is one of the Italians' businesses. I've never been here before, but I rarely eat out anyway. Ruslan and Katia never join me at the table and remain on guard, and I hate having them alert in public places. I'm not surprised that Kyle is close enough with the Lucianos' underboss, Nicolo, to the point of using his name for favors. He's a snake that way, and he has the best connections to the heads of crime organizations through Adrian.

The waiter guides us to a table that's out of view near the wall. No window is close by, and the other patrons are far away. This is why I don't like eating out; the entire experience is tarnished by security measures.

I order pasta with seafood and Kyle orders some complicated Italian dish that I'm sure will taste like shit. He then asks the waiter for a 1979 Chateau Grand-Marteau wine.

The waiter brings the bottle back, smiling as he carefully opens it. "Excellent taste, sir."

After the waiter pours him a glass, Kyle swirls the wine and inhales before nodding. "Thank you."

The waiter places the bottle on the table with extra care, as if it's some sort of a national treasure.

While we wait for our food, Kyle pours me a glass.

"What's the occasion?" I ask.

"There doesn't need to be an occasion for us to drink good wine."

"I didn't know you liked wine."

His sharp stare pins me in place over the rim of his cup. "Know?"

Shit. This is why spending more time with him is dangerous. I fall into easy conversation with him and forget about my amnesia plan. Thankfully, I recover quickly. "You look like the strong-stuff type."

"I actually prefer wine, but it doesn't suit my killer image so I've been hiding it."

I mask a smile behind my napkin. Who knew Kyle was more of the wine type?

"What are you laughing at, Princess?"

"Your love for wine."

"Those who have not tasted wine—good wine, not the cheap stuff—are missing out."

"You just don't look like a wine person."

"And what type of person do I look like?" He places the glass close to his nose and inhales deeply.

"I don't know. Maybe Jack Daniels."

"Well, the last time I bought Jack Daniels, we had so much fun on our wedding night."

My cheeks feel like they're on fire. "I don't remember that."

"I do, and that's enough." He pauses. "For now."

I take the glass, attempting to drink it all in one go, but Kyle places his hand on the top of mine. His touch is soft, almost like he's trying to touch not only my hand but also other invisible parts of me.

His eyes gleam as he speaks in a seductive tone. "You have to smell it first."

"Is that a rule?"

"No, but you'll enjoy it much better, believe me."

I'll be damned if I believe another word out of his mouth,

but I do as I'm told anyway and take a sniff of the wine. It does smell good, fermented and a bit old. It's like I could get drunk on the smell alone.

I take my first sip, closing my eyes to relish the taste that fills my throat.

"How does it feel?"

At Kyle's voice, I open my eyes, not realizing I closed them for long.

"It's fine."

"It's more than fine. It's exquisite." His eyes never leave mine as he speaks and sips from his own glass. Then he licks the wine off his lips as his gaze slowly slides to my breasts.

I clear my throat. "I'm up here."

He doesn't break eye contact. "You're also down there."

Jerk.

He really has an infuriating type of confidence that can't be either measured or contained. An asshole through and through.

My phone vibrates before I can give him a piece of my mind.

Vlad.

He wouldn't call unless it was an emergency. I abandon the glass on the table and stand up. "I have to take this call."

"Who is it?"

"Work-related." I leave before he can question me any more.

I round the corner toward a small back terrace and make sure no one is around before I answer. "Is everything all right?"

"No. Rolan called Sergei and told him if he doesn't retreat, he'll bring in the Albanians and it'll be a bloodbath."

"That fucker."

"We need to move before they do. The one you mentioned—will he be useful?"

"Yes."

"Is he someone I know?"

"More than know."

"Who?"

"Kyle."

There's a pause on the other end before he repeats, "Kyle?"

"I'll tell you all about it later. I have to go back before he suspects me."

"Are you sure about this, Rai?"

A part of me isn't, but that part is the same one who cried for the bastard after he left me. That part is the one who's broken after I listened to Kyle's plans for my family.

So no, that part won't handle this.

"Yeah, I'm sure."

I slip my hand in my bag and grab the small bottle of medicine. Drinking wine won't be the same again for him.

I've heard stories about the black widow spider who kills her mate after mating, and I always found it fascinating how she followed her instinct, even if it meant killing her own husband.

I guess we're the same that way.

EIGHT

Kyle

RAI SAYS SHE'S A BIT TIRED AND WANTS TO GO home.

I insist on dropping her off even though her guards follow after us. I have developed the habit of not leaving her side. It's not only a control freak trait. Whenever I do leave her, I feel like something disastrous will happen to her in my absence.

It doesn't help that I've been getting the feeling she's hiding something from me. I don't know what it is exactly, but it's there in her bright gaze sometimes.

I'll eventually figure it out even though Rai always has her walls up around me. The fact that she lost her memories doesn't change her personality.

She doesn't spare me a glance during the entire ride, focusing on her phone, replying to work emails and whatnot. Her workaholic nature is still the same even with lost memories.

As soon as we stop in front of the house, she climbs out without saying a word.

I follow after and grab her by the arm. She swings around so fast, her hand lays on my chest for balance.

"What?" There's subtle wariness in her tone that I wouldn't have noticed if I weren't so attuned to her physical reaction. It's almost as if she's scared, but of what? Who?

I palm her cheek and she remains as still as a statue, her breathing crackling before she whispers, "What is it?"

"Do you remember when I told you there are times when you have to make drastic decisions?"

She gulps, her throat working with the motion. It takes everything in me not to grab her by that throat and kiss the fuck out of her until I bruise her delicate lips. I should really get a fucking trophy for abstaining the past week. Having her by my side and not touching her is bloody blasphemy. However, she's been weak and doesn't eat properly, so I will wait until she's in better shape. Because the next time I fuck her, she'll be all in like usual.

"I don't. I have no memories, remember?"

The fucking memories.

I try telling myself I'll make her learn everything about us and, with time, she'll remember me, but the fact remains: I loathe this feeling.

I was never a nobody in Rai's life, not even when we lived continents apart, so being a nobody to her now is like a black hole. With every passing day, that hole gets bigger, wider, deeper, and it'll eventually drag me to its bottom if I let it.

That's why I've been telling her pieces of my life I didn't offer before. I'm even mentioning my real parents when everyone else thinks Igor is my father. My logic was simple: if she gets to know me better, maybe she'll understand my motives and eventually remember me.

"I once said that when you're cornered and have no way

out except if you hurt others, that's exactly what you should do, Princess."

"What made you have that philosophy?"

"I've been in such a situation before, and I figured the only method to get out of it alive was if I kill my way out. Sure, I could've come up with a more traditional method, but that's not how the world works."

"So you solve all your problems by using that philosophy?"

"Most of the time."

"But there are some times where you don't use it?"

Yes. There are times like these where I want to throw everything into the air, carry her in my arms, and go far away from this world and all the tragedies associated with it.

Instead of telling her that, I brush my lips against hers for the briefest second before I claim her mouth. Her taste is both an aphrodisiac and an adrenaline wave. She makes me feel like everything is possible, including the part where I will whisk her with me once my mission is complete.

Rai doesn't kiss me back or wrap her arms around me, but she opens her lips the slightest bit, allowing me to feast on her tongue and drink in her scent.

Jesus fucking Christ. She's the best thing I've ever had the pleasure of tasting, and if the bulge in my trousers is any indication, I'm more than ready for more.

I pull away to not fuck her over the hood of the car. While I'm completely fine with the public setting, I might have to gouge out the eyes of every fucking guard who looks at her, and that's just extra work with no pleasure.

Rai stares at me funny as if she's searching for something on my face or relearning my features all over again.

I allow her explorations, but only because I also want to study her and engrave her expression to memory so whenever I think of her or crave to touch her, I'll have this image of her in the corner of my mind.

"Don't you have to go back to the company?" she murmurs.

"One more moment. I haven't gotten my fill of you."

"Do you ever?"

"Nah, not really. So stay still." I brush her hair behind her ear, letting the golden strands fall between my fingers. She's been wearing it down lately, probably because she doesn't remember her cold, stern phase, and while I love how she looks, I'm constantly in the mood to snipe down every fucker who looks in her direction.

"How long am I supposed to stay here, Kyle?"

"As long as it takes, wife."

"Aren't you tired of calling me your wife when I said I don't remember the marriage?"

"Aren't you tired of denying it when it's the truth?"

"I can never win with you, can I?"

"You can try. I love it when you try, especially that other time when you sucked me off to snatch some power back."

Her cheeks heat. "I did not."

"Yes, you did, and it was hot as fuck. Mmmm. Thinking about it makes me hard." I press the evidence against her stomach. "How are you going to deal with it, Princess?"

"If by dealing with it, you mean I'll get rid of your dick, then sure, I'll deal with it."

I laugh, my head tipping back with the motion. "You're fucking crazy."

"And that's funny because…"

"Because you're only this way with me, whether you have memories or not." I brush my lips against hers one final time. "Rest well and wait for me."

"Why would I do that?"

"Because I'm staking my claim tonight." I wink and she swallows, heat rising to her cheeks, before she turns around and heads inside.

After I make sure she's safely in the house, I go back to my car.

Peter, the useless guard Igor planted at my side, taps on my window. I lower it and stare at him, not bothering to hide my irritation.

He's holding a weird gun, twirling it between his hands as he speaks. "You want me to come along?"

"No. Stay put."

"You never take me with you these days."

"Because you're useless."

"Not so useless." He points the gun at me. "You know what this is?"

"No, but I'm sure you'll bore me to death about it."

"It's an anesthesia gun. It can be very powerful."

"A bullet is more powerful, kid." I put my window up and drive out of the property.

I have some sort of a company meeting, but I don't give two fucks about V Corp and their nonsense strategies.

My actual meeting is with Flame. We need to plot the next attack, which, if it all goes well, will be the last.

At this point, both the Russians and the Irish have lost many soldiers and exhausted their powers. Even the fucker Damien who thinks he has endless destructive energy can't be on the attack forever. Actually, he's a bull who doesn't stop unless he's dead. If this were an ancient war, he would be the general who wouldn't raise the white flag, even if all the other units did.

But even he can't do one consecutive attack after the other.

At this rate, Rolan or Sergei needs a large-scale attack that will wipe out the other party's army.

I know exactly who I want to lose the most in this war.

After a twenty-minute drive, I notice a black van following me, so instead of going to the rooftop where I agreed to meet Flame, I stop the car at the back of an abandoned warehouse.

Wires and industrialized waste are scattered all over the site, as if this place was used as the set for an apocalyptic film.

I pretend this is my final destination and lean against the car, retrieving my phone.

Kyle: I have company.

His reply comes in a second.

Flame: How could you let them follow you? What are you, an amateur?

Kyle: I didn't let them. I stopped, didn't I?

Flame: After they followed? Amateur.

Kyle: Piss off, arsehole.

Flame: All the better. I can't be away from the boring club for too long. Let's reschedule.

I'm about to hide my phone when it lights up with another text from him.

Flame: Don't taint my name by telling anyone I trained you, amateur.

That fucker.

Though, it is weird. I should've noticed it at the beginning, but it's like some of my inhibitions are muted.

Slipping the phone in my pocket, I draw my gun and make sure the magazine is full.

That's when the first one comes out.

In the beginning, I don't recognize the face of the guard. They all wear black like members of some secret society who judge each other for not having the same grim dress code.

When the second man steps beside him, my hold tightens on the gun even though it's still by my side.

"What the fuck are you doing here, Vladimir?"

Five more guards join him, and the seven of them surround me in a circle, all with weapons. I know for a fact Vladimir doesn't move without a prior plan. He might seem like a stupid burly bear, but he's far from it. He knows exactly where to hit and how to do it with the least damage possible.

The fact that he brought in so many guards for me is alarming.

"Is this some sort of a late welcome party?" I keep my tone light, jokey even. "Please tell me you brought presents."

I grin as I stare at their faces and behind them, discreetly searching for an escape route. Since this warehouse isn't where I intended to meet Flame, I'm not familiar with the area and, therefore, my options are limited.

What makes matters worse are the guards Vladimir brought with him; his three senior soldiers, the ones he uses for extreme torture, and there are two of Sergei's merciless guards as well.

If he went as far as to gather the strongest he has, this is more serious than I originally anticipated.

"No presents? What happened to the Russian hospitable nature? But fine, whatever. Do I at least get something to drink at my late welcoming party? I'll even settle for your beloved vodka today. See? I'm not so difficult."

"You're going to answer our questions, and you're going to answer them truthfully." Vladimir's no-nonsense tone booms in the silence of the space.

"I'll happily answer. What are your questions?" I maintain my smile, making sure it's neither taunting nor threatening.

I don't want to kill them, because it'd be a fucking hassle to hide the bodies and come up with excuses, but if they keep getting on my nerves, that's exactly what will happen.

"Come with us." Vladimir motions at the warehouse.

"I would rather we talk here. I have a thing against rusty ware-houses. Do you know how many germs are in places like these?"

"Cut the sarcastic attitude and follow us."

"I vote no."

"This is no fucking democracy. You don't have a choice."

"I beg to differ. I do have a choice. In fact, I choose to walk away from here without answering any questions. You lost your chance, Vladimir."

I attempt to leave but the guards close in on me, and I tighten my hold, calculating who to shoot first. Probably the bald head, one of Vladimir's closest soldiers and possibly the strongest. If he's gone, I'll have a better chance of finishing off the others.

Vladimir shakes his head and they stop in their tracks.

What the fuck?

They don't even retrieve their guns, remaining frozen in place.

"I said I'm leaving." I try again and pause at the slur in my voice. I'm not the type who drinks until I get drunk, because that's equivalent to letting my guard down and signing my own death certificate.

Back in the restaurant, I only had two glasses of wine, which I can tolerate perfectly, so what's with the slur at the end of my speech?

"The fuuuck are you doing?" I point my gun at the bald head. "Geeet youuur weapon."

The slur is getting worse, not better.

"Don't waste a bullet on him," says Vladimir—or the twin that just appeared by his side. "Our work has already been done for us."

The gun slips from my hand and drops to the ground. It's the first time I've lost control over my weapon. It's like my hand has no strength to hold a gun.

Our work has already been done for us.

My vision blurs, and the seven men turn into fourteen. That's when the dooming realization hits me.

I've been poisoned.

My body swings back and I slam against one of the guards before I fall on my knees to the ground.

As the world spins around, the pieces slowly come together.

There's only one person who could've poisoned me today: the one who poured me my second glass of wine.

My wife stabbed me in the back and threw me to her pack of wolves.

NINE

Kyle

MY EYES OPEN SLOWLY, MY LIDS STICKING TO EACH other.

The first thing I notice is that I'm sitting down and completely bound to a metal chair.

Plain gray walls surround me, and rusty metal machines flicker in the corners. I shake my head; no, they're not the ones moving—it's my vision.

I try to move, but thick ropes hold me in place. I'm sitting on a metal chair, my hands bound behind my back and feet strapped to the metal.

This isn't a new experience for me. With enough wiggling about, I can flip the chair backward then bend one of its legs, and once I free my ankles, I'll have more leeway to release myself.

Before I can act on my plan, I'm surrounded by the lucky seven who captured me. They didn't even bother to take me to one of their compounds and just moved me inside the warehouse. If the location holds no importance, then it should mean my life or death doesn't matter.

Vladimir steps forward, handing his jacket to one of his underlings, and makes a show of rolling his sleeves to his elbows and revealing his Bratva tattoos. While doing so, he watches me with his usual grumpy, brooding expression that makes him such a bore.

"I didn't know we were close enough to play kinky games, Vladimir. Before we start, my safe word is *Let me go.*" My tone is humorous, but it doesn't camouflage the taste of betrayal burning down my throat and over my chest.

Rai didn't only poison me, she also handed me over to her men so they'd finish the job.

I'm supposed to be mad, to let my anger take over, but any semblance of it is squashed by that fucking burning feeling.

"You're quite edgy, aren't you?" I continue in the same joking tone. "Is this place similar to where you usually live?"

"This will be your grave if you don't answer our questions."

"I don't like knife play either. All that blood is a hassle to clean."

"Are you done being a smart fucker?"

"I'm just communicating legitimate concerns, Vladimir. We need to have ground rules for these things."

"*Rules?*" He scoffs. "Since when do you believe in those?"

"Since the Bratva. Your rules are no joke, mate."

"I'm not your *mate.* Now either answer me or we'll start with the knife you hate so much." He pauses to drive the information home. "Who's your insider with the Irish?"

"And I should tell you because...?"

"Because if you don't, you'll regret it. That's your final warning, Hunter."

"I know we're doing kinky stuff, but we're not exactly at the point in our relationship where we'd have a cheeky heart-to-heart, eh?"

Vladimir raises his fist and punches me across the face so hard, I flinch in my seat and blood explodes from my upper lip.

Motherfucker.

"This will only get worse with every wrong answer." He tightens his fist. "What are your plans?"

"Going home to my beautiful wife. Do you think she'll mind whatever kink we're exercising here since she's the one who set us up together—"

I'm cut off when he jams his fist into my face, nearly breaking my fucking nose. I gasp on air, spitting away the blood that's gathered at my mouth.

Vladimir doesn't seem bothered by the red that's smudging his fingers, but then again, he specializes in torture, so this entire scene is his playground.

"I repeat, what are your plans?"

"I just told you. It's not my fault you don't believe me."

He punches and kicks me in the stomach at the same time. I fall backward with the chair and hit the ground with a loud thud.

I spit blood on the ground as Vladimir's henchman lift me up so he can hit me again, this time using both his fists as if I'm his punching bag.

While Vladimir isn't the most reckless like Damien or the most ruthless like Adrian, he's the most brutish and doesn't hesitate to use his force to get what he wants.

I need to do something before he smashes my face into the ground and walks all over it, but I have no clue how much they've figured out. This could be a ploy to make me talk, but that's improbable since Vladimir doesn't move without concrete evidence.

Until I figure that out, I can take torture. Having my background comes in handy at times like these. I had torture training, which was basically being tortured until I was hallucinating and feverish and on the verge of death. After all, the only way to survive torture is to go through it.

Physical torture is nothing. I lived through it and know exactly how to handle it. Pain is concentrated in nerve endings, and the best way to get past that is to numb it. If you don't think about it, the agonizing sensation eventually vanishes.

The pitfall in my plan is that I can't forget the reason I'm here in the first place, the reason I am now serving as Vladimir's punching bag.

My wife.

That type of torture is way different from a physical one. That type of torture is what has led countless men to their breaking points.

Sucking in a breath, I meet Vladimir's gaze. While it seems like he's watching me with a neutral expression, deep down it's anything but. He must be celebrating the chance to finally hit me. After all, he's hated me ever since the day I came back and snatched Rai from under his protective shield.

It's not actually jealousy since I don't think he's capable of feeling romantic things, but it's more that he thought Rai was his responsibility after he pledged to Nikolai that he'd protect her.

"How did you get me, Vladimir? Because we both know it wasn't strength."

"Do you want to feel my strength, Kyle? I've been taking it easy on you, but if you insist, I have no reason to refuse."

Easy? He disfigured my face and calls it *easy?*

"I just want to know why you have to be so difficult by tying me up and stuff."

"You're here to answer for your sins."

"Sins?" I laugh through the blood. "Have you suddenly turned into God or something? But it's useless since I don't believe in holy things."

"Just because you don't believe in them, doesn't mean you

get to escape them." He drives his fist into my face until a crack of bones echoes in the air.

It hurts like a mother, and I grit my teeth against the constant pulsing of pain.

"If you want to play..." He shows me his fists, which are now dripping with blood—my blood—all over the ground. "I'll indulge."

"Where is she?" I murmur, staring at the door opposite me. "Is she there? Or are there cameras through which she can watch the show?"

He grabs me by the collar, nearly lifting me and the chair off the ground. "You answer to *me*."

"I answer to no one."

"Then would you rather die?"

"Come out, Princess!" I call, my voice straining. "Don't you think you've watched enough?"

"Shut the fuck up." Vladimir hits me again.

"I thought you wanted me to talk—now you want me to shut it? Make up your mind, you grumpy-arse fucker. Come out, Princess. I thought we shared things," I say with humor, which is my usual way of deflecting reality, but the words stab me inside my bloody soul. I really thought we shared things, but she went ahead and stabbed me in the back.

"You don't speak to her. You speak to me." Vladimir's strong voice booms in the silence of the room, his accent getting thicker.

"I won't talk unless I see my wife, so if you want to kill me, then go right ahead. But as you know, you won't get anything out of my corpse."

"You think I won't kill you?" Vladimir pulls his gun from his waistband and points it at my temple. "You've always been a pest who didn't belong in the brotherhood. I don't care what Nikolai or Sergei see in you, or that you think you're all that just because you eliminated some targets like a fucking dog for hire. You have no loyalty, know no principles, and follow no morals, and because of that, you don't belong here."

"Finally. Your true fucking colors, Vladimir. Aren't they nice and bloody shiny?"

The reason he respected my presence is because the bosses were the ones who ordered it. If it was up to him, he would have kicked me out a long time ago. So now that he's finally getting his chance to get back at me, he's using it to the fullest.

I have no doubt he will pull the trigger.

"Are you going to talk or should I turn those fucking eyes dead?"

"The only person I'll talk to is my wife."

Why do I keep calling her my wife when she betrayed our vows?

But I guess I betrayed those first when I turned our wedding into a bloodbath.

No idea how it happened, but I was taken by surprise. Being blindsided by an aspect of my life has weakened me, and this doesn't even seem like a phase.

The door opens and I remain still as the sound of heels echo on the ground.

I raise my eyes up. They're swollen and one of them is half open, blood dripping over the lid. And yet, I make out Rai standing in front of me. She puts enough distance between us so I couldn't reach out for her even if I somehow had my hands free.

She's still wearing the black dress from earlier, which means she must have come here as soon as I dropped her off.

The traitor wanted to see her handiwork for herself. Well played, Rai. Well fucking played.

But instead of divulging my true emotions, I grin, showing her my bloody teeth. "Vladimir here seems to have a misconception, Princess. Save me from his kinky games."

"Stop being a smartass," she says in a monotone voice, crossing her arms over her chest. "That won't work on us."

Wait a fucking second... "Does this mean you never lost your memories?"

"No, but I fooled you, didn't I?"

Bloody hell.

She did. She *really* did, and I had no way of focusing enough to uncover the lie because I was worried about her safety. I completely let go of my logical side in favor of the fucking thing beating inside my chest.

"Well played, Sokolov. Nikolai must be so proud of his little devil creation."

"I don't care about your games."

"You don't care, huh? Figures, after you poisoned my drink."

Her expression remains the same, as if she abandoned her emotions somewhere and came here void of anything. "Tell Vlad what he wants to know and maybe I'll have him spare your life."

"What makes you think I have something to say?"

"I heard you talking on the phone the day I fell down the stairs, Kyle. I know what you're planning."

Fuck. Was I too loose? Usually, I wouldn't let my guard down, but I was still on painkillers at the time. Not that blaming the meds will solve the issue at hand.

"Did you think I would stand by as you destroy my family?" Her tone turns lethal. "I'll protect them with everything in me."

"Go right ahead."

"You think I'm bluffing?"

"No."

"Then why the fuck aren't you talking?"

"Because it's pointless."

"Don't test me, Kyle. I'll have you killed."

"Do it then. You already poisoned me, so killing me wouldn't make a difference."

A blush covers her cheeks, but it's not out of embarrassment—it's anger, or rather, rage. Why the fuck is *she* angry? I'm the one who's supposed to be boiling.

And yet, all I feel is the cut of her betrayal in a place I thought was long dead with my parents.

"You're ready for death, aren't you?"

"I was born ready for death. I had my resurrection in death and to death I shall return. Isn't that poetic?"

"You're sick."

"I think we've already established that."

"Let me finish him off." Vladimir digs the muzzle of the gun into my temple, causing my head to tilt back.

I don't stare at him—he's not important. My gaze stays locked on Rai's, caught by how her eyes darken then lighten, flitting around as if she's not sure whether to take the gun from Vladimir and shoot me or if it'll be better if she kills me with her bare hands.

A few seconds pass before she shakes her head. "Leave me alone with him."

Vladimir's shoulders snap back. "No."

"I can take care of this. Just wait for me outside." When he doesn't make a move to go, she touches his arm, her voice lowering but not softening. "Trust me."

Vladimir punches me one more time for good measure, and I groan even though I smirk at the fucker. He motions at his guards to follow him, then places the gun in Rai's hand. "We'll be right outside."

The door sliding shut traps me and my wife together.

Our marriage started by blood, and with blood it will end.

TEN

Rai

MY SPINE HAS BEEN SNAPPED IN A LINE SINCE I stepped inside.

Even though I told Vlad to leave, I don't feel like I'm completely in control of the situation. He, Ruslan, and Katia are waiting outside, and I can call them back in, but that would defy the reason why I came inside in the first place.

I try not to stare at Kyle's beaten-up state for too long, but his bloodied lips, eyelids, and nose are hard not to notice. Vlad has beaten him to a pulp, which isn't a surprise considering Vlad's merciless personality when he sets out to punish someone. He made Kyle's handsome face unrecognizable. It should feel better this way. He deserves every bit of pain he's now going through. In fact, he deserves more.

That's what I tell myself anyway, because as I stare at him, that stupid part who had my heart broken when I listened to his phone conversation is now in pain, too.

That fucking part feels as if I'm the one who's been beaten and has swollen eyes and bleeding lips.

But why should it? Kyle's injuries might be physical, but mine run deeper. He slammed into my chest and broke my heart, then walked all over it to the point that I'll never be able to mend it back together again.

And all of that was because I trusted him. Against my better judgment and doubtful personality, I trusted Kyle Hunter, and he smashed that trust to the ground.

Now, my loyalty, my oath, and my duty toward my family are put to the test. Everything I've fought for so far is thrust to the forefront, and I have no way to ignore it.

"Now what?" His voice, although calm, is emotionless, as if he doesn't want to speak at all.

"Now what?" I repeat incredulously, and it takes everything in me not to shout and hit him. I want to hurt him as much as he's ripping me apart from the inside out. "You have the audacity to ask me *now what?*"

"What am I supposed to ask then? You brought me here and got me beaten up, so I suppose you have the rest of it figured out."

I remain silent for a beat, then ask with a calmness I don't feel, "Why me?"

"What?"

"You obviously married me for a reason, so I've been wondering, why did it have to be me? Am I the easiest way in? Is it because you already knew me seven years ago? Or have you been planning this ever since we first met?"

I hate the emotions in my voice; the hurt behind it all translates to painful anger.

Kyle lifts a shoulder. "You were the most convenient way in, Rai Sokolov."

My hands fist on either side of me, and it takes all of my willpower to not surrender to the agitation. If anger consumes me then I'll commit mistakes, and he'll win without even making an effort.

So I hang on to my apparent calm with chipped nails and bloodied fingers. "Was anything you ever told me true?"

"Depends on what I told you. Which part?"

"You have no remorse whatsoever, do you?"

"If you're expecting me to feel sorry for going after the people who slaughtered my fucking parents in front of my eyes, then no, I have no bloody remorse whatsoever."

Up until now, I kind of had the idea that his parents were ghosts. He mentioned that they died, and I thought that was the end of it.

"I was five," he continues with a distant voice. He's staring at me, but he's seeing straight through me. "My mother was killed when she attempted to take me and leave. Then, my father was shot in the back. Both happened in front of my eyes."

The weight of his words strikes me in one brutal blow. It's not only about his parents' tragic deaths, but also about the way he calmly spoke about witnessing their murder when he was only five.

There are no emotions whatsoever behind his voice, as if he's numbed himself to those feelings.

"I don't recall their faces anymore—their alive faces, at least. The only thing I remember of my parents is their vacant eyes and their blood. That's been my driving force ever since I was a boy, but that's not the worst of it. Remember the organization I told you about? It's not a school for killers, it's a fucking torture chamber called The Pit. Since we were able to kill, we were forced to carry out hits for money or for our superiors."

I'm stunned into silence as I piece together what he's told me. Not only did he lose his parents as a boy, he was also made into a killer. All of this happened to him while he was just a child.

No wonder he became the ruthless machine he is today.

No wonder he doesn't hesitate when he kills.

His own life was finished a long time ago, so he finds it fair to step on others and murder them.

"That's how far I've come, and I won't stop until those who reduced my parents into vacant eyes pay."

"And I assume they have something to do with the Irish?"

"Everything to do with the Irish."

"Who from the Irish?"

"Why do you want to know?"

"You already told me the story, so you might as well tell me the perpetrators."

"No. It's my revenge."

"Then at least tell me this. What does the brotherhood have to do with your revenge?"

"Everything."

"What is that supposed to mean?"

"You don't need to know."

"Of course I do!"

"All that concerns you is that I'm after both the Irish and the Russians, so it's better to get rid of me now." He motions with his head at the weapon in my hand. "Just a single shot of that gun will do the job, or would you rather Vladimir do the honors?"

"Stop provoking me. You think I wouldn't do it?"

"I'm pretty sure you'd do it. After all, you poisoned me. Way to go, Princess. I'm proud of you."

"Stop saying things like that."

"Like what? That I'm proud of you?"

"Yes. I don't want you to be proud of me."

"Well, I am. I told you that, once cornered, you need to hurt, bite, and kill your way out, and that's exactly what you did." He coughs, blood dripping down his chin and soaking the collar of his shirt further. "You've come so far since Nikolai passed away. You didn't let his or your parents' deaths affect you. You just held your head high and forged ahead."

Frustrated, angry tears gather in my eyes, but I inhale deeply, refusing to let them out so he won't see how much his words affect me.

Not only by what he just told me, but the entire story about his parents and his upbringing.

No matter how much it rips my heart into pieces, I have a duty and I can't carry on with that duty if I'm this tangled up in his emotions, if I feel them as if they were my own.

"Who knew we would find ourselves in this situation?" I ask slowly.

"What situation?"

"Me holding a gun and you tortured."

"Our marriage started in a bloodbath, did you really expect it to end any differently?"

A pained sigh leaves the depths of my soul. "Were you really always ready for death?"

He nods once then winces. "I've been ready for thirty years. The time I lived until now has been a ticking timer until I get my revenge."

"Then what?"

"Huh?"

"After revenge, what were you planning to do?"

He shrugs as if that's not important. "Go back to England and take on contracts. That sort of thing."

"Then go."

"What?"

I place the gun on the ground and remain hunched down to undo the ropes at his ankles, then release his wrists and torso. Kyle doesn't move, even when he is completely free.

After I'm finished, I step away from him, but I'm not far enough to stop feeling his presence or smelling him.

His signature clean scent fills my nostrils, but it's now accompanied by the stench of blood, strong and poignant.

"What do you mean by *go?*"

I suck in a sharp breath so I can speak with a sliver of calm. "I'm giving you the only way out."

"What way?"

"Forget about revenge and just leave. Go back to England or wherever you want to go. Just don't show your face around here again. I'll make everyone believe you are not made for the Bratva and that we amicably split up." He opens his mouth to speak, but I cut him off. "You can go through the back door over there where there are no guards."

Kyle staggers to his feet and steps toward me.

I step back, my voice turning harsh, like *Dedushka's* when he issued orders. "If I see you again, I'll kill you."

Not waiting for his reply, I gather the gun from the ground, turn around, and march toward the front door.

My legs are heavy, screaming at me to stop and face him again, to take one last look, one last touch.

One last kiss.

Walk away. It's done, Rai. Just walk the fuck away.

Dedushka once told me sacrifices need to be made for the family and that not all of them would be easy; in fact, many would hurt. He said there's no honor without pain.

Now I understand exactly what he means.

As soon as the door closes behind me with a slow click, I brace myself against the wall for support. My chin trembles and my legs are about to fail me.

I'm breathing so violently, as if I'm about to stop any second now. That's when I hear it—the sound of something breaking in my chest.

At first, it's quiet, almost unnoticeable, but it gets louder and louder until it's the only thing I hear.

Ah. This must be what it means to have a broken heart.

The most daunting part is, I don't think this feeling will ever go away.

ELEVEN

Rai

I DON'T FEEL SO GOOD.

That's an understatement. I can at least admit that I'm the worst I've been since…*Dedushka*'s death.

A weight perches on my chest, confiscating my air supply and replacing it with a harsh, merciless gloom.

It's draining me.

Asphyxiating me.

And all I want to do is just…scream.

But at the same time, I don't have the luxury of losing myself to that feeling. It's over. Everything is…done.

It's been exactly two hours since I freed Kyle. Just two hours and it feels like fucking years already.

I was never good at letting things go. I never get used to the feeling with time like most people. Instead, I hold on to it and keep replaying it in my head during every waking moment. I didn't let go when Mom died or when I was separated from

Dad and Reina, and I definitely didn't let go when *Dedushka* left me all alone with this pack of wolves.

I lost too many things and became horrible at moving on. So it's not a surprise that I keep replaying Kyle's words and seeing his bloodied face over and over. At this rate, it'll consume me and eat at me from the inside out little by little.

So instead of getting lost in my own head, I choose to go back to V Corp and busy myself with work. Kai called to schedule a meeting, and I asked him to come today. I need all the distractions possible.

Ruslan and Katia accompanied me silently. They've been sulking ever since I freed Kyle. I left before Vlad could catch me because he'd have my head on a platter, but I'll deal with him later.

Ruslan even told me that Kyle isn't the type who will disappear just like that, but he forgot that Kyle has no choice because if he comes near my family or the brotherhood again, I will have to kill him.

Kai shows up on time, as usual, gives a firm handshake, and joins me in the lounge area. His guard remains outside with Ruslan and Katia.

While I wanted this meeting to happen so I could distract myself, I should've prepared more for it. Kai is a bit like Adrian. He doesn't give up and runs a lot deeper than his nonchalant façade. So when he plans something, he goes the extra mile that not many people know exists.

Kai is the brain of the Yakuza here and has strong ties to their counterparts in Japan. In fact, he has often been asked to go back to lead one of the clans in his country, but he prefers staying here.

At one of the parties we attended, he once told me that New York is more fun with all the warring clans and organizations. A man who gets off on chaos should never be taken lightly, because you never know when he'll get bored and instigate said chaos.

He sips leisurely from a cup of green tea while I opted for a coffee. Truth is, I prefer to just throw everything out and hit the bar.

If it were a few weeks ago, I would've spent ample time studying Kai's movements and trying to hold the upper hand in any negotiations.

But now my mind feels kind of blank, and instead of shooing it away, I hold on to it. The blankness means I don't have to think about what happened in the warehouse. About Kyle's bloodied face and tortured about. About whether or not he already left the country now.

"I heard you're having problems with the Irish," Kai starts nonchalantly.

"A little."

"Isn't that an understatement?"

"Perhaps, but it'll end one way or another."

"Don't you think it's taking more time than it should?"

"It is."

"It's natural, though."

"Natural, how?"

"You and the Irish were always on bad terms."

"How do you know that?"

"I might have heard tales."

"What kind of tales?"

"The interesting kind."

Ugh. He'll keep dragging me along before he finally divulges it. "Care to elaborate?"

"Let's say that you were friends once upon a time."

"We...were?" The brotherhood and the Irish have always been at each other's throats for as long as I can remember. Damien's dispute is only the straw that broke the camel's back.

"Yes. Nikolai never mentioned that?"

"Not really. I know our Bratva counterparts in Russia, Boston, and Chicago can get along with the Irish, but that was never the case for us."

Kai's eyes twinkle as he takes a steady sip of his tea. "You got along with them a long time ago."

"How long are we talking about?"

"Decades."

"How would you know? You couldn't have been present at the time."

"No. But I have birds."

A bird is Kai's word for a spy. He has lots of them. *Birds*.

"And what did your *birds* tell you?"

"Birds talk a lot and make so much noise, so I don't always take their word for granted."

"You wouldn't have mentioned it if you didn't already suspect something."

"This is why I like you." He snaps his fingers. "You're quick-witted and understand the situation just like that."

"Does the compliment mean you'll tell me?"

His lips move in a soft smile, which completely contradicts the tales I've heard about how he mutilates his opponents with his sword. He takes his love for *kendo* to another level that I'm sure isn't instilled in the noble form of the Japanese martial arts.

"What if I told you there are some illegitimate ties?"

"Illegitimate ties?" I repeat.

"As you said, I wasn't present. I've only heard passing birds talk about things that might not be true."

"What type of things?"

"Things that include secret alliances and meetings in the dark."

"Between who and who?"

"Someone Irish and someone Russian, and by someone, I mean they held—or hold—some importance in both organizations."

"And I guess you're not going to divulge the names?"

"I'm afraid my birds aren't *that* talkative."

More like *he* is not that talkative. He's keeping his cards to himself and won't reveal them unless he deems it necessary. "Why are you telling me this?"

"You seem quite stressed about this situation, and I don't like my partners stressed. See, that takes away from their efficiency."

I raise a brow. "Am I supposed to take that as a jab or a compliment?"

"I prefer the latter. I don't mean to offend you."

"Then there's no offense taken."

"Good, good." He savors his tea. "Now to the reason I'm here."

I place one leg over the other, getting comfortable. "Pray tell."

"Are you going to sell me more shares at a price fit for partners?"

The clever jerk. Kai knows V Corp's net profit will keep on rising, and he's one hundred percent behind profit. He will keep his octopus hands around us as long as it keeps doubling and tripling his initial investment.

"I would love to, but I Igor mentioned that you're not very sure about our partnership. I heard the meeting with Abe didn't go so well."

"Yes, that. He came to ask us for help, but we don't offer help. We believe partners benefit each other. In a partnership, you give as much as you take."

"Does this mean if I give you a profitable price, you will send your men over?"

He takes a sip of his tea before his sharp, dark eyes meet mine. "This means it'll be a good start of a partnership."

"And you'll personally see to it?"

"Definitely."

That's a good sign, because even though Abe, the head of the Yakuza, isn't open-minded, he listens to Kai. Not only is he the second man in command, he's also quite cunning.

"In that case." I raise my coffee mug. "I'll ask my secretary to send you some drafts."

"I will be waiting."

The door opens and I grit my teeth. The only people who would barge in like that are either one of the elite group or Sergei. Since my granduncle has an appointment with a doctor today, my options are narrowed down.

Sure enough, Vlad saunters in, eyes flaming and face tightened in a permanent scowl. Of course. It was only a matter of time before he followed.

Kai smiles at him. "Vladimir, long time no see."

"Kai." Vlad greets back, barely tipping his head in the Japanese's direction.

He looks like a man on a mission and in no mood for small talk. Not that he ever is.

Kai's smile remains in place as he stands up and buttons his jacket, then shakes my hand. "I'll be in touch."

"Looking forward to it."

His hand remains in mine for a second too long. "Before I go, may I give you a piece of advice?"

"Yes, of course."

"History does repeat itself, so you might want to look closely at that."

And with that, Kai releases my hand and steps out of the office.

As soon as the door closes behind him, Vlad is in my face. "Why *the fuck* did you let him escape?"

I sit down and continue drinking from my coffee even though it's turned cold. "Because he was useless."

"Useless? You had to feign amnesia for *useless?*"

"I overestimated the information he has. Turns out it holds no value to us."

"We get to decide that after we torture him. Besides, since he obviously kept things from the Vory, he deserves death."

That asshole has too many enemies to count. Vlad would be the first person to shoot Kyle in the face if he got the chance. Damien, Mikhail, and even Kirill would follow. None of them actually like him because he rose in the ranks so fast and didn't work hard enough like the rest of them.

And while Kyle's sin—the fact that he plotted the brotherhood's demise—is punishable by the worst form of death, I just couldn't do it or let anyone else do it for me.

The breaking of my heart that I heard earlier is still resonating in my chest like an echo. Even though I tried to ignore it during the afternoon, now all I want to do is curl up in a ball in a dark place and stay there.

"Just let him go, Vlad."

"I can't just let the motherfucker *go*. He needs to pay in blood."

"Have you forgotten that he's still my husband?"

"That doesn't make him untouchable."

"No, but if everyone else finds out he's a traitor, it'll reflect badly on me. Kirill and Mikhail are already plotting my fall, and if I give them this chance, they won't hesitate to chop my head off. So…just let it go. For my sake, Vlad."

His lips twist and I'm sure he has a thousand objections, but I played the card he can't refuse—me. It's a low blow, but it was the only way he'd ever agree. Besides, none of what I said is a lie.

"Fine, but if he shows up again, I'll fucking murder him."

"If he shows up again, I'll do it myself."

Vlad gives me an undecipherable glance as if he doesn't believe me, but leaves it at that.

I leave work late and barely check on Anastasia before my numb feet lead me to my room.

When I open the door, the first thing that hits me is his distinctive scent, and I hate that. I hate that his presence is a breathing being in every corner of the room.

It's not only about his jacket that's casually flung on the chair or the masculine traces he left behind. That's only the beginning of it, because everything in this place reminds me of him.

It reminds me of how he sneaks up on me from behind and picks me up just so he can fuck me on the bed.

Or when I wake up to him either spooning me from behind or eating me out until I scream.

Or when we wrestle to see who gets the upper hand and I end up losing—mostly on purpose—just so he'll fuck me roughly.

Or when he thrusts toys into me, his gleaming eyes never leaving mine, because we both love the depravity of it.

It hasn't been a long marriage, but he's became such an inseparable part of my life. Now that he's gone, I have no clue how the hell I am going to pick up the pieces.

I wish I really had amnesia so all of this would be easier.

But would it, really?

I don't bother with a shower or with changing my clothes.

Removing my dress, I kick it and the shoes away and flop on the bed in only my underwear.

Even the damn sheets smell like him, clean and masculine.

It won't be long before his presence completely vanishes. It's for the best. I know that, but a tear slides down my cheeks as I close my eyes.

God, it hurts. It's not supposed to, but I can almost hear my heart shattering to pieces all over again.

The pain is so raw, I gasp for air. It's like I caught a nasty disease with no cure.

I try telling myself it'll be better with time, but I said that lie seven years ago and it never worked. If anything, I kept thinking about him day in and day out like an addict.

I hated it.

I hated myself back then.

So why am I repeating it again?

No answer comes to mind, but tears do. They won't stop, and I fall asleep with my eyes wet and my heart in shreds.

Soft fingers wipe them away before they slide down my body.

I startle, eyes snapping open.

A large shadow looms over me. I scream, but his hand muffles any sound I might make.

I pause as his scent fills my nostrils and seeps into my bones.

Is this a dream or a nightmare? Perhaps it's both.

"You didn't really think you would get rid of me, did you, Princess?"

TWELVE

Rai

Aᴛ ꜰɪʀꜱᴛ, I ᴛʜɪɴᴋ I'ᴍ ʜᴀʟʟᴜᴄɪɴᴀᴛɪɴɢ. Pᴇʀʜᴀᴘꜱ this is another play of my imagination, or maybe I'm still asleep and lost in the dreamland where everything is possible.

However, when my eyes clash with his in the darkness of the room, something inside me shatters, and it's not the same sensation I had the entire day ever since I left him in the warehouse. This one is harsher and leaves me gasping and finding nothing but the distinctive taste of his hand.

His hold on my mouth forbids me from saying anything, but I couldn't speak even if he allowed me to. It's like being trapped in an out-of-body experience where I keep levitating with no plans to come down to the ground.

In the dark, his face is shadowed by the night, but due to the small light coming through the balcony, I can still decipher the bruises on his lids, the diagonal cut across his lip, and the smudges of blood all over his face. But even with those, strangely, all I see is the Kyle I knew from before, the arrogant handsome jerk who infuriated me most of the time.

I didn't think I would forget his face this soon, but isn't it odd that I can recall exactly how he looked? Or that I can easily imagine that face while I'm sleeping or in my darkest hours?

When he speaks, his voice is quiet, but it feels like being slammed into a sturdy, impenetrable wall. "Here's the thing. I'm not leaving."

I mumble against his hand, my body arching off the bed to fight him off. Not that it works. He pins both my wrists above my head and his thighs are caging mine. The position is so familiar to my starved body, but that's not what I force my brain to focus on.

It's his words.

What the hell does he mean by saying he won't leave? I already broke my heart for this, and it needs to be done for everyone's sake.

I attempt to lift my leg, but his thighs tighten, holding mine in place, and he digs his fingers into the soft flesh of my wrist.

"Stop fighting."

"Mmmm…" I mumble what is supposed to be a 'Let me go.'

"You should know by now that the harder you fight, the more ruthless I become, so *stop it*."

I open my mouth and bite his hand. Kyle groans but doesn't release me.

"Go ahead, Rai. Do whatever you like. You can bite me, shoot me, or bury me in a construction site, but that won't change the decision I made. Do you know what that decision is?" I shake my head frantically against his palm, and he lowers his head so he's speaking in a low tone against my lips. "We made vows, and I intend to keep them. Till death do us part."

No.

Why can't he understand that this isn't only about me? It's about the brotherhood and his unforgivable betrayal. If Sergei or any of the others find out about what he's done—and what he's planning to do—they will execute him Bratva style. I gave him a way out no one would have offered him. I gave him the chance to leave the brotherhood alive, but he just bounced right back.

I buck against him, trying to hit him in the crotch, but he releases my mouth and catches my knee. "I think you got me beaten enough for one day after you betrayed and poisoned me."

"I didn't poison you." They were sleeping pills, and I read the instructions a thousand times before I slipped them in his drink.

"You only handed me over on a platter so Vladimir could do the job for you." His voice is calm, but I sense the rage beneath it. "You *betrayed* me."

"You betrayed me *first*. You stabbed me in the back first! So excuse me if I stopped your master plan and stood up for myself!"

I wiggle against him with everything I have. I'm well aware that he's stronger than me and can subdue me easily, but I don't stop squirming until I free my wrists. I punch him in the chest where he's already injured, and when he winces, I use the chance to push him down and get on top.

Unlike what I expected, he doesn't fight me or try to wrestle me down. I'm breathing harshly, the sheets tangled around my feet as my thighs splay wide on either side of his taut abdomen. My palms are fisted in his shirt, nails digging into his skin, but Kyle's hands remain inert on either side of him, as if he doesn't want to touch me in this state.

It's for the best, because I feel like I'm one breath away from combusting, and my voice translates the pent-up energy. "Pretend this is seven years ago and leave without looking back."

"I'm not doing that again."

"Why the hell not? You did it just fine before."

"I can't do it again." The quiet in his voice, the vulnerability in it shatters my walls one by each damn one.

"You said I'm nothing. I heard you talking on the phone and you said you'll leave me behind, so do it!"

"Those were lies to misguide my insider."

"Do you expect me to believe that?"

"Do you think I would've come here and risked death if you were nothing?"

"Why can't you just leave?" My voice breaks and an onslaught of tears blurs my vision. "I already let you go."

"But I didn't."

God, he really needs to stop saying shit like that because I can't hold in the influx of emotions hitting me out of nowhere.

"If you stay, they will kill you."

"They?"

"The elite group of the brotherhood."

Both his palms wrap around my hips, and it feels familiar, his touch, the sensation of his hand on me. "Not you?"

"I'm part of the brotherhood, Kyle."

His grip tightens on my hip. "My question was clear. Will you do it?"

"Why can't you just leave?"

"You just answered your own question. I can't just leave."

My fist tightens in his shirt and the first tear falls on to his cheek. The vow I made to Mom to never cry in front of others, to never show weakness to any other human being starts crumbling right in front of me.

I can't even stop the tears because I've been so brutalized in the course of one day. Not only was it the goodbye, it was also the unbearable depression that came with it.

And I guess I'm exhausted. I'm just too *exhausted*, and that allows me to freely admit that a large part of me is relieved

That relief burns.

Because even though he's here, he has to leave so he can stay alive.

Kyle flips me so I'm lying underneath him, and I squeal, holding on to his shoulders. The sound slowly disappears when he slides his fingers under my eye, wiping the tears away.

"Why are you crying when I was the one beaten up?"

"You think I liked that? You think I enjoy seeing you like this? You asshole. Jerk—"

My words are cut off when his lips capture mine with raw hunger that confiscates my air. I taste metal from his cut lip, and I attempt to push away so I don't aggravate it, but Kyle thrusts his tongue between my teeth and twirls it with mine as if he's been starving for my taste.

The pungent smell of lust and something more potent permeates the air as he robs me not only of my breath, but also my sanity. He smashes every brick I carefully placed around my heart to the ground and walks all over it.

He nibbles down on my tongue, and the sharp sting of pain quickly heightens my arousal before his head pulls back. "You don't fucking push me away."

"You…don't understand…" I'm panting so harshly it's a miracle I manage to get those words out.

"I understand perfectly. It's you who doesn't. You're my wife. My. Fucking. *Wife*. Do you understand what that word means? It means we belong together, not far apart."

"But—"

"No fucking buts." His fingers latch onto the corners of my underwear and he pulls them down my legs.

I could fight or push him away, but what's the point when I'm burning for his touch? There has always been an explosive chemistry between Kyle and me. I denied it, tried to escape it, but the fact remains that it's existed since the first time *Dedushka* introduced him to me. Back then, I thought he was only a conceited killer; I had no idea he'd invade my whole world in no time.

Maybe if I have, I would've acted differently and avoided being tangled up with him. But even as I think that, a small voice whispers that I wouldn't have been able to change anything.

Kyle's fingers tease my clit as he kisses my throat, his teeth nibbling on the sensitive skin before he sucks it into his mouth, no doubt leaving a mark. I wrap my arm around his back, clawing with every sharp bite of his. That only makes him pick up his pace until my whole body is stimulated to the point of no return.

"After this...you'll leave," I manage to murmur, not sure whether it's directed at him or to reassure myself.

The sound of his zipper echoes in the silence of the bedroom and I drag in a breath, repeating, "You'll leave...right?"

My voice catches when he thrusts balls-deep inside me. Even though I'm soaking wet, Kyle is big and the stretching is real. God, how could I forget the way he's able to fill me until he's the only thing that matters in the world?

He slides a hand underneath me and lifts me up so he's sitting and I'm splayed all over his lap. *Holy shit.* If I thought he was filling me earlier, the depth right now is nothing like I've felt before.

I wrap my legs around his waist and dig my nails into his shoulders. I think I'm going to orgasm and he hasn't even moved yet.

When he does move, every powerful stroke feels different, almost like he's touching me for the first time. His thrusts leave the confinements of my body and hit something different inside, almost as if he's fucking my soul.

"There will be no more goodbyes between us, Princess." He speaks against my neck, his voice raspy, aroused, but also angry.

I pull back, still looping my arm around his nape, and stare at his face...his beautiful, ethereal face that's now bruised and bloodied.

Kyle powers into me with the same depth, but his pace isn't fast. Maybe he also wants to stare at me. Maybe, like me, he feels that our joined bodies are only a bridge for our battered souls.

My fingers stroke the skin of his cheek lightly to not hurt him. "I'm sorry."

"For what?"

"For what happened to you. No child should ever go through that."

"I thought you were sorry for poisoning me."

"You know I did what I had to do for the brotherhood."

He wraps a hand around my throat and cages me firmly in place. "How about your fucking husband?"

"It's because you're my husband that I wanted you gone." I strain against his hold, and before he can say anything else, I seal my lips to his. I kiss him slowly, tentatively, as if I have no clue how to kiss. Truth is, before him, I never took the time to learn. I hardly had interest in the other sex or sex in general, but he somehow became my deepest, darkest desire—the one I can't survive without and the one who might also kill me at the same time.

Kyle's rhythm picks up and he rams inside me with the urgency of a man who has nothing behind him or before him so he can only live in this moment. Our tongues and teeth clash together, and I keep tasting the metal of his blood, but if it hurts, he doesn't pull away.

His urgency matches mine. I can taste the desperation in his kiss and feel the unbound obsession in each of his thrusts.

It doesn't matter that I said goodbye or that this is only temporarily. At this moment, all I can do is get lost in him and pray there will be no way out.

His fingers tighten around my throat and I feel my walls clenching around his dick at the same time. He's all over me, inside me, around me, and it's impossible to escape his hold.

The piercing blue of his eyes captures mine as his touch leaves the confinement of my skin and shoots straight into my chest.

He said I poisoned him, but he's the one who poisoned me. He's the one who's firing an arrow at my heart, and I have no way to stop it because he destroyed my fortress.

The orgasm hits me like a slow-burning explosive. I moan, shaking, as tears slide down my cheeks.

Kyle kisses them away as his abs tighten and he spills inside me. I'm tempted to close my eyes to soak in the sensation, but I don't. I prefer watching him instead, even if his face isn't the same as usual.

We're both panting, his breaths mingling with mine, and a sheen of sweat covers our skin.

I lay my head on his shoulder, but I remain silent because the moment I speak, everything will end and I will have to return to the bleak reality where he really has to leave.

And this time, I don't know if I can handle it.

THIRTEEN

Kyle

RAI IS FAST ASLEEP, HER LIPS PARTED SLIGHTLY AND her golden locks splayed all over the pillow.

I've spent the last hour watching her; the slight flutter of her thick lashes, the steady rise and fall of her chest under the blanket, and how peaceful she looks—safe almost. Her fair complexion appears bluish in the darkness, ethereal, and so fucking appetizing I want to take her all over again. But at the same time, I love how she drowns into me as she sleeps. How she wraps her hand around my torso and intertwines her legs with mine.

She's so beautiful, it's maddening.

My obsession with this woman runs deeper and darker than I originally calculated. The thought of putting distance between us felt like ripping my heart out from between my ribs.

I think it started when I first met her. When Nikolai introduced her to me with a gleam in his usually bland eyes, I wondered what could have made the merciless leader of the New York Bratva so proud.

At the time, I thought she looked normal like all American-born Russians with her head held high and her eyes sparkling like she wanted to discover the world and all of its galaxies in one lifetime.

The only difference was that Rai didn't seem like she only wanted to discover the world. Even at that age, she was set on conquering.

The part that stayed with me other than her expressive eyes was her smile. Unlike other spoiled mafia princesses, Rai was too mature for her age.

She might have been spoiled by Nikolai, but she always knew her place and strived to be more for the brotherhood.

Back then, I didn't realize I was obsessed.

After I left Godfather and the others back in London, my aim was to stay by Nikolai's side. Not having a place to belong to ate away at my soul, but I couldn't stay just anywhere; I had to be where I could somehow plot my revenge. So I figured if he trusted me enough to protect his granddaughter, he would keep me around.

My plan worked, but I didn't count on this woman getting under my skin.

The first time I noticed how much of an effect she had on me was after I left. That morning I woke up and didn't have someone knocking on my door demanding that I teach them how to shoot or accompany them on a walk.

I went into withdrawal with its buried screams, its burning memories, and its silent breakdown.

And I remained in that fucking withdrawal for seven years. But it's not withdrawal if it lasted that long; it's an obsession. As soon as I returned, that obsession grabbed me by the throat like nothing ever had.

It's different from the obsession pulsing under my skin that's been demanding I avenge my parents' death.

One is bloodlust with the need to hurt. The other is still some sort of lust, but it's like a never-ending ache, the type that carved its place into the very marrow of my bones.

Stroking her hair behind her ear, I brush my lips to her forehead, lingering for a second too long so I can inhale her. Then I carefully untangle her from around me and stand up.

I slide my boxer briefs on and head to the bathroom. I hit the light switch and stand in front of the mirror.

My hands grip the marble counter as I stare at the galaxy of colors. Scarlet red, violet, bluish. That fucker Vlad made a painting out of my face—a chaotic one at that.

My eyes are swollen and the cut on my lip has dried blood all over it.

I should have probably taken care of it a bit more before I got here. Peter had a fright when he saw me. The kid shouldn't have joined the Bratva at all.

Instead of thinking of mundane things like cleaning my face, the only thought in my mind was that I needed to see her before she completely erased me.

I have no doubt she would live a perfectly normal life without me. I'm the one who kept having withdrawals for seven fucking years.

Reaching into the cabinet, I retrieve the first aid kit so I can clean the wounds.

Vladimir, the fucker, should start picking his funeral song, because he'll pay. Not only for hitting me, but for taking my wife away from me.

The condescending piece of shit always made it clear that I shouldn't be with her. She's a mafia princess and I'm a nobody, a killer who should remain in the shadows and only come out when he's needed to take care of extracurricular activities.

He's not wrong, but fuck him and everyone who thinks of me as a bloody shadow.

The padding of feet comes from behind me. I don't turn

around, not wanting her to know I feel her, even when she's far away.

She already thinks I'm abnormal, and I cemented that fact by telling her about my bloody past.

I never divulged those memories to anyone except for Godfather. With her, the words tumbled out of my mouth so easily, as if I was always meant to tell her about it.

Rai stops behind me and tilts to the side so she can peek at me through the mirror.

Her brows furrow when she makes out the cotton filled with alcohol in my hand. "Does it hurt?"

"It looks worse than it is."

She slips under my arm so she can stand between me and the counter. The only thing that covers her is a flimsy white gown that teases at her rosy areolas and hardened nipples.

Fuck me. She always looks like sin waiting to happen.

"You don't have to be modest about it. I know Vlad's punches hurt like hell."

"My punch hurts worse." My tone is flat. I'm being petty, but I don't like that she thinks any other man is stronger than me.

"I'm sure it does." She takes the cotton from my fingers and dabs it with some yellow liquid instead of alcohol.

Feeling the need to further prove myself, I say, "I was the best sniper in my group."

"Your group?" she asks without taking her attention from the cotton.

"At The Pit, we were divided into groups of approximately ten. We trained together and basically lived in the same space."

"Did you go on missions together?"

"No. We went in pairs of two. We usually had a permanent partner."

"Did you?"

"Not really, but I guess I spent a long time with Celeste."

Her movements pause and she stares up at me. "Celeste? That sounds like a girl's name."

I hide my internal smirk. "It is. She's crazy but fun to have around."

"Then why aren't you with her?"

"Because I'm with you, Princess." I try to kiss her, but she places a hand on my chest.

"You're hurt. Stop it."

"It'll hurt less if I kiss you."

"No," she scolds, going back to dabbing the cotton, not meeting my gaze. "Was she a sniper, too? Celeste."

I feign nonchalance. "She can be, but she's not at my level. We had better chemistry on groundwork."

She presses the cotton to my lip and I groan, but her expression remains neutral. "Glad you had *chemistry*."

"Are you jealous, Mrs. Hunter?"

"I'm not Mrs. Hunter."

"But you're jealous."

"Why would I be? Because of the *chemistry*?"

"Don't worry. You and I have better chemistry."

"Screw you."

"Finish cleaning me up and I'd be happy to oblige."

"Why don't you hit up *Celeste* for that?"

"And have you jealous?" I attempt to pinch her cheek and she swats my hand away.

I chuckle, and it ends on a grunt when my cuts sting.

"Stay still." Rai rises on her tiptoes so she can reach up. I grab her by the hips, lifting her, and she squeals as I plant her on the marble counter. I open her legs and settle between them so she's eye level with me.

She looks so soft right now, tempting, edible, and everything in between. Cleaning my wounds becomes the worst idea possible when all I want to do is to lay her down and pound into her until she screams. Then I would bite that pink nipple through the transparent cloth and suck on it until she's writhing in pleasure.

Rai aborts the image when she diligently cleans my face. She starts with my mouth then moves to my nose. Her fingers pause when she's about to take care of the cuts near my eyes. "It might hurt a little."

"It's nothing."

"Have you been hurt like this before?"

"Of course. Being shot makes this look like a child's game."

She strokes the pads of her fingers over the scar on my chest. "How did this happen?"

"That was because of Godfather—Ghost."

"Was Ghost part of your group?"

"He trained us. Godfather is one of The Pit's first generation. They're called Team Zero and all have weird names. My group is considered part of the second generation."

She continues to carefully clean my wound. "What's the difference between the first and the second generation?"

"The first generation are now old men—and women. We're younger and prettier, I guess?"

She shakes her head. "Is that the only difference?"

"Well, that and the fact that they were drugged. Their loyalty was ensured by a special type of drug."

"Is there a clear criterion on how to be in the first or second generation?"

"Not really, but the first generation lost most recollection of their previous lives. We didn't."

"That's sad. Are there many of them?"

"Not really. About a dozen."

"How do you differentiate between them and the second generation?"

"They all trained us so all second gen know them. Besides, they have weird names: Ghost, Crow, Shadow, Mist, Flame, Scar, Poison, and so on. It's like a den of vipers. Needless to say, it's not their real names, but even they don't remember their actual names."

"What about you?" Her eyes hold mine hostage, appearing darker in the late night. "Is Kyle your real name?

"It is. This is the name my mother gave me."

"How about your last name? Is it Hunter?"

I could lie to her, but what's the point? She already knows my plan, and I'm in no mood to keep her in the dark any longer. I slowly shake my head once.

"Then what is it?"

"Fitzpatrick. My real name is Kyle Fitzpatrick."

She freezes, her hand remaining suspended in midair as the realization settles in.

"You...are you related to Rolan Fitzpatrick?"

"He's my uncle."

"You're..."

"Irish? Yeah. Half, though. My mum was Northern Irish and she considered herself British."

"Oh."

"What type of 'Oh' is that?"

"It's an 'Oh, that's what the accent change means.'"

"Accent change?"

"You sometimes speak in a different accent during sex."

"I do?"

"You do."

"Mmm. I didn't notice that."

"Do you slip into it subconsciously?"

"I guess. I shed it away a long time ago, but it keeps coming back."

She gently strokes the cotton on my skin. "Why?"

"Why what?"

"Why did you shed it away?"

"Godfather is British and I was raised with him speaking in an English accent, so I picked it up."

"That's all?"

"And I didn't want the memories related to the accent." I don't know why I'm telling her this, but now that I've started, I can't stop. "I did speak in a Northern Irish accent when I was with Godfather because it reminded me of Mum and how my father wanted me to speak more like an Irish person. He was a snob about all his Irish lineage and what-the-fuck-ever."

"Your father was Niall Fitzpatrick, right?"

I nod.

"I heard about him from *Dedushka*. He said he was a good leader and that his brother, Rolan, is worse than him."

"I don't know about good. He was like a lot of the crime organization leaders—blinded by profit and power. Still, he didn't deserve to be shot in the back by his own brother."

A soft gasp leaves her lips. "He was?"

"He died by the hands of the one person he trusted the most. Isn't that ironic?"

"Unfortunately, it happens more often than you think in our world." She strokes my cheek. "So now you want to destroy your uncle?"

"And everything the fucker stands for. He's the one who sold me in the black market and made me into this, but he's not the only one. The ones who contributed that night will pay too."

"Oh, Kyle."

"Save your pity, Princess."

"I'm far from pitying you." Her expression is determined, hard, and holds no doubts. "I want to murder him for you."

FOURTEEN

Kyle

I *WANT TO MURDER HIM FOR YOU.*

Her words take me by surprise even though they shouldn't. If there's anything I've learned about Rai after staying with her this long, it's that she has a strong sense of justice and she doesn't back down when she decides to protect someone.

Maybe back then, if Mum had someone like her by her side, she wouldn't have died the way she did.

Maybe then, Rai and I could have met under different circumstances. Me, as the Irish's heir, and she a Russian mafia princess. Maybe then, I wouldn't have been the shadow who sometimes doesn't know whether I want to be seen or simply disappear.

A fiery gleam sparkles in her eyes as she speaks with con-

"Kill Rolan for you."

"I could've done it myself a long time ago, could've sniped him down while he was walking the streets, but I didn't. Because death is a way out for that scum."

"So what's your plan exactly?"

"Make him suffer first. Toy with him first. Only then will he be granted death."

"That means you'll keep using the brotherhood, and I won't allow you to hurt anyone in my organization."

"You're awfully loyal to people who keep trying to chase you out."

"So what? That doesn't mean I didn't snatch my rightful place. I may not be a"—she makes quotation marks—"'brother', a fact they won't stop reminding me of. I might hate Mikhail's sexist ass and despise Kirill's slippery nature. I might distrust Damien's recklessness, Adrian's mysteriousness, and Igor's secretiveness, but my loyalty lies with what those men stand for. I will not allow you to destroy them."

"And how do you intend to stop me?"

"With my life. Kill me first, then you can do whatever you want."

"Fuck, Rai. You'd put your own life on the line?"

"If it's the only thing that would stop you, I wouldn't hesitate to use it."

Touché, Princess.

Maybe she really knows me more than I thought possible. At this moment, the only thing that's able to stop me is her. I even came back here, risking being shot to death by that fucker Vladimir if it meant seeing her one last time.

Godfather and all the fuckers from The Pit—especially Flame—would be so unimpressed with the way I chose to die. By a Russian. For a woman.

I would laugh if I could. They would tell their children tales about how pathetic I've become, how the mighty have fallen.

And yet, I'd still come back here in a heartbeat.

"Instead…" Rai trails off. "I will take revenge against Rolan on your behalf."

I raise a brow. "You will?"

"You have my word."

"What to do? My revenge might start with Rolan, but it doesn't end with him."

"Then how does it end?"

"There was a Russian there that night—the one who betrayed my mother. Unless he dies, my revenge won't end."

"Is he one of us?"

"I believe so, but I'm not sure if he's one of the existing ones or if he went back to Russia."

"So you decided to attack us without concrete evidence."

"Russian Bratva in New York was all the evidence I needed."

"Are you serious? You would've destroyed an entire organization for one person?"

"I would've done more. I told you, I was raised for the sole purpose of destruction. I'm a killing machine and all I know is how to kill."

"That's not true."

"Not true? You called my hands filthy, remember?"

"That's because you hurt me, you jerk. I bite back as hard as I'm bitten."

"Isn't that the fucking truth," I sigh, lips twitching.

"Let me ask you something."

"Anything." I wrap my hands around the small of her back, because touching her feels critical right now. Like if I stop touching her, I will stop breathing.

"What took you so long to start your revenge? Surely you could've done it in your twenties or somewhere during that time."

"It took me a long time to track things down. I always

knew my parents were killed and the scene was vivid in my head, but I lost lots of details during The Pit. I lost sense of time and space and didn't know if it happened in Ireland or in England or in the States."

"When did you remember clearly?"

"It didn't happen in one go. I recalled Rolan's involvement after I joined Nikolai when I was in my mid-twenties. That came to me as clear as crystal the first time I saw the fucker, Rolan, at one of your grandfather's parties. I thought, 'hey, being kicked out from Godfather's side wasn't so bad, after all.'"

She smiles a little. "Troublemaker."

"Always have been, Princess."

"You're not supposed to be proud of that."

"You like that about me."

"No, I don't."

"Yes, you do, but I digress—slightly."

"Then?" She uses another cotton ball to wipe at my brows. "Then what?"

"You said your memories didn't come in one go. When did you recall one of the Bratva's involvement?"

"Before I came back, I had a job in Northern Ireland, and maybe it was being there and hearing people talk in Mum's accent is what had triggered a memory from that night. At the time, my mother was carrying me in her arms while she was talking on the phone. I remember hearing the Russian accent from the other end, and he ordered some people in the background while he was talking to her, which means he had some rank in the Bratva.

"Before that, I spent most of my time investigating Rolan's background and boring Irish internal affairs. He's not easy to track down, but that was expected since he didn't only kill his own brother and sister-in-law then sell his nephew. He also beheaded his own wife and buried his son alive when he learned he was not his biological child."

"Wow. So the rumors about him are true."

"They're probably worse than you've heard. He's a heart-less fucker who never gets enough. That's why he's after your territories."

"I thought you instigated this."

"I did, but there's no smoke without fire. Rolan always had eyes for your territories, but Nikolai was too strong for him. He thinks he can win now that Sergei is the *Pakhan*. Igor believes Rolan has an ally from the inner circle."

"Igor? Your *fake* father?"

I smile, then wince when my cut lip burns. "How did you know?"

"I ran a DNA test."

"Smart, though I thought you wouldn't be able to get Igor's sample."

"It wasn't easy."

"I'm sure. That was still smart."

"And you're cunning to use Igor."

"Yeah, well, I had to get access somehow."

"Why did you choose Igor?"

"We chose each other. I thought he was the Russian from that time and mentioned my mother's name in front of him to gauge his reaction. Surprisingly, he didn't act like he didn't know her and told me she was a famous prostitute in one of Brooklyn's notorious clubs. Not going to lie, it was no fun to learn my mum was a prostitute."

She grimaces. "Sorry."

"Don't be. It made sense why Dad always looked down on her and often called her a whore. Anyhow, Igor also mentioned that she was 'acquainted' with most of the brothers at the time, so the person I'm looking for could, in fact, have returned to Russia throughout the years."

"And he decided to help you just like that?"

"Not just like that. It was an exchange. I bring the traitor he suspects down and he gives me an in to avenge my mother's death."

"Traitor?"

"Yeah, Igor believes there's one among you."

"What made him think there's even a traitor? Does he have evidence?"

"I don't think so. He's following his instincts on this one, and he strongly suspects someone."

"Who?"

"I guess it doesn't matter if you know. Igor doubts Damien."

She laughs, the sound throaty. "Not Kirill or Adrian, but Damien?"

I narrow my eyes. "What's so funny about *Damien?*"

"That man thinks with his fists and would never be sophisticated enough to plot betrayal. Besides, he's so Russian and hotheaded that it's exhausting sometimes. He would never, and I mean *never*, choose another clan over us. He might be reckless, but he's no traitor."

My hold tightens on her waist. "Are you done defending the fucker in front of me?"

She swallows, her lips parting. "I'm just stating facts."

"Too *many* facts."

"Just enough to prove that Igor is wasting your time and his. Damien isn't the traitor—that is if there is one in the first place."

"Are you going to stop saying his name or should I fuck it out of you?"

"Stop saying things like that." She tries to fight the blush creeping up her cheeks and fails.

"Not until you stop talking about other men in my presence. I don't like it and it's the best way to send me on a murder spree."

"You're crazy."

"You just figured that out?"

"I guess I keep forgetting about it."

"I'm happy to remind you."

"I'm sure you are." She gives me a dirty look. "Anyway, just tell Igor he's wasting his time."

"But you do have a traitor."

"What's your proof?"

"When you approved V Corp's recent finances, didn't you notice something off?"

"Adrian asking for them?"

"Why do you think he's purposefully putting his hands into your business?"

"Because he's a control freak?"

"Because he suspects you."

"Suspects me of what?"

"Theft."

"Theft? Ha, he should corner Mikhail about that, not me."

"He's cornering everyone in his own way. Sergei and Adrian are the only two who know someone is stealing from the brotherhood. Igor must be in the know, too, and that's why he's trying to weed the traitor out."

"Wait…but the numbers I have from the financial team match. I would've figured it out if there was a theft."

"Adrian must've ordered them to submit fake numbers to gauge your reaction. If you caused a ruckus, he'd have caught you, for you wouldn't have known the numbers were fake unless you were the one who had been strategically stealing."

"That motherfucker."

"Do you expect anything less from him?"

"No, but the fact that he has insiders in my damn company makes me livid. I'm going to weed them all out."

"Good choice, but remember that V Corp is the brotherhood's company. Not only has Adrian been around longer than you, he also outranks you, so his roots run deeper."

"Are you worried about him?" she snaps.

"I'm worried about *you*, Princess. He's not someone you should make an enemy out of. If you're going to hit him, be discreet about it."

"I know that."

"And if you want to reduce his power, strike where it would hurt him the most."

"Adrian doesn't have a weakness."

"Yes, he does. I'm actually surprised you didn't figure it out."

"What is it?"

"The question is who, not what."

"It's a person? Wait, if you mean his son, I'll strangle you. Do you think I'd use a child to gain power?"

I chuckle. She'd sure as hell strangle me if she got the chance. "No, not his son."

"Then who?"

"His wife."

"Lia? Have you seen them together? He doesn't care about her and is only keeping her around because she's the mother of his son."

"Or that's what he likes you and everyone else to think. Didn't you see the way he almost lost it when she was shot at? Even *you* thought that was uncharacteristic of him."

She remains silent, probably turning the information over in that smart head of hers. I shouldn't have revealed the weakness I'm supposed to be using against Adrian, but if it keeps Rai in the position she loves so much, I'll sacrifice all the information I have.

Taking advantage of her moment of absentmindedness, I pull her closer. "So?"

"So what?"

"How are you going to reward me for all the information I gave you?"

"I already did by cleaning your wounds." She reaches to the

side and closes the first aid box. "You only have to apply the ointment about three times a day."

"Or you can do it."

"Fine," she says distracted, focused on the box.

"Does that mean you're my nurse now? Kinky."

She stares up at me with wild eyes before she hits my shoulder. "Do you always have to come up with some porn scenario?"

"When it comes to you, I sure as fuck do. Now, answer my question. Are you going to be my nurse?"

"Does this mean you're intent on staying?"

"Till death does us part."

Her inquisitive eyes meet mine. "Promise there will be no more secrets between us."

"Depends on whether or not you'll take that fucker Vladimir's side over mine again."

"Vlad has the brotherhood's best interests in mind."

I scoff. "I'm sure the fucker does."

"Stop being jealous, you idiot." She leans over and brushes her lips to mine, softly, carefully, away from my cut. "None of them is my husband."

None of them is her husband.

Those words stab me straight in the bones. When she attempts to pull away, I grab her by the throat and deepen the kiss.

Time to fuck her on the counter as I originally planned.

FIFTEEN

Rai

A WEEK LATER, WHEN I WAKE UP IN BED ALONE, A thousand ominous thoughts rush into my head.

It takes me a few minutes to grab my phone due to the shaking in my hand. The message I find there instantly calms my breathing.

Kyle: Morning, Princess. I'm off with Adrian for business with the Italians. Don't forget to eat breakfast. Oh, and come home early so I can make up for not fucking you first thing in the morning. P.S. Wear that red thing from the other time.

I smile, imagining his exact tone as if he said those words aloud. Ever since that night where he barged back into my room, bloodied and bruised, and announced that he was staying, I've felt like I'm in an alternate reality, one that's shrouded by fog. I figure the mist will eventually wear off and he'll realize staying is dangerous.

Not that Kyle is afraid of danger. If anything, the life he's lived thus far might have gotten him addicted to it.

Every night, after he fucks me until I scream, he gathers me in his arms and answers any questions I have. We have no trouble talking now, and it feels new—exciting, even—for every day I look forward to what he'll tell me about his life in The Pit or the countless adventures he's been through.

I feel closer to him now more than ever, to the point that I'm impatient to go back home just so I can see him. All the chaos in the company and my secret search for the embezzler all fade to the background when I'm with him.

In Kyle's arms, I feel light, protected, and...peaceful.

I tell myself that's why I long for his merest touch, and not the fact that my sexual drive has become insatiable lately. Sometimes, I want to restart as soon as we finish, and that's not normal, especially since he exhausts me to the point of no return.

To say I completely trust him now would be a lie. After everything he's done, it's hard to take his word for granted. He didn't only lie to me, he also used me, and that doesn't just go away.

I might be unable to kick him out of my life, but I can't completely accept him. At least not until I make sure everything he said is true or that his intentions are no longer nefarious.

I need to get to the bottom of that, even if keeping this whole thing a secret from Sergei is eating at me. Not only do I not like keeping him in the dark, it'll be dangerous if he finds out I'm hiding critical information. When it comes to choosing between family and duty, the latter always comes first for the *Pakhan*.

But I'm sure he'll forgive me if he knows I'm doing this for both my husband and the brotherhood. I already told him and everyone else that I regained my memories, so he has to wait a bit longer for the rest.

They all wondered how Kyle got beat up, and he came up with a lame excuse that some 'brute' thug and his 'stupid' minions ganged up on him. He said they looked worse than him, something for which Vlad nearly shot him there and then.

After showering and dressing in a white shirt and a black pencil skirt, I sit at my console to do my makeup. I'm starting to miss the toy between my legs—or more like, the feel of Kyle with me at all times. While I meant that I will kill him if he embarrasses me by using it in front of the Vory members, I did like the added excitement. Or this could be another manifestation of my weird sex drive.

After finishing, I stand up. My heel catches on the ground as the world starts spinning. I hold on to the console with shaky fingers and close my eyes for a brief second in order to regain my composure.

When I open them again, my room comes back into focus. That was weird. I need to eat in case some vitamins are missing from my body. I'm generally not the best when it comes to self-care.

I step out of my room and stop at the bottom of the stairs at the sound of hushed tones. I'm not one to eavesdrop, usually, but the two people speaking hold more importance than that principle.

My back flattens against the wall as I slowly peek around the corner. Kirill and Damien are standing toe to toe by the balcony's door that leads to the garden. They either forgot the door was open or they don't care.

Damien is shoving a cigarette in his mouth with clear detachment in his green eyes. He has flecks of gray in them when you look close enough, but they're not visible from this distance.

His posture is nonchalant, but not hunched or completely detached. Damien is the type of person who's always ready to punch someone here, shoot someone there, and bury someone somewhere.

Kirill, on the other hand, is an erect wall, standing with

his hands lying limp by his sides. It's the body language he usually feigns to make the other party believe he is approachable, harmless, even. That fox is cunning even when it comes to his body language. He's fully aware of every move he makes, unlike Damien who doesn't care what image he projects on the world as long as he gets to inflict violence.

The reason I'm standing here is the utter weirdness of the view. Damien and Kirill have never gotten along, not in *Dedushka*'s time and not now. They were always reprimanded for the endless fights they caused at the table.

Kirill leans more toward Igor and Adrian. Damien is a lone wolf who doesn't get along with anyone—except for maybe Vlad a little. Well, and me when he wants to be a pain in the ass.

The fact that they're talking one-on-one is suspicious. The absence of their closest guards who follow them like shadows is one more reason why I should be privy to this conversation.

Kirill readjusts his glasses with his middle finger. While they're thick-framed, they don't hide the intensity of his gaze. "What's your deepest, darkest desire, Damien?"

"Aside from spilling your brains on the ground and pretending to mourn at your funeral?" Damien lights his cigarette and blows the smoke in Kirill's face, fogging his glasses.

The latter doesn't flinch or show a hint of annoyance. He doesn't even remove his glasses to clean them and lets the smoke disperse on its own. "Yes. Aside from that."

"Hmm. Why are you asking?"

"I might make it happen."

"There, there, since when did you start to think you're all that? If I want something done, I will do it myself. I don't need your fucking help."

"I'm faster."

"I'm stronger."

"Speed is more important, Damien." His words turn

slower, agonizingly so—taunting, even. "Surely, it'll come in handy for your current *quest*."

One second, Kirill is standing, and the next, Damien is grabbing him by the throat against the balcony's glass door. I hide further behind the wall in case they notice me.

The gray flecks in Damien's eyes that I couldn't perceive earlier expand until they nearly cover the entirety of his irises.

The black bull.

It's the side of him that only comes out when he's on a violent spree. I contemplate going out there in case the crazy bastard actually kills Kirill, but the smirk on the other asshole's face stops me.

What am I thinking? Kirill is well aware of Damien's unhinged nature, more than anyone else. He signed up for this and he knows exactly what he's doing.

"How the fuck do you know about that?" Damien snarls in his face, pointing the lit part of his cigarette at Kirill's cheek as if he's planning to burn holes in it. I wouldn't be surprised if he went on with that plan.

"Does it matter?" Kirill pushes him away with what seems like ease but must've taken a lot of effort. He readjusts his glasses with deliberate slowness. "Something else matters more. Pardon—some*one*."

"I'm going to fucking kill you, Kirill."

"You can try, but that would be a waste since we can have an agreement."

Damien takes a long drag of his cigarette and lets out a cloud of smoke. "What the fuck do you want?"

"I'm glad you asked." Kirill smiles, dusting off Damien's jacket. "Let's get together in a more private place after the meeting."

Shit.

I can't lose track of their conversation after that. Kirill is clearly planning something. First, he got his octopus hands on

Adrian, and now he's going after Damien—whom I at least thought couldn't be swayed.

My phone vibrates and I swiftly pull away to check the text.

Vlad: Sergei wants you in his office.

With a groan, I go back upstairs. Kirill and Damien won't leave yet since they were called by Sergei. I need to figure out what they're plotting, or at least Damien's fixation. If I can get him that instead of Kirill, I can convince him to switch to my side.

I knock on Sergei's door before I step inside. Vladimir and Igor are sitting with him in the lounge area. I nod at my supposed father-in-law, and he nods in return before focusing back on the paperwork splayed in front of him.

Vlad doesn't spare me a glance. His jaw is tight and his beard appears thicker today, casting an ominous shadow on his face. He's been in a pissed mood since I released Kyle that day, and he completely stopped talking to me when he found out I took Kyle back.

He tried to shoot him the following morning. Needless to say, Kyle got his own gun, ready to murder him as well. So I stood between them to stop their madness and told Vladimir he has no evidence against Kyle and, therefore, he can't shoot him. Something for which Kyle smirked at while he pulled me possessively to his side by the waist.

"I don't even know you anymore," Vlad told me. "When you go back to being the Rai I recognize, come talk to me."

That was about a week ago, and to say I don't miss Vlad's companionship would be a lie. If it were the old days, he would've been the first to help me brainstorm about Kirill and Damien.

Sighing, I greet Sergei by kissing his hand and then remain standing. "You asked for me?"

"Yes. You did well, Rai."

I stare at the three men present. "Concerning what?"

"Kai," Sergei explains with a proud gleam. "His leader, Abe, is open to negotiations, and it's all thanks to you."

I smile. "It's my duty."

I knew Kai's profit-oriented brain would be favorable for a lucrative partnership.

Vlad grunts under his breath, but he says nothing. He's like a grumpy large bear who finds it a chore to speak.

"If there isn't anything else, I'll go to work," I tell Sergei.

"No, no. Since you started this, you have to take it to the very end."

I halt in my tracks and face him. My granduncle appears healthier lately, his face less darkened and his coughs seldom making appearances. It gives me hope that I don't want to have, like the hope I had when *Dedushka*'s heart condition got worse. I thought he was stronger than the world, but he left me. Sergei will leave too.

Everyone does.

I shoo those thoughts away and ask, "What do you mean?"

"We have a meeting with Kai and Abe today."

"And?"

Sergei exchanges a look with Igor, who speaks on his behalf. "Abe specifically asked for you, Kirill, and Damien."

"He did?" I stare incredulously. "Wouldn't it make more sense if Igor goes?"

"That's what I said," Kyle's fake father agrees. "Damien, of all people, shouldn't be anywhere near a strategic meeting."

He can say that again.

"It can't be helped." Sergei stands. "Can I trust you, Rai?"

"Of course."

"Keep that wild dog on a leash," Igor tells me, appearing uneasy as if we're heading straight to a disaster, which might as well be the case.

Kirill, Damien, and me in a meeting all on our own?

Yeah, this needs a word stronger than disaster.

SIXTEEN

Rai

Tʜᴇ ᴍᴇᴇᴛɪɴɢ ɪs sᴇᴛ ɪɴ ᴀ ᴛʀᴀᴅɪᴛɪᴏɴᴀʟ Asɪᴀɴ restaurant with private rooms.

It's one of the places where the Yakuza conduct their outside meetings. If I remember correctly, they own this one.

Our guards remain outside as we agreed on beforehand.

Damien, Kirill, and I arrive a bit early, so the three of us are sitting on the floor. Damien is beside me to the right, and Kirill chose to sit opposite me even though there's room on my left.

The table is empty except for a ceramic teapot that rests in the middle. Every five minutes, a waitress comes to refill our teacups.

"Don't you have some vodka in here?" Damien barks, and the slim woman flinches at the strength of his voice. She'd probably piss her pants if he showed any hint of his Russian accent. He's really a bull.

"No need to yell at the lady." Kirill smiles, speaking in a smooth, suave voice. "Can you please get us some vodka? Our friend here lacks class and is not a fan of tea."

She mirrors his smile, falling right into his fake charm. "Right away, sir."

As soon as the wooden door slides shut behind her, Kirill's smile vanishes. "How long are they going to keep us waiting? Is this a tactic?"

I take a sip of my tea and relish the relief it creates at the bottom of my stomach. "The question should be *why* they chose the three of us."

"Especially you," Kirill says with condescension.

"Why should that be a surprise when I'm the one who brought Kai around?"

"Did you use some lady skills?" Kirill taunts. "Does that tool husband of yours know?"

"No, but if you really want him to know about something, I can tell him about your own set of *skills*."

Kirill readjusts his glasses with his middle finger, glaring at me, but he drops the subject.

The waitress brings us a bottle of vodka and glasses, smiles at Kirill, then leaves. Damien uncaps the bottle, ignores the glasses, and drinks straight from it like the savage he is.

"Stop it." I try to take the bottle from him, but he pushes me away.

"Drink your tea and leave me the fuck alone."

"I can't leave you the fuck alone when the brotherhood depends on this meeting." I grab the bottle and yank it away, causing droplets to fall on his shirt. "You're hard to handle sober, so there's no way in hell you're getting drunk on a day like this."

He licks his mouth, wiping away the droplets of vodka that stuck to his upper lip. "Are you this bossy in bed, too? That lucky bastard, Kyle."

"More like poor bastard," Kirill mutters.

"Lucky or poor is none of your business."

"Tell me, I'm curious." Damien leans his elbow on the table. "What made you settle with Kyle, of all the men who surrounded you all your life? You had much better options. Hint: *me*."

"He understands me better than anyone else," I say without even thinking about it. That's what always made Kyle special. He sometimes understands my needs before I do.

"How does one even begin to understand a witch?" Kirill asks.

"You would never know because when you start, you're already under my spell."

"Holy fuck, that must've hurt." Damien barks out a laugh. "You okay there, Kirill? Want me to get you something for the burn?"

I smirk at Kirill and he flips me off. Damien uses my distraction to try to reach for the bottle of vodka. I swat his hand away, clasp the bottle, and place it in front of me under the table so he doesn't have access to it.

Even though he's sitting still, his eyes are shifty and agitated. I'm ready to bet it's because of whatever seed Kirill planted in his head back at the house.

The door slides open again, and this time, it's not the waitress. Kai walks in, followed by an old, short man who wears a pressed suit.

Abe Hitori. The leader of the Yakuza branch in New York.

Kirill and I stand in greeting, but Damien remains planted in place. Not only that, he also uses the chance of my standing up to grab the bottle of vodka.

I glare down at him, but he just sips from the bottle. "What? Surely they know how I am if they specifically asked for me. Right, old man?"

The motherfucker.

I curse inwardly, but I pause when Abe laughs, wrinkles forming around his eyes, then speaks in a subtle Japanese accent. "Always a black sheep, Damien."

"I will drink to that." He swallows another gulp of his vodka, then wipes his mouth with the back of his hand. "Now, spare us the suspense and let us know why we're here."

"Patience, young man." Abe sits beside Damien, and the asshole doesn't even attempt to give him room.

Kai smiles at me in greeting before he kneels beside me in an upright posture that somehow appears reverent. He places a hand on my thigh. "Have you been well?"

"Yes," I murmur as I remove his hand. "And that question doesn't need to be asked while you touch me, does it?"

He chuckles softly. "I didn't expect anything less from you."

After the food arrives, a mixture of soups, noodles, and an exquisite fish dish, Abe and Kai unhurriedly dig into their meals. Kirill and I join, mimicking their pace. *Dedushka* taught me how to use chopsticks a long time ago. He said respecting other people's cultures goes a long way.

Damien, though, digs in with his bare hands, still sipping from the bottle every other bite.

We need to finish and get the hell out of here before he disrespects them anymore.

"Sergei sends his regards," I tell Abe.

He merely nods, still focused on Damien. "Say, are you betrothed?"

"What's that? Some type of food?" Damien asks between mouthfuls of fish.

"Marriage. Ever thought of it?"

"Why would I?"

"Maybe you should."

"Well, maybe *you* should."

"I *am* married."

"No kidding. And here I thought you were single for life."

"I'm going to propose something."

"Why are you looking at me?" Damien motions at me and Kirill. "They usually do the talking thing."

"I'm not interested in talking."

"Then why have you brought me here in the midst of my busy schedule? I have people to kill, old man."

Abe smiles again. "What if I said I have an offer to make?"

"Then make it already and spare us the bullshit."

"Damien," I scold under my breath.

"What?" he shoots back. "I have shit to do."

"It's fine, fine." Abe motions at me with a dismissive hand. "Damien?"

"Yes?"

"I'm offering you my daughter's hand in marriage."

"Why would you do that to her?" Damien stares incredulously, then whispers, "Is she not really your daughter, so you're punishing her?"

Abe laughs, the sound genuinely amused. "I like you, Damien Orlov."

"Believe me, your daughter won't," I say before I can measure my words.

"Yeah, I agree." Damien is still chewing on his food while he speaks.

"Let me be the judge of that." Abe takes a sip of *sake*, a traditional rice wine. "The marriage is part of the deal. Take it or leave it."

"Leave it." Damien attempts to stand up, but I grab his thigh and force him to sit down, my nails digging into his pants.

I smile at Abe. "What he meant to say is that we'll think about it."

"We will?" Damien asks.

"Yes, we will." I give him a knowing look, then direct it at Kirill, who takes his time savoring the fish before he speaks.

"We would be honored by such an alliance," Kirill says in his suave voice. "I'm sure Sergei will be thrilled."

"Yes, yes." Abe slides a cup in front of Damien and pours sake in it.

"No thanks, old man. I prefer vodka."

I pinch Damien's thigh and he groans, but I don't let go, mouthing, "Do it."

It's extremely disrespectful to refuse a drink, especially if it's from someone older than you.

Damien rolls his eyes and takes the cup, downing it in one go before he shoos my hand away and stands, clutching his vodka bottle. "I'm out of here." When neither of us move, the brute grabs Kirill by the collar. "You waiting for an invitation or something? We have shit to do."

Kirill follows Damien's lead and bows.

Dammit. They're leaving together. No way in hell.

I follow their lead, bowing before I stand up. "I apologize for Damien's behavior."

"No, no." Abe raises his hand dismissively, a small smile on his lips. "He's an interesting man, yes?"

"You could say that," I speak slowly. "May I ask why you wanted Kirill and me to join?"

"Kai said you and Kirill are more rational and would convince him."

My gaze slides to Kai, and he smiles at me with a knowing nod. I don't know if I should be thankful or wary of his ulterior motives.

"Thank you for the meal." I nod and slowly retreat out of the room.

As soon as I'm out of Abe and Kai's view, I sprint in the direction of the parking lot. Thankfully, I catch a glimpse of Damien and Kirill heading to the latter's car, followed by their horde of guards.

Katia rushes in my direction, but I shake my head. Then, I retrieve my phone and shoot a text in the group chat.

Rai: You and Ruslan follow me from afar. I need to go back with Kirill and Damien.

My guard nods and retreats to join Ruslan.

"Auntie!"

I freeze, the phone nearly clattering to the ground at the small voice. My head jerks to the left and my gaze lands on my nephew's little face. On his dreamy green eyes and soft features.

Gareth.

He's a few feet away, smiling up at me with pure innocence, showing his baby teeth.

Shit. Fuck.

My eyes frantically search around. If he's here, Reina is too. Kirill and Damien cannot, under any circumstances, know she exists. Especially Kirill. He would destroy me and her.

My fingers tremble when Kirill's closest guard, Aleksander, stops. He stares at me over his shoulder, his critical gaze sliding to Gareth.

There's nothing I want to do more than shoot Aleksander in the face, grab Gareth, and run away, but that will only hurt him and his parents.

"Auntie?" he repeats, tone unsure.

Aleksander stops walking and turns around fully to watch the scene. Any move from my side will cause a disaster. If I talk to Gareth, Aleksander will make it his job to find out exactly who he is, and that will lead him straight to Reina.

If I leave, my baby nephew will be all alone and unprotected in this place.

I can't even tell Katia and Ruslan to take care of it because that will lead back to me.

A man crouches and picks Gareth up. "There you are, troublemaker. I told you not to call strangers auntie."

A breath heaves out of me at seeing Asher. He gives me an impersonal smile as if it's the first time he's seeing me and nails the role so well. "Sorry about that."

"Don't worry about it." I make sure Aleksander sees my fake smile.

Seeming to lose interest, he turns and joins his boss.

"I'm sorry," I whisper to Asher, who nods in understanding before he takes a protesting Gareth inside.

My chest aches at the inability to hold my nephew or kiss him. It's better this way, for his sake.

Once again, I type in the group chat.

Rai: Gareth and Asher are in this restaurant, and Reina must be here, too. Follow them from afar and make sure they get home safe and no one suspects anything. Do not under any circumstances make direct contact unless they're in danger.

Ruslan: Yes, boss.

Katia: On it.

I half-jog to Kirill's car just before Aleksander closes the door. I push past him and sit beside Damien.

"What the fuck are you doing?" Kirill watches me as if I grew a second head.

"Take me back with you."

"You have your own car."

"It's broken down. Ruslan is trying to fix it."

"Do I look like a taxi to you?"

"Well, you could be one."

"Leave, Rai." Damien sips from his vodka. "Kirill and I have a meeting."

I'm well aware, but if they think they can get rid of me this easily, they're mistaken.

"Then do it after you drop me off."

Kirill shrugs a shoulder. "Or I can just throw you out."

"You just wasted a minute. We would've arrived faster if we'd taken off already, besides…Abe told me something after you left."

"Who cares what that delusional old man says?" Damien mocks.

Kirill does because he motions at his driver to go. Aleksander gives me a peculiar glance from the passenger seat, then immediately conceals it. *Please tell me he doesn't suspect anything about Asher and Gareth.*

As soon as the car rolls out of the parking lot, followed by another vehicle that's full of Kirill and Damien's guards, I try to get comfy. As comfy as it gets with two large men dwarfing the back seat.

"What did Abe say?" Kirill asks.

"It's about Damien," I say, slowly gauging his reaction, but he appears completely uninterested. "Don't you want to know?"

"I do want to know why you said I'll think about it. You want to marry me off, Rai?"

"If it benefits the brotherhood, why not settle down?"

"*Settle down?* What are you, my mother?"

"First of all, eww. Second of all, just go with it."

"Just like you went with your own marriage? It's so boring if we're all so sacrificial like you, Rayenka."

"Does that mean you won't do it?"

"I don't see why I should."

"You can't disrespect Abe that way, Damien. He's one of the strongest allies we can have."

Kirill readjusts his glasses. "And he will become our worst enemy if this bull kills his daughter in one of his violent episodes."

"You hurt women?" I snap at Damien.

He continues sipping from his vodka before he lowers his mouth to my ear. "When they get close, yes. Why? You want to test it?"

I push him away, glaring. "You will control that side of you and treat Abe's daughter well, and if I find out you hurt any woman, you'll have me to answer to."

He grins. "Will it be kinky?"

I'm about to gouge his eyes out when the car swerves and comes to a screeching halt. The force is so strong that I bump against the back of Aleksander's seat.

"What is it?" Kirill barks at his driver in Russian.

"Don't know, sir. There's something on the road—"

His words cut off when a shot lodges straight in his chest. Aleksander gets his gun out, cursing, but it's too late.

Gunshots erupt from all directions.

We're under attack.

SEVENTEEN

Kyle

THIS ISN'T EXACTLY WHERE I WANT TO BE.

It's not where I should be either. Who gives a fuck about the Russians' business? Certainly not me.

The only things I would rather be doing right now is either shooting the fucker Rolan in the face or eating my wife out. There's no in between.

The first part is out, for now. I asked Flame to stay on standby—an option he wasn't so thrilled about since the lack of action bores him.

That makes two of us. Flame and I are the types who won't accept a mission if we don't deem it exciting enough. The adrenaline wave is our bitch and we ride it every chance we get. Now, the only one I want to ride me is Rai.

I like how adorable she looks when she thinks she has the upper hand before I flip her on to her back and tease her

"Focus." Adrian speaks low enough so only I can hear. "Or try to appear as if you're focusing."

We're sitting in one of the Bratva's empty clubs downtown with the Lucianos' underboss, Nicolo. He brought a dozen guards with him, and they are currently watching the sparse staff buzzing around.

Since it's not opening time yet, the workers are in the prepping phase. Nicolo is known for his distrustful nature, and he's the reason why Lazlo was reluctant about an alliance, but even he can't ignore the danger to his boss's life—who also happens to be his eldest brother. So in a way, his hand was forced by me.

Adrian should thank me. If it weren't for my very convenient interference, he wouldn't have Nicolo exactly where he wants him. I can be such a good sport when need be.

Nicolo sucks a drag of his cigarette and blows the smoke upward. When he speaks, he does so with a sophisticated Italian accent. "Rolan has been teaming up with Albanians."

"Is that so?" Adrian twirls the ice in his whiskey as he exchanges a glance with me.

He told me to look into it and I said the Albanians aren't dangerous. They aren't. They're very few in number and barely have any territories.

"Yes, those fuckers go after women." Nicolo crushes his barely finished cigarette and retrieves another one, shoving it in his mouth before lighting it.

"Don't they all?" I sip my drink, unable to hide the boredom in my voice.

"I don't mean prostitutes." Nicolo gesticulates with his lighter. "But our women, wives, betrothed—those types. They like to know they can turn them into whores, sell them on the black market, and tarnish our honor. We've been keeping our women out of the public eye, and I would do the same if I were you."

"Adrian doesn't need to." I grin. "His wife is always hidden away like Sleeping Beauty."

Adrian hides the clenching of his jaw with a smile. "Your wife, on the other hand, is very forthcoming about getting out."

"Cheers to my wife, without whom the brotherhood wouldn't have legal money to funnel back to your deep dark secrets."

"I'll drink to that." Adrian takes a sip of his glass and turns back to Nicolo. "Do you have anyone following the Albanians around?"

My phone vibrates and I place my glass on the table to check the text from Kirill. He doesn't usually get in touch unless it's to use his cunning nature to extract information. Since it never works, he gave up some time ago. The break of pattern turns my suspicious meter on.

Kirill: I have interesting scenery in front of me, so I thought I would share.

My hold tightens on the phone when he sends a picture taken in a traditional Asian restaurant. Rai is smiling, sitting between Damien and Kai, and the latter has his fucking hand on her thigh.

That's it. That fucker's date of death is only a matter of time now.

I know Sergei sent her to meet the Japanese with Kirill and Damien. She called me as soon as she was out of her granduncle's office, happiness bursting through her words. I made sure to tell her not to get too comfy in the fucker Kai's company. I clearly said to stay away from the sod, Damien, too. I didn't have to warn her about Kirill because she wouldn't go near that cocksucker even if her life depended on it.

But here she is being all comfy with those two. My mood flips from bored to murderous in a fraction of a second.

I'm vaguely listening to Nicolo talking about the Albanians. All I want to do is fly to wherever they're having the meeting and snatch Rai away—after I put a few bullets each in Kai and Damien.

"Lazlo and I were young at the time it happened." Nicolo takes a drag of his cigarette, his eyes darkening and accent thickening. "The capo at the time was my grandfather. He was fearless, ruthless, and didn't hesitate to cut any fucker who thought they could get past him. After we confiscated one of the Albanians' territories fair and square, they kidnapped my grandmother. But those motherfuckers didn't stop there. They sent pictures and videos of her repeated rape to Grandfather, my father, and my uncles. At first, she cried and fought. She kicked and scratched. Then, as the days went by, she just went silent. She used to call out *Nonno's* name, but then she didn't. She tried to kill herself, but they strapped her to a bed and used her like she was a filthy animal." Nicolo pauses to light another cigarette, his jaw turning as hard as granite. "It was the worst time in my family's history. A stain of dishonor."

"Your grandfather didn't look for her?" Adrian asks.

"Of course he did. He turned New York upside fucking down and went on a killing spree where he murdered anyone who stood in his path, but the only things he could find were the tapes they sent. And do you know what those fuckers did next?"

"I assume they killed her?" Adrian speaks calmly, almost as if he's sympathetic. He's not; he's just good at emulating the emotions needed for such situations.

"In cold fucking blood. When my grandfather finally succumbed to let them have their territories back, they said they would return her. That moment when she saw *Nonno* was the first time her expression changed. She sprinted in his direction, but the motherfuckers shot her in the back before she could reach him. They didn't need the territories anymore. The sadistic fucks only wanted to inflict pain and break *Nonno*, which eventually happened, you know. After *Nonna's* death, *Nonno* assassinated every last motherfucker he could find. He even went after them when they scattered all over Europe, but that turned him into a crazed dog who didn't work or sleep. He survived on vengeance, and that eventually destroyed him. He couldn't forgive himself for he was larger than the world, but he still couldn't save his wife. A few years later, he shot himself in the head with the same bullet they shot *Nonna* with."

"May they rest in peace," Adrian says.

Nicolo nods, crushing his unfinished cigarette. "Point is, don't underestimate that bunch of motherfuckers. They may not have much territory to speak of, but they don't hesitate to fuck you up in ways you can't survive."

He's speaking as if the Italians don't go around kidnapping women for payment. The Russians would've done that too—if Rai let them. It's the modus operandi of every crime ring since the beginning of time, but they still act victimized when they're the target.

Pathetic.

Adrian pretends to sympathize with Nicolo, but he's the biggest hypocrite. From the little information I've managed to gather about his closed-off life, he got his wife in a similar way. He's the last person who should judge the Albanians' methods when his are even more nefarious.

Adrian retrieves his phone and pauses at Kirill's name flashing on his screen before he answers. "Volkov."

I'm close enough to hear the gunshots through the phone.

Pop. Pop. Pop.

Shouts in Russian and another very familiar language filter through.

"Motherfucker!" Kirill curses in Russian before he yells, "We're under attack! Send backup!"

The line goes dead.

Adrian and I exchange a look as I feel the blood draining from my fucking face.

There's no doubt about it. The other voices, the ones who are attacking them, were Albanians.

EIGHTEEN

Rai

"This won't do." Damien checks his gun, then curses in Russian. He only has a few bullets left.

I'm not any better.

My gaze trails to Kirill, who's firing over the car's hood. The three of us are behind the vehicle, caught in the midst of a gun war that has lasted only a few minutes but feels longer.

I thought it would be the Irish, but it's worse. Their Albanian allies have joined the war and they have absolutely no fear. They'd readily step into direct gunshots as long as it meant they killed their targets. *Dedushka* once told me that if a soldier dies, the Albanians' leader honors him and makes sure his name goes down in the organization's history in a reverent kind of way.

The ambush was smart. Not only did they get Damien, Kirill, and me together, they also got us without many guards.

Since they greatly outnumber us, it's easier for them to take us out now.

We have been trying to stall as much as possible before backup arrives.

"How much do you have left?" I ask Kirill.

"Five." He fires a bullet, hitting an Albanian in the chest. "Four."

"They keep multiplying like fucking cockroaches." Damien kills two more, but the others continue approaching, using the cars as shields.

They probably know we will be out of ammunition soon so they don't mind sacrificing a few soldiers to empty all our guns.

At this rate, our death is a matter of when, not if.

"Stop firing," I tell them. "Try hiding more."

"When I need your help to tell me how to shoot, I will ask for it," Kirill says without looking at me.

He's distracted, gaze straying to Aleksander, who's a car ahead with Damien's senior guard. They, and a few other soldiers, work as our front line.

"No offense, Rayenka, but leave this to me." Damien's critical gaze flits ahead, probably trying to figure out how to turn this into a fistfight.

"They want us out of bullets." I stand between Kirill and Damien, and although I'm crouched, I try peeking through the car's window at the scene.

There are still a lot of them, and Aleksander is most likely out of bullets, his feminine features creasing with exertion. He stares back at us—or more like, at Kirill—and mouths, "Prosti menya."

Forgive me.

"No!" Kirill completely ignores the bullets and barges to his second in command.

I try grabbing him by the jacket, but he yanks my hand away and runs to the middle of the battlefield.

I lose my balance from the force of his push. Before I hit the ground, I make out one of the Albanians coming. "Careful!" I scream at Damien. He shoots him in the face, creating a bloody hole, and grabs me by the arm to keep me upright.

"Fuck. I'm out." He throws his gun away. "And stay still. You're going to get yourself killed."

"I'm fine. Kirill, however..." I don't get a chance to look at him when another guard rushes toward us.

"Let me take care of this sucker." Damien steps in front of me.

"Don't be an idiot—he has a gun."

He winks at me over his shoulder. "Didn't stop me before."

"You're not bulletproof, asshole."

"I love your tough love, Rayenka." He grins. "Besides, I need to stay alive for that marriage and shit."

He goes straight for the guard, and I attempt to shoot on his behalf, but I don't get the chance.

Two others gang up on me. I shoot the first, but before I can do the same to the other, he kicks my gun away, nearly breaking my wrist with it.

Instead of shooting me as I expect him to, he comes at me. I grab him by the arm and knee him in the crotch. My skirt tears at the bottom, but it's a small price to pay.

He howls in pain and I use the chance to try to snatch his rifle. A black bag is shoved over my head from behind. My nails dig into the fabric, but it's strapped so tight that no air comes in.

Worse, I'm breathing some sort of a funny smell.

I kick my leg up, but it connects with nothing. I buck against the one holding me, but two other pairs of hands join in immobilizing me.

No. I'm not going to die.

I still have a lot to do and...Kyle and I didn't even get our proper start yet. *I can't die.*

I elbow the body behind me, but his hold on the bag doesn't loosen. I feel lightheaded and my movements slow. My harsh breathing withers away and I fall slack against meaty arms.

No.

No…

I try to kick, but my limbs don't move.

Soon enough, darkness swallows me whole.

NINETEEN

Kyle

I BARGE OUT OF THE CAR BEFORE IT FULLY STOPS MOVING. The scene in front of me is nothing short of a battle-field. A few men are lying on the ground, their blood leaving splashes and forming pools on the filthy asphalt. Others are hiding from the gunshots behind cars.

But there's nothing to hide from.

More accurately, we're late.

Fuck.

Adrian motions at his guards to check the perimeter, and they comply with sharp nods. I remain in place, feet planted solidly on the ground, as my gaze roams the cars and the people left behind, whether they're alive or with their heads down.

Every time I see a motionless body, my heartbeat explodes in my ears until I make sure it's not Rai.

There's no trace of her.

None. Nada.

My hand trembles around the gun, and it's a fucking first. After taking a life when I was ten, I've never had my hand tremble around a weapon. Guns, rifles, and knives aren't only weapons; they are an extension of my hand, a method to not only stay alive but to also eradicate anyone who stands in my path.

This is the first time my weapon isn't fulfilling its role. I failed her, and so it failed me.

"Where the fuck did they go?" Kirill's agitated voice grabs my attention, and I sprint in his direction.

Although he and Rai hate each other, he won't be out to kill her. Besides, as much as I loathe the fucker Damien, he would make it his mission to protect the *Pakhan*'s grandniece.

Adrian joins me, even though he's intently watching the scene, probably recreating it in his mind's eye as I suspect he does whenever he visits a place.

We find Kirill between two cars filled with bullet holes, and I mean completely fucked up with bullets like in some Middle Eastern war. Two bodies lie limp around him as he punches an Albanian to a pulp. Even though the man is not small by any means, Kirill has made a bloody painting out of his face. His features are unrecognizable, eyes swollen, lip busted, and shirt soaked with blood and dirt.

Every time he punches him, the man's blood sprays on Kirill's shirt, face, and even glasses. That's a first for someone who's so meticulous and never gets his hands dirty.

"I said…" He breathes harshly. "Where the fuck is your nest of cowards? Where do you rats hide? Huh?"

The man groans with obvious pain but says nothing. If anything, he smirks, and that gets him a brutish punch to the skull.

"He won't talk." Damien leans against a car as his closest guard fusses with a wound in his bicep. "The others didn't before we killed them."

"Where's Rai?" I don't recognize my voice, the rage in it and…the fear. A fear so deep I can taste the bitterness of it.

Damien shakes his head once. "They took her."

His words strike me like a thunderbolt in the middle of a raging sea.

They took her.

The Albanians took her.

Nicolo's words from earlier and his retellings about what they did to his grandmother wrap a tight noose around my throat. It keeps suffocating me with every gruesome detail he mentioned.

I storm in front of Damien and grab him by the throat. "How the fuck did you let them take her? Where the fuck were you?"

His guard steps in to push me away, but stops with a dismissive motion of Damien's hand. "Not that I have to fucking answer to you, but they wouldn't have taken her if I were there. I was fighting one of them off, and when I turned around, they were carrying her and Aleksander into a van."

"Aleksander was taken, too?" Adrian's suspicious gaze slides to Kirill, then goes back to Damien. "Why would they take a guard?"

"Fuck if I know." Damien dismisses the soldier who won't leave his bleeding arm alone.

"In my place." Kirill pants, still clutching the Albanian by the collar. "They took Sasha in my place."

Sasha? Ah, right. Russians and their weird nicknames. How they even associate Sasha with Aleksander is a mystery.

"Still doesn't make any sense that they'd take you or Aleksander." Adrian stares at me even as he speaks to Kirill. "They're usually interested in women."

At his words, the retelling of Nicolo's grandmother's story hits me again, and this time, the images—the rape, the breaking, the murder, the tapes—all of them are too vivid and my hold instinctively loosens from Damien.

Bloody hell.

"He…" the guard in Kirill's hold croaks, smiling to show bloodied teeth. "He…looked…like a woman…that guard…"

"Fuck! Fuck!" Kirill roars, then takes a few breaths, smoothing his voice even though he appears ready to murder a town. "Listen to me, cockroach, if you don't tell me where you took him, I'm going to have you raped. I'll assault you with so many objects until I fucking break you. Maybe then you'll know how it feels, yeah?"

"In the meantime…your girly guard's ass will be broken."

Kirill swiftly yanks Adrian's gun and points it at the Albanian's head.

"No." I sprint toward him and place a hand on his arm, then whisper so he's the only one who hears. "He's our only card to find them and he's provoking you on purpose so you'll kill him."

Kirill is breathing through his nostrils even though his face remains stone cold. Instead of releasing the gun, he shoots the guard's leg, and blood splashes onto the Russian's glasses.

The Albanian screams like a chicken being slaughtered, but he soon goes back to smirking.

"Let me." I slightly push Kirill back and he complies, wiping blood off his glasses with the hem of his shirt.

The Albanian is kneeling on the floor, so I crouch in front of him and adopt the tone that got me through everything, the slightly light one, the one that hides how much I want to shoot this scum's brains out. "Hey there, I'm the good cop among all of them. Damien there would snap your neck in a second. Kirill here would torture you to death, and Adrian, well, you must have heard rumors about how he puts people in a white room, then drives them crazy without laying a hand on them. So aren't you happy you got me?"

"She's…your wife…isn't she? The…blonde beauty. I bet they can tear her cunt in one day—"

I drive my fist straight into his face, and even though the need to finish him off is stronger than anything I've felt before, I smile and continue in a semi-restrained tone. "Focus. That was not my question. But, anyway, since I'm a good cop, I have good-cop methods." I grab his cheek, wiping the blood with my thumb as if I'm worried about it. "What's your name?"

"David."

"I bet that's not your real name, but don't worry, part of my good cop arsenal is that I can take a picture of you, send it to my hackers, and receive an email back with all your details. Your real name, age, and even face if you went under the knife. But that's not all. They will also find out *things* like where you were born and how. Were you in the gulags? Or were you perhaps ex-military turned mercenary before you came here? Did you run in Eastern European circuits, do some burglaries here and some there? All of those will be in the records, and then, I will know about your family. Surely, you didn't come all the way here for yourself. You guys always have a sick mother living in a cottage-like home on a mountain, waiting for a check from you so they can fight off the merciless winters. Perhaps you have a girl on the side, too, or an offspring you're hiding."

Even though his expression doesn't change, David swallows. One of those is correct. The mother, the woman, or the offspring.

Jackpot.

"So here's the thing, David. For every hair hurt on Rai's head, you're going to watch that mother and woman of yours being raped and know you won't be able to save them until they spit their last breaths. Only then will I grant you death. How does that sound?"

David stares between the four of us, probably searching for someone who'll tell me not to do this, but he's fallen among the wrong crowd. Damien doesn't give a fuck about the methods we use as long as it gets things done. Kirill would've come up with this idea himself, and Adrian…well, he stands still and expressionless, almost as if he doesn't care what's going on.

I'm probably the only one who wouldn't use that option. Innocent women have nothing to do with this. However, I have to make him believe I would because, no matter how much they prefer this method, they wouldn't want it used against them. If anything, considering the horror they inflict, they know it will stab tenfold worse if it's directed at them.

"What's it going to be, David?" I wipe the blood from his face. When he says nothing, I stand to my feet, retrieve my phone, and direct it at him. "Smile for the camera."

"N-no…I…will tell you," David whimpers. "I'll tell you."

"Glad we agree." I glare down at him, my voice darkening. "Now fucking talk."

As soon as he finishes giving information and we make sure it's true, I shoot him between the eyes.

Every second I don't go to her, she's in danger.

With every second, they might hurt her in ways she can never come back from.

I'll get Rai back. I have to, even if I have to resort to methods I've never used before.

TWENTY

Rai

A FUNNY TASTE LINGERS AT THE BACK OF MY THROAT as I slowly open my eyes.

My surroundings gradually come into focus. I'm lying on a dark floor that appears like old, abandoned asphalt. A rotten smell like a public toilet in a forgotten gas station nearly causes me to gag.

I sit up and the world starts spinning like it did this morning. The gray stone walls have some industrialized red numbers on them, but they're faded, washed away by the merciless hands of time. The few cracks invading the solid surface and a metal bed in the corner are the only things in sight. Its white sheets are yellowish and appear to not have been washed in an eternity.

How did I end up here? After the bag was thrown over my head, I don't remember anything. Back then, the only thought I had was that I was dying and I couldn't just die.

The sense of relief at being alive doesn't hit me as strongly as it should. I might not be dead now, but that could change. Besides, it's worse if they take me alive. They could use me to try to force Granduncle's hand on something. It took so much for me to get to where I am, so there's no way in hell I'll be the brotherhood's weakness.

I try to stand up, but I fall back on my ass immediately.

"It's useless." The quiet voice coming from beside me startles me. I didn't know I wasn't alone.

Aleksander sits by my side, his legs outstretched in front of him and his arms limp by either of his sides. There's a cut in the shoulder of his jacket and his soft features appear strained, numb, even.

"They injected us with something," he continues, still staring at the wall across from us. "I don't know what it is, but it's robbing me of energy."

Now that I focus on my body, it feels hot and kind of numb, like I can't control my limbs. I try to stand up again, but I fall back faster than the first time.

"Better save your energy, miss."

"Shit," I pant.

"Shit, indeed."

I stare at him sideways. His lips are dry and cracked, which could mean he's dehydrated. I motion at his jacket where there's a red hole. Stains of blood cover his cheeks, too, giving him the look of a wounded warrior. "Did you lose a lot of blood?"

He stares at his injury as if he forgot it's there. "No. This should be fine."

"How did you end up here too?"

"They took me in place of Boss."

"Kirill?"

"Yes."

"Why would they want to take Kirill?"

"I'm not sure. I just knew I had to protect him."

The amount of blind loyalty Aleksander has for Kirill is insane. He'd literally die for him. As would Katia and Ruslan for me, I guess. I hope they didn't get caught in the gun war.

"We need to come up with a plan to escape," I tell him.

"Our best option is if one of us causes a diversion and the other escapes."

"I will do it."

"No. You're the *Pakhan's* grandniece. I'm disposable, so I'll do it."

"Even though you're Kirill's guard, you're not disposable. None of our men are, even if you hate me."

"I don't hate you."

"Your boss does."

"That's because you're threatening him, miss."

"Only to protect myself. I won't cause any of you harm if you don't cause me harm."

"Does that mean you're not..." He clears his throat. "You know, against his preferences?"

"Why would I be? They're his preferences and no one's opinion matters. As I said, I will only use his sexuality against him if he threatens me. I would rather not, but that's the only thing I've got on him, considering how closed off he is. If you tell me something else...I can ditch it."

"Nice try, miss." He smiles a little. It's the first time I've seen Aleksander smile, and I hate to be like the other guards who compare him to a girl, but he really looks like one right now.

"Doesn't hurt to try." I smile back. "Let's escape first, then we'll talk."

The door bangs open and both of us stiffen against the wall. We don't try to scramble away because that's not only use-less considering whatever they injected in our systems, but it also would drain our energy sooner rather than later.

Five men walk inside, all tall and broad with mean features.

The bald one, who appears to be their leader, approaches me with a gleam in his light eyes.

He has a scar that cuts across his bald head and ends right above his eyelid. When he speaks, it's in a thick Eastern European accent. "We should start with this one. You'll scream for your uncle and husband, won't you, kitten?"

Two men charge toward me, each trying to grab me by the arm. I kick and push at them, but not only am I outnumbered, my body also doesn't feel like mine. My movements are slow, and every time I punch them, they laugh and speak in their language, which I don't understand.

Aleksander tries to help me, but the other two hold him down on his knees and press down on the wound in his shoulder. He bites his lower lip to not release any sound of pain.

"Get her on her knees," the bald one orders. "I want those lips around my cock."

The guards get me in position, lust shining through their eyes. The sick assholes must've been promised a share after their leader is done.

The bald one gets his short, fat dick out and places it at my mouth. I don't open, glaring up at him. I'm going to fight tooth and nail before I let them touch me. I'm a Sokolov, and we don't go down without a fight.

He motions at the other guard, and they punch Aleksander across the stomach. He groans, falling to the ground, but they hold him upright, one of them grabbing him by his injured shoulder.

"For every second you don't suck me off like a good whore, that girly faggot will be punched. How long until he dies, I wonder?"

The guards hit him again and blood explodes from his mouth.

"Wait a second." One of the men holding Aleksander

crouches in front of him and feels at his chest. Aleksander tries to shoo them away, groaning and bucking until his face turns red.

The guard unbuckles Aleksander's pants and boxers. I don't want to watch the assault, but if I close my eyes, how am I a leader? Aleksander is one of our men, and if I let him go through this alone, it's no different than betraying my role.

Gritting my teeth, I force myself to stare at his face, to tell him it'll be fine even if I, myself, am not so sure of that. Aleksander isn't focused on me, though. He's lost his cool head and is blindly trying to ward them off, which only gets him hurt more.

I'm about to call his name, but pause when his pants and boxers are pulled down to his knees. Instead of the penis I expected to see, there are…female genitals.

"Fucking shit. Jackpot, boss." The guard grins. "It's a woman."

My incredulous gaze meets Aleksander's, who lowers his eyes, a tear sliding down his cheek—or more accurately, *her* cheek.

She's a woman. Aleksander has a been a woman all along.

I should've suspected it since the beginning considering her features, but she's such an excellent guard, stronger than many of her male counterparts, that no one dared to question her gender, even when they joked about her looks.

"Have fun with her while I have fun with this one." The bald guy runs his meaty fingers along my cheek.

The two other men flip Aleksander on her back, and something inside me snaps.

I grit my teeth, but I don't open my mouth, not until I make sure Aleksander meets my gaze.

Now, I tell her.

Then I swallow the clog in my throat and open my mouth. Ever since that day I first gave Kyle a blowjob, I swore to never do it to any other man after him. Ever since that moment, I felt like every part of me belonged to him and him alone.

Now that I'm in the midst of this situation, I can only think of him and how much I wish he were here, because if he were, no one would ever touch me.

But since he's not, I need to get this done myself.

As soon as the bald guy's dick is inside my mouth, I bite down on it as hard as I can. A metallic taste explodes on my tongue. The guard by my side kicks me in the stomach so I release his boss.

I grunt as I push away from him. The bald man wails and I back up, using their distraction with their leader to reach Aleksander.

They're too busy to notice me, one imprisoning her down and the other trying to shove his dick inside her. I use all my energy to kick the one holding her down and steal his gun.

Aleksander kicks the other one, then holds him in a headlock. As he screams, she steals his gun, then breaks his neck, the sickening crack echoing in the air.

I shoot one of the bald man's minions in the leg, turn to the leader, and shoot him in the dick. Then one more time in the forehead, for good measure. We run out of there, back-to-back in case the others follow.

Aleksander holds her pants up with one hand and buttons them.

Wait, it's not Aleksander, though.

"Is your name Aleksander?" I ask. "Do you prefer I call you that?"

"It's Aleksandra," she whispers, not meeting my gaze. "Thank you for helping me."

"Any time."

We sprint toward the nearest exit even though it feels like I'm about to collapse. My breathing is harsh and irregular, and the slightest movement feels like climbing a mountain. Both of us are panting by the time we hear distorted voices. They're after us, and by the sound of the thudding footsteps, it seems as if the number doubled from when they first barged inside.

Aleksandra and I exchange a look and then we each hide behind a wall, across from one another. If we have to fight to the death, so be it.

We fire at the ones following us, then move positions so they don't catch us. Our bullets are running out, though. At this rate, they will catch us again and it'll be worse than the first time.

Bang!

Aleksandra and I freeze at the sound of the explosion. That was some sort of bomb. Sure enough, soon after, a multitude of gunshots follow.

No one is shooting at us anymore or following us, but the sound doesn't cease.

Pop. Pop. Pop.

Then, we hear Russian voices. Aleksandra and I stare at each other and smile.

They came for us.

We carefully slide out of our hiding spot and follow the sound of the guns. Sure enough, Kirill and his men are at the front, eliminating anyone in their path. Damien is there, too, shooting out bullets like they're candy, an ammunition belt slung casually over his shoulder.

My heart leaps out of my throat when I catch a glimpse of Kyle pushing a guard to the ground. He usually prefers sniping positions that are far away from any conflict. This is the first time he's willingly gone into a battlefield.

He has three of the Albanians kneeling in front of him when his gaze meets mine.

They're still as hypnotizing as ever, but they're dark and enraged as if he's been thrust into a different state of being. One where his main purpose is to kill and maim.

He places a gun at the back of the first guard's head. "Did he touch you?"

I nod. He's one of the two who held me down.

Kyle doesn't blink as he pulls the trigger. The body falls to the ground as he moves to the next. "Did this fucker put his hands on you? Did he touch what's mine, Rai?"

The guard is about to piss his pants, lips trembling and pale. It's the first time I've seen his face, so I shake my head.

Kyle shoots him anyway. "He participated."

And then he goes on to finish the third one without even asking me. Their bodies lie lifeless at his feet, but he still watches them as if he's contemplating a way to bring them back to life just so he can kill them all over again.

It's one of the rare times Kyle lets me see this side of him up close and personal—the merciless killer. The one who will finish a life as if it's a fly's. And he did it for me. For some reason, it's like he learned everything up to this point so he could kill for me.

I should feel bad or be struck by some sort of remorse for being the reason behind so many people's deaths, but I don't. They're sick motherfuckers and they made many other women's lives hell. If Kyle hadn't come in time, Aleksandra and I would've met the same fate.

And then, I wouldn't have seen my husband's face again.

I don't allow myself to think as I run toward Kyle and jump on him. My body crashes into his, arms wrapped around his neck and legs caging his waist.

He staggers back a little at the force of the impact but loops both his arms around me, including the one with the gun. He inhales me in and I do the same, allowing myself to let my guard down, just for a second.

When in his embrace, I'm protected and safe. I probably shouldn't feel this way around someone I don't fully trust, but I can't ward off this strange feeling of belonging.

"Are you okay?" he whispers slowly.

"Yeah."

"Really?"

"Really. I'm glad you came, Kyle. I'm *so* glad." I don't know how it would've ended if he weren't around.

I try to get to my feet, but he doesn't release me, at least not until Ruslan and Katia rush toward us. I squeeze his bicep so he sets me down, but he does that reluctantly and keeps an arm around my waist.

Katia watches me with moisture in her eyes. "Miss…we're so sorry we weren't there."

"What are you sorry about? I'm the one who sent you off."

"But—"

"I'm fine, Katy. It takes much more than this to hurt me."

"But you look pale," Ruslan says.

Kyle places two fingers under my chin and lifts it up so I'm staring at him. "You do."

"It's nothing." I smile, forcing Kyle to release me so I can assess the situation around us.

The Albanians are completely wiped out, at least the ones here. And judging by Damien's expression, he's not very amused that it ended so soon.

Kirill is barking orders at his guards, probably to clean up, since we don't want the authorities at our backs. Aleksandra stands to the side, and when she attempts to help, Kirill dismisses her.

Her eyes meet mine, and I smile at her. She approaches me and clears her throat, adopting her 'male' voice. "Thank you."

"Likewise, Aleksander." I take the hint to call her by the name she goes by in public. If she doesn't want people to know, I won't tell.

"You can call me Sasha, miss." She bows and heads to Kirill, who has been watching us the entire time while wiping blood off his glasses.

As soon as Aleksandra—Sasha—joins him, he gives me an 'I'm watching you' gesture. He then pushes Sasha to walk in front of him on their way out.

The asshole doesn't deserve a diligent worker like her. I didn't like her guts and her loathsome loyalty to Kirill when she was a man, but now that I've found out she's a woman, I'm sure dire circumstances pushed her to hide her gender. Maybe I can steal her away.

"What are you thinking about?" Kyle turns me around to face him and I stumble. The room starts spinning and my vision blurs.

Kyle clutches me by the small of my back and his hand digs into my arm to keep me upright. "What's wrong?"

"I…I don't know."

"You should see a doctor."

"There's no need. I think it's because of whatever they gave us." I stroke his collar, lowering my tone. "How about you take me home?"

"I'm taking you to a doctor, Rai," he says in his non-negotiable tone.

I shake my head as I let him carry me toward the car.

A doctor is the last thing on my mind right now. All I want is Kyle for myself.

TWENTY-ONE

Rai

KYLE DRIVES ME TO THE NEAREST HOSPITAL. I tried arguing that I feel great and don't need medical care, but Kyle being Kyle, he didn't listen to those protests. Why can't the mule understand that I would rather be in our bed right now?

While I did fight, there was a moment where I thought I would be raped then killed and would never see him again.

It doesn't matter that none of that happened. The thought is already planted in the dark recesses of my psyche, and that idea killed me slowly. That thought broke my heart, which only beat back to life after I saw him again.

So no, a hospital isn't where I want to go right now.

I want him to take me, to make me forget about the scum who put his limp dick inside my mouth. I want him to wash away everything and everyone so he's the only one who remains.

But we obviously have different ideas of what I need. For someone so smart, Kyle can be such an idiot sometimes.

He's currently driving. One of his strong hands is on the steering wheel, and the other lies motionless in his lap. Even his side profile exudes a potent type of masculinity. I've always loved watching him while he's quiet and in his element. While Kyle usually has a huge amount of energy, it's mostly camouflage. Now, he's more relaxed, and I feel at peace when I look at him.

Well, aside from the tingling at my core that didn't stop once we left the Albanians' compound.

It should be wrong and demented that I want him this much after what just happened, but I do. I'm not even deterred by the stains of blood on his white shirt from when he murdered those men.

I have no right to judge when I'm a killer myself. Besides, he was strangely attractive at that moment when he showed his actual nature for me.

Kyle's gaze keeps flitting back to me every now and then, as if he's checking for something.

"What?" I ask.

"Are you really okay?"

"I am. And I would really rather we go home instead of to the hospital."

"No. You're pale and you almost fainted earlier."

"It's because I haven't had a proper meal all day."

"Why didn't you?"

"I was in a hurry in the morning, and I wasn't exactly focused on food during the meeting with the Japanese."

"Fuck, Rai. You need to take care of your health."

I suppress a smile at how worried he sounds. Why do I like this feeling a bit too much? "I'll pay extra attention in the future. Happy?"

"I'll only be happy when you start acting on it. In the meantime, we're going to the hospital."

"Ugh. You're infuriating."

"Glad to be." He pauses, his voice decreasing in volume as if he doesn't want to speak. "Did they do anything to you?"

"They didn't rape me," I say quietly. "Or Sasha."

"Then what did they do?" A muscle clenches in his jaw as though he's struggling to hold on to his cool. "Don't leave any detail out."

"They...well, one of them tried to force me to suck him off." My voice chokes at the end and I swallow. What the hell? I thought I was fine, so why do I feel dirty all of a sudden?

"Fuck!" Kyle hits the steering wheel, and I flinch at the sudden sound, even though I don't usually get affected. I guess I'm more emotionally distressed than I thought.

He takes my hand in his and kisses my knuckles, then speaks against them. "I'm sorry I wasn't there sooner, Princess. I'm so sorry."

The feel of his lips on my skin triggers something raw inside me, and I shake my head even though a tear slides down my cheek. "The only thing that matters is that you did show up."

"Not soon enough."

"It was for me. Besides, Sasha and I saved ourselves."

"What if you couldn't?"

"But I did. I'm here, Kyle."

"Was the fucker who touched you one of the guards I executed?"

I shake my head.

"I'm going back in there to burn him alive."

"No need to. I already finished his life." I puff my chest. "I shot him straight in the dick after I bit it off, and then I also shot him in the forehead."

Kyle chuckles softly. "I wouldn't expect anything less from my beautiful wife. I'm so proud of you, Princess."

His words make me want to purr, to snuggle into his side

and hug him—among other things. I've always been strong and independent and didn't allow people close. *Dedushka* taught me that I needed to protect myself because no one was going to do it for me, but there are situations like these where I realize just how much I love having Kyle around.

It's not only about how he came for me, but also the fact that I know he has my back as much as I have his.

And for that, I want to show my gratitude. Slipping my hand from his, I undo my seatbelt and fumble with his. It takes me seconds I don't have to spare to undo his belt and free his cock.

It jumps to semi-erectness at my first stroke. I had it in me last night, but the size still gets me all hot and tingly whenever I study it.

"What are you doing, Princess?" Kyle stares at me with fiery lust.

"Just keep driving," I murmur as I lower my head and take him down my throat as far as I can. He's too big for me to have him all in, so I make up for that by stroking his balls.

Kyle groans, eyes momentarily closing before he focuses back on the road. His hand tightens on the wheel as the other gets lost in my hair. "Fuck, Princess. Your mouth feels like sin."

His words get me working harder, teasing his balls and bobbing my head up and down at the speed he prefers. I may have been a newbie that first time I gave him a blowjob, but I have learned to adapt to his rhythm. Kyle likes rough and fast, even when it comes to blowjobs. He gets off on the endless flow of movement and has converted me to the dark side with him. Or maybe it's been there all along, and he just yanked it out.

With every second, he grows bigger in my mouth, and I'm sure he's close to the finish line. I increase my speed, even though my jaw hurts from his size.

Kyle pulls me back by the hair, making me release him, a streak of precum sticking to my lips.

"But…why…" I pant.

"First of all, I can't drive like this." It isn't until then that I realize the car has stopped on some unknown, deserted road. "Second of all, I love your mouth, but I'm not coming inside it today."

He jumps me—literally. One moment, he's sitting; the next, he's on top of me, fumbling with my seat so it falls backward. I squeal, hands pressing against his chest, but the sound is stolen when he captures my lips in an animalistic kiss.

There's nothing gentle about his touch right now. Not when he kisses me, sucking and nibbling on my lips like he's drunk on the taste, and certainly not when he yanks my dress up and then my panties down. His fingernails dig into my skin with a tangible urgency while he fuses his body with mine.

He's like a beast with nothing in his sights but me.

I could cry with gratitude.

If he treated me differently, as if I were a broken doll, it would hurt so much. I would think he no longer wanted me, that what I experienced today made him hate me.

But that seems far from the case now when he kisses me with so much wildness I can't keep up. It's like he's sucking at my life essence and giving me his in return.

He lowers his hand down my body until he grabs the globes of my ass. "I'm going to own this soon, baby. You better be ready for that."

I don't know if it's his words or the strange rush of arousal, but a tinge of impatience grabs hold of me. I want him inside me. Anywhere would do, even if it hurts—especially if it hurts.

His cock nudges against my entrance and I spread my leg wide, locking my ankles around his waist as he slams inside me with one brutal thrust. I cry out, flattening myself against the hard ridges of his muscled chest.

"Fuck, Princess." He strains at how my inner wall tighten around his length.

I gasp for air, and he only leaves me a second to breathe before he claims my lips again. That's the only second he allows me to adjust to his size, too—not that I need it. Yes, it hurts, but I want to hurt right now because that means I'm alive, it means I survived and Kyle is right here with me.

His tongue dances against mine as he thrusts into me hard and fast, his hips jerking with the motion. The seat creaks with the force of his hips. If someone passed by, they'd think a war was going on in here, and that might as well be the truth.

We're both fighters in this war, and at this moment, we only have each other.

I kiss him with renewed energy, pushing my hips up when he rams down. My arms wind around his neck and his hand grips me by the throat.

Surprisingly—or not really—that's all it takes to push me over the edge. I come with a gasp, my legs trembling around his waist.

Kyle joins soon after, cursing in what I now recognize as a Northern Irish accent. I find it strangely erotic that he switches to his original accent when he's this turned on. It's like he can't think straight enough to switch accents, and I like being the cause of that.

Both his hands rest on either side of my head to not crush me, even though his head lies on my shoulder.

I dig my fingers into his shirt, feeling the hard muscles underneath my touch.

"I'm sorry," he murmurs.

"For what?"

"For being such an animal right now. I should've taken it easy on you."

I tilt my head, kissing his cheek, and then tighten my arms around his broad back. "There's nothing to apologize about. It was…fine."

"Fine?" he teases. "I should up my game."

"More than fine. It was perfect."

"You're a masochist, aren't you, Princess?"

"Only with you, Kyle."

He pushes back, his intense gaze shining with unhidden possessiveness. "Only with me."

"Mmm." I smile. "Now, can we go home? I would love a shower. I can also wear that red nightgown."

"You're killing me, Princess."

"Is that a yes?"

"Doctor first."

He pulls out, cleans me with tissues, and then takes care of himself before he drives to the hospital. Why did I think he would forget about it after the sex?

Wishful thinking.

We sit down in one of the examination rooms, waiting for the test results. Kyle's words were, and I quote, "Check all of her." The nurse smiled, and I had to apologize for his overbearing nature.

"I'm going to be fine." I sigh, throwing my head back on the hospital bed. The pillow feels soft to the touch. After the nurse drew blood, she told me to rest and not attempt to stand up too soon.

"Then we will just confirm it." Kyle smiles in that infuriating way from his sitting position on the bed beside me.

"We're wasting time here when we could be doing other stuff."

His gaze gleams. "Other stuff like what?"

"You know."

"No, I'm afraid I don't. How about you enlighten me?"

"Do you want me to say it?"

"Fuck yeah, baby."

My cheeks heat at the way he calls me that.

"So what type of stuff?" he asks when I don't say anything.

"Husband and wife stuff."

"Husband and wife stuff, huh? You're surprisingly very horny tonight. Not that I mind."

"Shut up," I tell him, even though it's definitely true. I don't know why I feel like I want to jump him and let him fuck me all night long.

Part of it is because of the rush of life that invaded me after the whole shitstorm today, but the other part is something else I can't put my finger on.

Kyle cups my jaw before his fingers slide to my throat and he closes his hand around it. The position has become so familiar that my heart leaps whenever he does it. It's not helping my libido, though, because my body associates this gesture with sex, and he obviously won't do it while we're waiting for the test results.

"Once I make sure you're all good, I'm going to fuck you until tomorrow, Princess."

"Until tomorrow?" I whisper.

"It'll be rough, too just how you like it."

"Really?"

"Absolutely, so don't beg me to slow down or stop."

"I won't tonight."

"Mmm. Does that mean I get to do whatever I like?"

I nod once, biting my lower lip.

The door opens and I pull back against the pillow, but Kyle doesn't release me.

"Let me go," I murmur as the doctor approaches us.

Kyle tightens his hold around my throat for a second before he does as he's told. My face must be all red as the doctor stands beside us. He appears to be in his fifties with some white strands in his ginger hair.

If he noticed the scene, he doesn't comment on it, just busies himself with the papers in his hand. "The tests came back normal. There were traces of propofol in your system, but thankfully, it's not a dangerous amount that could harm the baby." His gaze slides to Kyle. "There are a few bruises on your stomach that aren't critical either, but if you'd like to talk to someone, please let me know."

My mouth hangs open as one word he said stays in my mind. "Wait—go back. Did you just mention a baby?"

The doctor's gaze doesn't change as he flips between the papers. "Yes. You're pregnant."

TWENTY-TWO

Rai

PREGNANT.

I think the doctor just said I'm pregnant.

"I can't be pregnant," I blurt. "I'm on the pill."

The doctor double-checks the papers in his hand. "You are, miss."

"There must be a mistake."

"No. Your blood tests came back with a considerable amount of hCG, which is the pregnancy hormone."

I stare at his face, my mouth falling open. "Then…then… how can I get pregnant if I'm on the pill?"

"If you missed a day or so, it could happen."

"I never have." Because the brute Kyle keeps coming inside me all the time and is so vehemently against wearing a fucking condom, I take them religiously.

My gaze slowly slides to his. He's grown quiet, his face expressionless. What is that supposed to mean? Is he also shocked?

I'm going to put a baby in you.

My eyes widen as his words from before slam back into me.

No, he didn't.

He…wouldn't.

"Is this the first time you're finding out about the pregnancy? If so, you should see an OB-GYN," the doctor continues. "It needs to be done as soon as possible."

I'm unable to answer him, so I nod as a response. The doctor watches us peculiarly for a second, then takes his leave.

As soon as the door closes behind him, I face Kyle, trying as hard as hell to hold on to my cool. A volcano is raging inside me with the intention of sweeping me under.

"Aren't you going to say anything?"

His eyes meet mine, and I see it, the cunning, the fucking victory. If I had any doubt, it's now eradicated.

The asshole.

The fucking asshole.

Kyle takes my hand in his and brings it to his face, but I yank it away before he can kiss it.

"Is something the matter?" he asks nonchalantly, almost *innocently.*

"Something the matter? Something the fucking matter? I was on the pill. I shouldn't be pregnant."

Kyle keeps his cool. "I've heard it's only ninety-nine percent effective."

"Or zero if you switched them out."

"Possibly."

"What the fuck is wrong with you?" I jump up from the bed, ready to punch him, but the world spins, putting a halt to my plans.

Kyle clutches me by the arm, but I yank it back, facing away from him to grip the bedpost. I want to scratch and claw at his damn face. I want to kick and hit him, but I feel too physically weak to inflict any pain.

"Why are you so angry? It would've happened at one point or another."

My lips part. He's not even trying to deny it or defend himself. He's openly confessing that he switched out my fucking pills.

"Wow. I really want to kill you right now."

"That will leave you alone with our baby, so I vote against that option."

I turn around and punch him across his slowly healing face. He doesn't attempt to avoid it, even though he must've seen it coming. "It's not *our* baby."

"You and I made him or her, so that makes the baby ours."

"*You* made this happen."

"Fine, but don't get too agitated. It's not good for your health."

"How can you be so calm about this?"

"Why wouldn't I?"

"Right, why wouldn't you?" My voice rises with a sense of mockery that's so close to rage. "You're the one who plotted for this all along, and it's simply working according to your plan. Now what? What's next in your grand plan? Are you going to put a few other babies in me?"

"If you want to."

"I don't want to! That's why I took the damn pills."

"Are you done?"

"I'm not fucking done! You know, this is why I can't trust you, Kyle. This is *exactly* why. One moment, you make me feel as if the world is at my fingertips, then you go and stab me in the damn back."

"Don't be so dramatic."

"Dramatic? You think this is dramatic? Oh, I will show you what dramatic is really like." I push at his chest. "You and I are no longer on speaking terms."

"Fine."

"Don't talk to me!"

"I'm not, you are."

Frustration bubbles in my veins, but I bottle it up and storm out of the room. I'm well aware of Kyle following right after me. I stand in front of the car because I have nothing on me, not even a phone to call Ruslan and Katia. As soon as he opens the door, I slide in the passenger seat and stare out the window.

I try to ignore the memories that come with being in this seat. Less than an hour ago, he made me feel over the moon. Now, he's done it again in a completely different way.

A sigh leaves him and I feel his eyes watching me. "Do you feel nauseous? The doctor gave me a prescription."

I don't respond and continue staring at the other cars through the window.

"So this is how it's going to be? Silent treatment?"

Exactly.

Until I figure out what to do with the life growing inside me and the man who put it there.

Because there's no way we'll ever be the same after this.

TWENTY-THREE

Kyle

THE DRIVE HOME IS SPENT IN UTTER SILENCE—THE suffocating type.

Rai erases me completely and focuses her entire attention on the world outside.

I clench my fist around the steering wheel to keep myself from grabbing her and knocking some sense into her. That will only escalate things for the worse, so I stop myself.

After all, it's not like she's mad for no reason. I may have played it down at the hospital so she didn't pop a nerve, but even I know her anger is legitimate.

As soon as we arrive at the Russians' compound, she barges outside. Katia and Ruslan greet her at the entrance, and she merely nods in their direction.

I walk beside her, keeping up with her angry strides. Anger is good sometimes. It means she cares enough to be angry. It's the lack of reaction that grates on my nerves.

We're only two steps inside when Anastasia jerks up from her position at the bottom of the stairs and quits clinking her nails against each other. Was she sitting there all along? She's in her pajamas, her white-blonde hair is barely brushed, and the dark circles under her eyes hint at many sleepless nights.

We stop when she runs and clasps Rai in a hug. "Are you okay, Rayenka? I heard what happened and was so worried about you."

My wife fakes a smile for her grandcousin's sake, even though she's been sulking around me. "I'm totally okay, Ana."

"But Papa said the Albanians got you and took you and…" She trails off, sniffling.

"Anastasia Sokolov, don't cry for something as trivial as this," Rai scolds like a loving mother, and the analogy hits me with the image of her carrying her own son or daughter. *My* son or daughter.

My gaze trails to her stomach, and although it's flat, the doctor said our child is there. Our. Mine and Rai's.

Holy fuck. I never thought it would feel this…euphoric. Fascinating, really.

"It's not trivial," Anastasia argues. "You were in danger."

"But I'm not anymore, you crybaby."

"But you were in the past and you will be in the future." Something flashes in Anastasia's gaze, something I never thought a soft, sheltered thing like her would ever show.

Grudge. An angry grudge.

Is that interesting, or what?

Rai pulls her into an affectionate hug. "Don't worry, Ana. I'll always be around to protect you."

"But for how long?" the younger woman murmurs, her gaze on nothing in particular.

"For as long as it takes." Rai pulls back. "Okay?"

She nods, her gaze sliding toward me, then back to Rai. "I…I want to talk to you about something."

"Can it wait until tomorrow?"

"Yes, of course." She kisses her. "I'm so glad you're safe." Then, Anastasia smiles at me. "Thank you for bringing her back."

"She's my wife. I would do it any time." I try to reach for Rai, but she steps away from my reach.

As soon as Anastasia disappears up the stairs, Rai's smile vanishes.

I suppress my reaction as we head to Sergei's office so we can give him a report of what happened.

"He will let you know the rest." She makes a vague gesture in my direction without looking at me. "I'm tired, so I'll retreat to my room."

"Of course, of course." Sergei's brows furrow. "Take care of yourself and the baby."

Her lips thin in a line at that. She didn't have a problem lying about her pregnancy all this time, but now that it's become true, she's in the mood to kill me.

She tells Sergei good night and storms out of the office as if hell is on her shoulders.

I contemplate the best way to summarize the situation to him before I join her. There's no way I'm letting her sleep in that state tonight. It takes me twenty minutes of answering Sergei's questions before I've had enough.

"I don't think we killed all the Albanians since that's not their only hideout. Kirill and Adrian will give you a full report come morning."

I'm about to excuse myself when Sergei cuts off my attempt to flee. "I'm going to need you to carry out a hit."

"On who?"

"I'll let you know soon." He pauses. "Just be ready for it and keep it between the two of us."

"Got it." No idea who he's trying to eliminate, but if he's keeping it a secret, something is definitely up. I will look into it as soon as he gives me a name. Did they perhaps figure out the identity of the traitor who's been stealing from them?

The wrinkles ease at his eyes. "And thank you."

"For what?"

"For saving Rai from an atrocious fate."

Why do he and Anastasia think I did it for them? I only did it for her, and myself by extension.

"There's no need to thank me. She's my wife."

After saying my good nights, I retreat to our room. I stop at the threshold when I spot her sleeping form on the bed. She's curled up in a ball, which is the last position I would expect Rai to sleep in.

The vulnerability of it doesn't escape me. She has been through so much today, from the attack to the kidnapping, and she ended the day by finding out about her pregnancy.

Recalling what those fuckers did to her makes me want to go back in time and slice the throat of every last one of those bastards.

If Kirill didn't catch that guard or if I were a little too late, she wouldn't be sleeping in our bed like this. I could've lost her for fucking good.

A long breath heaves out of my lungs as I shake those thoughts away. It's over. She's here, and I'll make sure nothing like that happens again, even if it means keeping her in my sight at all times.

She certainly won't like that, though.

The covers slide down her body, revealing her nightgown that rides up her bare thighs. It's a plain white one, not the red I was promised tonight, but, oh well—I didn't expect her to wear it after the fiasco in the hospital.

Her hair is slightly damp, which means she took a quick shower.

I'm tempted to lie beside her like this, but I don't want any of the blood marring my clothes and skin on her. She has the ability to make me feel like I do have filthy hands, and those hands keep on tarnishing her over and over again.

If I were sane enough, I would've stopped this vicious cycle of tainting her every step of the way, but I'm fucking insane when it comes to this woman.

I strip on my way to the bathroom and take a quick shower, letting the blood cascade down the drain.

When I return to the room, Rai is still curled on her side, but this time, a frown is etched deep between her brows. My chest tightens at what she must be dreaming about—the memories from today.

All I want to do is erase them and protect her, not only from those heinous memories, but also from the world.

Not bothering with clothes, I lift the covers and slip in behind her. My arm snakes under hers and I place my palm on her stomach and stroke it over the cloth, searching for what, I don't know. It's not like I can feel the life growing there this early.

I never thought about becoming a father before. I was like Rai and found the idea of a kid ridiculous. But ever since I saw this woman again, all I've wanted to do is put that life inside her.

It was a way to keep her with me, bind her to me so she'd never think of leaving me. Did I go overboard by switching out her pills? Probably. But I don't seem to have a moral compass when it comes to this woman. Most of the time, I'm acting on pure instinct like a fucking animal.

"Mmmm," Rai mumbles, the sound pained. Her brows furrow further and her breathing turns harsh. "No... mmmm...n-no..."

"Rai," I softly call her name.

"M-mmm...no..."

"Rai." I grab her face, and while my touch is gentle, my voice is anything but. "Wake up."

"Mmmm…"

"Come on, baby. Open those beautiful eyes."

"Nooo!" Her voice catches and a tear slides down her cheek and clings to her upper lip.

I shake her shoulder and she startles awake, her mouth agape and her bright eyes unfocused. Sweat covers her temples and her brows.

"It's okay. I'm here." I wipe the tears staining her cheeks.

Her chin trembles as she stares at me over her shoulder. "They…they were grabbing me…I didn't…couldn't…fight…"

"It's over, Rai. It's all over, okay?"

"They…they stripped Sasha in front of me and almost raped her and I…I couldn't help her."

So Rai finally figured out Kirill's second in command is actually a woman. About time someone did.

"But you did help." I plant a kiss on her forehead. "You did great. You were strong, Princess."

Her breathing slowly calms as she tilts her head further to get a better look at me. The sadness in those electric blue eyes bug me, especially since she seems sad about something entirely different than her nightmare about the kidnapping.

She attempts to face the other side. "Stay away from me."

"Not so fast." I grab her chin and force her to face me. "You said all night long, remember?"

"What?"

"I will make you forget about those scum."

Her eyes widen, but she doesn't get a chance to protest as my lips devour hers. She stiffens but doesn't attempt to push me away, her arms lying limp on either side of her.

Like me, she can't ignore the synergy that blossoms out of nowhere whenever our bodies are close to one another.

Wrenching my lips away, I whisper against her, "Tell me you want me."

"No."

"Rai...please."

She purses her lips before releasing them. "I'm not talking to you right now."

"But I want to talk to you. I want to touch you and make you forget. But if you don't want it, I can go to another room."

"Don't go," she whispers, and before I can be relieved, she continues. "This is only because I feel weird due to the hormones. It means nothing. I don't forgive you and I'm still not talking to you."

A muscle works in my jaw, but I bottle up my reaction for the dozenth time tonight. *We'll see if this means nothing.*

I trap her lower lip between my teeth as I pinch her nipple over the cloth. It hardens into a tight bud in no time, and Rai arches her back. Her pupils dilate and her arse grinds against my hard dick. I don't know if it's because of the hormones or what happened today, but the look of ecstasy on her face is like nothing I've seen before.

Still clutching her by the jaw, I slide my other hand down her body until I find the hem of her nightgown. I bunch it up to her waist and part her legs enough to push the crown of my dick inside.

"Fuck," I groan against her mouth at the same time she gasps. *Bloody fucking hell.* This is not normal, after all.

At first, I denied it because it didn't make any sense, but now, it's crystal clear. Being inside Rai is like finding home—which is bloody weird considering I've never had a home. And until her, I didn't think I had the right to covet it.

Now, I want it—*need it*—with everything in me.

I let her legs trap me in as I slide in and out of her in a rhythm I've never tried before—slow, moderate and too fucking deep. I take my time rotating my hips, pulling out almost completely then thrusting back in. I tell myself it's because I don't want to hurt the baby, but soon after, the pace grabs and drags me under.

My body has never been in synergy with hers as it is now. Rai holds her breath, then gasps, then holds her breath again.

She has never been good at controlling her air intake whenever she's turned on.

I place two fingers in her mouth and open it, using the chance to glide them against her tongue. "Breathe, Princess. *In. Out. That's it.*"

Her eyes never leave mine as she follows my lead.

I slide my fingers from her mouth and use them to part her arse cheeks. Rai gasps as I slowly push my middle finger inside. Her walls clench further around my dick as a moan rips from her throat.

Holy fuck. I want to own every inch of her here and now, but she's too damn tight.

Still fucking her in the arse, I pick up my pace in her pussy, and she bucks off the bed, murmuring, "There…there…"

"Here?" I rasp against her ear as I pull out then pound back in, hitting her sweet spot.

She shudders and her legs tremble as she shatters all around me. Rai might act like she needs no one on the outside, but she always, without a doubt, comes undone around me.

And in a way, she has the same effect on me. I've never wanted to own anyone as much as I crave her. I never thought about complete belonging before she came along. She's the only one who drives me crazy day in and day out.

I keep thrusting into her a few more times before my own orgasm sweeps me under. A groan spills from my lips as I empty myself inside her tight walls.

Rai slowly closes her eyes, lips pursing. I wrap my arms around her waist, holding her close. My head rests in the crook of her neck and I nibble on the hickey I left there yesterday.

She remains still for a minute and her breathing eventually goes back to normal.

I think she's fallen asleep, but then she whispers, "I'm going to abort the baby."

TWENTY-FOUR

Rai

KYLE ISN'T THERE WHEN I WAKE UP IN THE MORNING. In fact, he hasn't been there since I said those words. He pulled out of me, and although he didn't leave the bed, he didn't hold me either.

He was there in body, but not in soul. For the first time since we got married, he slept with enough distance between us that I shivered in the cold.

And in a way, it felt like he disappeared again.

I should've seen that coming when I said I'd get an abortion, but predicting something is entirely different from actually witnessing him withdraw from me. I guess a stupid part of me hoped he'd rectify his mistake by letting me have the final decision and actually respecting it.

Instead, he didn't talk to me, didn't fight, and didn't even make one of his distasteful passive-aggressive remarks. He just left as he usually does.

I try to ignore the soreness between my legs as I get ready for my day. I shouldn't have let him fuck me last night.

I really, *really* shouldn't have.

But hearing his soothing voice and feeling his warmth at my back loosened me up. It's the fucking hormones; I can feel them stealing my good judgment away and scattering it into the air.

That's why I said what I did right after we finished. I couldn't just allow him to take everything from me without a fight. He wronged me. He put a baby in me without my permission, so fuck him and fuck the way he withdrew from me.

Ruslan and Katia wait for me in front of my room, expressions concerned.

"Did you even get any sleep?" I ask.

Ruslan gives a sharp nod. "Yes, miss."

"No, you didn't. Look at those bloodshot eyes."

"They will eventually go away." Katia lowers her head. "We...we would've never been able to live with ourselves if something happened to you."

"If we were there, you wouldn't have had to go through that, miss," Ruslan agrees.

"Hey, you two, I was the one who told you to make sure Asher and Gareth were safe. Okay?"

"But—"

"No buts, Katia. It already happened, and we don't dwell on what's happened, so we'll just focus on the future." I pat both of their shoulders. "I feel so much safer knowing you two have my back."

"Always," both of them say, and I smile as the three of us descend the stairs.

Peter, Kyle's lonesome guard who's usually lounging around the house, is stuffing his face with a muffin. He's the most useless guard I've ever seen, and it's not only because of his bleached hair and brow piercings. It's that he truly lacks skills more than any guard I know, which makes me wonder why on earth Igor would recruit him. He talks back to Kyle all the time, which usually gets him smacked upside the head, and Kyle doesn't take him on dangerous missions either, so he's usually eating and being lazy.

Since he's here, Kyle could be around, too. My breathing shortens at the prospect of seeing him, and therefore talking to him. Considering everything that happened last night, it won't be pretty.

But I stand by my decision.

"Katia, clear my schedule for the afternoon."

"Done, miss."

"Will you need the car?" Ruslan asks.

"Yes." If I'm going to get an abortion, I might as well rip off the Band-Aid sooner rather than later.

I step inside the dining room for the usual morning meeting while inhaling deep. Who knows how the hell it will go with Kyle sitting right beside me…?

My train of thought scatters when I don't find him at the table. Everyone is here except for him and Adrian.

"Rai," Sergei urges when I remain rooted in place. "Come, sit. We were about to discuss the funds V Corp has been funneling into the brigades."

I force myself to stride to the seat and flop down beside Damien.

He nudges me and lowers his voice so I'm the only one who can hear. "Better today?"

"Yes," I reply meekly.

"The baby too?"

"Yeah." *Apparently.*

"Pity. I thought you'd leave the bastard Kyle if there weren't a baby."

"I can still leave him even when a baby is involved."

"That's my Rayenka. I vote for leaving him."

"Why are you so hell-bent on it?"

"You're matchmaking me with some Japanese girl who probably doesn't drink vodka. If I'm going to be miserable, I need to recruit you to my club." His brows rise. "How about an affair?"

"Maybe if you're the last man alive, Damien."

"I can make it happen," he murmurs with complete seriousness, as if he really is contemplating the best way to do that.

I shake my head, opting to not give him crazy ideas. More importantly, I'm in no frame of mind to focus on mundane conversations. My mood went from bad to horrible the moment I walked inside and didn't find Kyle. Where the hell is he? And is he really going to let me abort without talking about it?

The asshole's lack of reaction pisses me off more than if he had one.

Ruslan, who's standing behind me, leans over to whisper in my ear, "Aleksander keeps staring at you, miss. You want me to put him in his place?"

"No," I murmur and smile up at Sasha, who discreetly smiles back.

Kirill, on the other hand, glares at me as he readjusts his glasses. That manic look in his eyes can't be good news. The bastard really doesn't deserve Sasha by his side.

I wonder if he knows she's a woman. What am I saying? Of course he doesn't. If he did, he would shoot her dead. Since deceit is his modus operandi, Kirill takes offense at anyone lying or deceiving him. Besides, a woman passing as a man is a direct insult to the *Pakhan* himself.

Which is one more reason why I should bring her to my side.

It's a world ruled by men to the point that even female guards aren't allowed. *Dedushka* made an exception for Katia because I put my foot down for her. Everyone except Ruslan still looks down on her, despite her top-notch skills. They do it behind my back, of course, because I would rip them a new one if they badmouthed her in my presence.

During the meeting, we talk about the financing and that, due to the circumstances, I agree to release a higher percentage of V Corp's net profit. But I dig my heels in until Sergei agrees that we'll have a deadline for when the brigades will repay the money, something Kirill and especially Mikhail don't like. Kirill disagrees because he hates to be told what to do by me—or anyone, basically, but Mikhail is in a dire situation. I've seen his brigade's numbers, and they're more than shit.

After the meeting, I linger in the dining room after I find a text from my twin sister.

Reina: I can't believe you met Gareth and Asher, but not me. It's been months since I last saw you, Rai. Should I apply for next year?

I can almost hear the sarcasm and hurt in her tone.

My chest feels stuffed as I stare at her tiny picture at the top of the chat. It's one of her holding Gareth and laughing while Asher kisses her cheek.

It's so spontaneous and full of life, like everything about Reina. I miss her so much, now more than ever. I wish I could meet her even for a while and just...*talk*. I want to tell her about everything like we used to confide in each other when we were little.

"Leave us. I need a word with Rai." Kirill's voice pulls me out of my reverie and I quickly hide my phone.

I realize he's speaking to Ruslan and Sasha since we're the only four left here.

Ruslan doesn't move until I nod at him. Sasha hesitates, staring between me and Kirill, her lips parting in clear worry.

"Boss—"

"What part of fucking leave do you not understand?" He cuts her off without sparing her a glance.

She jerks upright as if his command is a whip, then gives a

sharp nod. Before moving, she chances one last unsure glance at me then slips out, closing the door behind her.

Kirill and I sit across from each other. I want to break his glasses and jam them in his eyes for the way he yelled at Sasha, but I remain calm since he's the type of freak who gets off on strong emotions.

"I didn't realize we were close enough to sit for tea after breakfast, Kirill." I take a sip of my coffee while continuing to stare at him over the rim of my cup. I feel like I always need to watch the cunning fox to somehow grasp him.

"We're not. Fortunately."

"Fortunately. So to what do I owe this *honorable* meeting?"

"I've been wondering."

"About?"

"When are you going to tell Sergei and the others about what you saw?"

"What I saw?"

"In the club. You remember now, don't you?"

I never forgot, idiot.

"Oh, you mean your sexual preferences? I told you, I don't want to use that against you unless you force my hand."

"I'm forcing your hand, then. Tell them."

"Why would you want me to tell them?" It doesn't make any sense for him to dig his own grave.

"Don't you want to destroy me? You have your chance, so fucking seize it."

"No." I was serious when I told Sasha I would rather never threaten him with that part of his life. Being gay is like being a woman in this world—though I suspect he's bisexual. Point is, they're an oppressed minority within any crime organization. Despite all his accomplishments for the Bratva, if this gets out, Kirill and his family would completely lose favor for something that shouldn't be treated any differently than normal.

"I said. Do. It."

"No, Kirill. What the hell is wrong with you?"

"If you don't, I'll kill your sister."

I freeze, but keep my expression neutral. "I don't know what you're talking about."

"Reina Ellis. Though, she's Reina Carson now, yes?"

I choke on the coffee, splatters covering the table. "How…"

"Did you really think I wouldn't find out about her with you holding something over my head? You hid her well, but I have my ways."

"Kirill," I warn.

"She's been married to her childhood sweetheart for seven years now, right? He's a lawyer and works for his father's firm. They also have a beautiful little boy who was named after your father. Should I start with the child first? Would that give you a good enough incentive?"

I spring to my feet, pulling my gun from my bag, and point it at his head. "I'll spill your brains here and now."

"Kill me and an unfortunate gas accident will blow up their house. And since it's the weekend, they're all home today. Can you picture the headlines talking about the tragic event?"

My hand shakes as the reality of what will happen to Reina slams into me. Kirill wouldn't hesitate to do it. He has a fucking talent for disguising every murder as an accident.

My worst nightmare is a reality. Everything I did to protect Reina from my life is biting me in the ass. Out of all people, it had to be Kirill.

"What the hell do you want?" I bite out.

"I'll pretend I know nothing about Reina's existence if you tell the brotherhood about me."

"Why don't you come out yourself?"

"That's none of your fucking business. Just do as you're told." He stands up and buttons his jacket, uncaring about the gun that's still pointed at him. "You have a day before the bomb goes off."

As soon as he leaves, my hand with the gun falls to my side. The only thought in my head is that of the sister who's the spitting image of me.

Reina.

I need to save Reina.

TWENTY-FIVE

Rai

I'M ASPHYXIATING ON AIR BY THE TIME I REACH REI'S house.

The architecture is modern and the building is two stories with an attic. At least they were mindful of security since they chose a property that's surrounded by tall, solid walls. Even their garage is inside the wall.

And when I say they were mindful of security, I meant I convinced them to buy something like this, because even seven years ago, I was sort of prepared for something like this to happen.

It's the second time I've been here. It should be weird that I'm visiting my sister's house for only the second time since she got married seven years ago, but for me, it was a perfectly normal decision.

I didn't want to come before in case Kirill, Damien, or Mikhail had someone following me around. I didn't trust that they wouldn't find and hurt her.

But now, it's over. Now, Kirill knows, and he won't stop until I either fulfill his callous demands or he hurts my sister.

The sister I promised Mom I would protect with my life if I had to. Reina is the last connection I have to Mom and Dad. She's one of the few people who make me feel as if I have a purpose in life.

Ruslan and Katia stand on either side of me as I hit the doorbell. Everything I did to protect her and her family doesn't matter now that Kirill is on the hunt for their lives.

I need to get them out of here, send them somewhere and—

The door opens, my mouth agape with it. The person standing in front of me is the last one I expected to find here.

Kyle.

What the…

He's nonchalantly carrying little Gareth on his shoulders. My nephew giggles, showing his missing teeth as he runs his toy car through my husband's hair.

"What…what are you doing here?" I sound as confused as I feel.

"I'm paying Reina and Asher a visit." His expression is as blank as his voice.

Why do I hate that so much? Kyle might have been away before, but whenever he's with me, I'm always the only one on his mind.

Ever since yesterday, I feel like he's slipping from between my fingers and, eventually, he'll disappear all over again.

"Auntie!" Gareth exclaims, waving his toy in the air.

"Hey, baby boy." I try to take him from Kyle's hold, but he lifts his shoulders and holds on to Kyle's neck.

"You know me now, Auntie?" he pouts.

"I do. I'm so sorry for yesterday, Gareth. I was tired and thought you were someone else."

"It's okay. Mommy said aunties forget sometimes."

"Rai!" My sister's exclamation reaches me first before she attacks me in a bear hug. "I missed you *so* much."

I wrap my arms around her as I push her inside, nodding over my shoulder at Ruslan and Katia to stand guard outside before I close the door.

Reina steps back to stare at me as if it's been years since we last met. She's wearing simple slim jeans and a tight blue tank top. Her hair falls loose to her shoulders, and her makeup is light but striking. She was always the beauty queen between the two of us. Ex-high school cheerleader, prom queen, and somewhat mean girl of her school.

If we'd gone to school together, I would've probably been the quiet twin who kicked everyone who dared to approach her. But I guess Asher fulfilled that role on my behalf.

She smiles, and it strangely feels as if I'm staring at myself in the mirror, though my smile isn't as bright as hers, or as carefree.

"Kyle was right."

"About what?" My gaze strays from her to him. He doesn't even make eye contact, pretending to be busy with Gareth, and when he does, it's as blank as his soul.

The asshole.

"He said you'd come to visit us today, but I didn't believe him." She strokes my cheek. "But here you are. You look so… different."

"I'm still me, Rei." I keep stealing glances at Kyle. How did he know I would be coming here before I even did it?

"Like hell you are." Her smile drops and she adopts a stern tone that's so similar to Mom's. "Don't you have something to tell me?"

"Like what?"

She grabs my hand and shoves the one with my wedding ring in my face.

"Oh."

"Right. *Oh*. I can't believe you got married without telling me." Her voice drops. "I was planning so many things for your wedding, but I wasn't even invited."

Shit.

I hate seeing her anguished like this. It feels as if I'm amputating a limb or something. I hold her to my side by the shoulder. "I'm so sorry, Rei. Everyone was there and I couldn't endanger your life." Her brows stay drawn together, not seeming convinced in the least, so I continue, "Your absence was like having an empty hole in my chest, but I couldn't bring you in. Not when your life, Gareth's, and Asher's are at stake."

That makes her wrap an arm around my waist. "I know, but it still sucks."

"I'm sorry."

"Sorry doesn't fix the fact that you hid it from me." She pushes back. "I can try to understand not being invited, but we talk all the time—how come you never mentioned it? If Kyle hadn't come to visit, would you have ever told me?"

I glare at him. The jerk is meddling in business that doesn't concern him.

His expression remains the same, and even though he's playing with Gareth, he's barely smiling.

"It was an arranged marriage. I didn't think it would last," I tell Reina. "I still don't."

If I expected a reaction from Kyle, I'm disappointed as he gives none, indulging Gareth by letting him run the toy car on his chest.

"But why?" Reina's brows furrow. "Kyle seems like a great guy. He was the guard who was protecting you seven years ago, right?"

Of course Reina would remember stupid details like that.

"Let's talk somewhere else." I take her by the hand. "I came here for something urgent."

Kyle brings out his phone and types while his other hand

holds Gareth. My phone vibrates and I check it while still holding Reina's hand.

Kyle: Don't alarm her for no reason. I already took care of the man Kirill sent to plant something in the house. Don't tell her to pack and leave because that will only put her in more danger. You can protect her better when you know where she is at all times.

I hate how right he is. Besides, knowing Reina, she'll also think I'm the one in danger and wouldn't budge from here, not to mention both her and Asher's lives are here. All their friends and her entire social circle are in this place.

Typing back, I don't look at him.

Rai: How did you know about this?

Kyle: Adrian told me about Kirill's plans. He owes me one.

"Rai, what is it?" Reina tugs on my hand.

"Nothing." I breathe out and smile. "Can't I visit my little sister?"

She grins. "About time you come to visit. Let me show you around."

Reina tells me about the renovations they did and how the fireplace is upgraded from the one I saw the last time I came here, which was years ago, as Reina likes to remind me.

We find Asher in the kitchen, picking beers, probably for him and Kyle. He smiles upon seeing me, and although he's in simple gray slacks and a white T-shirt, he appears groomed and ready to step into court any minute.

"I'm sorry about yesterday," I say.

"Don't worry about it." He offers me a beer. "Like you, I don't want my son near that crowd."

Although he doesn't say it in a condescending manner, I know exactly what he means. Asher was brought up by one of the most successful lawyers in the country, and while he's not the morality police, he's not entirely comfortable with Reina's criminal legacy. He just wants to live a normal life with his family, and I completely respect that.

"Thanks." I motion at the beer. "But I'm not drinking."

"Rai!" Reina grips me by the arm. "Are you—"

I place a hand on her mouth and drag her with me. "Excuse us."

Asher smiles knowingly. "Take your time."

As soon as we're in an adjacent dining room and out of ear-shot, I let Reina remove my hand from her mouth.

She stands in front of me, placing a hand on her hip and tapping her foot on the ground. She really acts like Mom sometimes.

"Spill, Rai."

"What?" I feign innocence.

"You're pregnant, aren't you?"

"What gave you that idea?"

"*Thanks, but I'm not drinking.*" She mimics the tone I used.

"Only that?"

"That's the exact same line I told Asher as soon as I found out I was pregnant with Gareth. Also, you're all radiant—your skin is glowing and your hair is shinier. That's what's different about you."

"You're imagining things."

"No, I'm not. You also look at Kyle as if you want to ride him standing. I did that during my first trimester. The position isn't exactly comfy, but it's fucking hot."

"Too much information, Rei."

"Stop being a prude."

"I'm not a prude. I just don't like talking about these things aloud."

"Which is the definition of a prude. So am I right or am I right?"

I can never win with her, so I sigh. "Yeah, fine, I'm pregnant."

She squeals, jumping up and down like when she won

whenever Mom played hide and seek with us. I guess Reina kept more of her child self than I did. That part of me died when I realized what it meant to be part of the brotherhood—that if I don't kill, I'll be killed.

"I'm not keeping it," I say, low enough that I'm almost sure she didn't hear me.

But Reina stops jumping, her expression more worried than judgmental. "Why?"

"Because...I just can't bring a child into the world I live in."

"What are you talking about? At this rate, you're just wasting your life away."

"I'm not wasting my life away. I'm *building* it. There's a difference."

"Okay, fine. But answer one question."

"What?"

"Do you want children?"

"I...don't know."

"Have you ever thought about motherhood? About Mom?"

"I think about her all the time." I clear my throat when my voice catches. "But I won't be her, Reina. I will not give birth to children knowing full well they will suffer in the crime world."

"Did you suffer?"

"No, but that's because I had *Dedushka*."

"And your child will have you and Kyle and his badass auntie, too. Ash and I started taking Muay Thai classes and we can totally kick ass." She steps back to show me a pose, and I smile a little. "So before you make any decisions, just think about it, okay?"

"I have, and my decision is final."

"Is Kyle fine with it?"

"No, but his opinion doesn't matter."

"He's the father, Rai."

"And this is *my* body. He had no right to plant his seed in there without my permission." My voice rises and I breathe through my nostrils to calm down. "I didn't ask for this. I'm not...I'm not *fit* to be a mother. I'm not you or Mom, Rei. What...would happen to my child if I somehow died? Huh? And Kyle? That bastard's lifestyle is even more dangerous than mine. Sooner or later, he'll leave, whether by choice or by a bullet. And then what? How am I supposed to carry that weight on my own?"

"Why can't you?" She rubs my arm. "You're the strongest person I know, Rai. You've been my hero since the moment you stepped in front of Ivan and said, 'I'm Rai Sokolov.' I was trembling in the corner like a stray kitten in the rain, but you didn't falter or look back. You took my place without hesitation and gave me your comfy life. You saved me, Rai, in more ways than one and continue to do so sixteen years later. Why would you doubt your motherly skills when you've had them since we were kids?

"Besides..." She wipes the tear that slides down my cheek. "We'll all die one day, so it's pointless to use that as an excuse. You're just scared, and it's fine. I was constantly afraid of what type of mother I'd be. I still doubt myself sometimes, but Ash and I hold each other through it all. It's like one of us would fall without the other. Gareth is the best gift I could've ever gotten. So I don't want you to make rash decisions without thinking clearly about it. That being said, if you still want to abort, I'll be right there, holding your hand through it."

"Reina..."

"Come here, big sis." She hugs me, and I close my eyes as I let her warmth envelop me. "Although, five minutes is too unfair. I should've come out first."

I chuckle, pulling away to stroke her hair. "I feel so much better after talking to you."

"That's what twins are for—though you're losing your privileges after you hid your marriage from me."

"Rei..."

"Fine, fine. You were protecting me and whatever."

"I would do anything to make sure you're safe."

"I have no doubt, but don't cut me out of your life. I *hate* that."

"I'll try to be more present."

"As you should. Now, tell me all about you and Kyle."

A deep sigh heaves out of my lungs. "There's nothing to tell."

"What do you mean there's nothing to tell? There's so much tension between you two that it can be cut through with a knife."

"Have you seen the way he looks at me?"

"Like he wants to hate-fuck you, then slowly fuck you?"

"No, like he's erasing me."

She stares at me incredulously. "Whoa. You're hopeless."

"What?"

"You're such a great judge of character in mafia things, but you suck in the affection department, Rai."

"What is that supposed to mean? He really looks like he doesn't care."

"No, he doesn't. He just seems a bit heartbroken."

"Because I said I would abort the baby that wouldn't have happened if he hadn't switched my birth control pills. Who between us should be heartbroken?"

"He did that?" she murmurs.

"Yes, so how about you go give him some lessons about communication?"

"That's such a dick move."

"Say it again for the people in the back."

"He must've really wanted the baby."

"Why would he?"

"You're the one who's supposed to know the answer to that question. He's your husband, after all."

"Don't you think I thought about it? But I keep drawing a blank. His type shouldn't even want a family."

"Why not? Even the most heartless people want families."

"Not him, Rei..." I trail off as his words about his family's death hit me.

He saw his own parents being murdered when he was only five. His only family since then were assassins who turned him into a killing machine. He's never actually had a family. Could that be why he yearns for one of his own?

I never thought about it from that angle. Not that it excuses what he did, but it at least somewhat explains his behavior.

"Just talk to him," Reina urges. "Without your walls up."

"My walls aren't up."

"There—they just went up now. Try not to be defensive."

"But he's the one in the wrong."

"He is, there's no doubt about it. But is the murderous tension how you want it to be for the rest of your lives? Because the lack of communication can turn toxic way too fast. Ask me how I know."

I rub her arm, recalling how she told me all about her history with Asher. "But you're here now and Asher proved he deserves you."

"Kyle didn't?"

"Not really."

"And fucking with your birth control pills doesn't get him any brownie points either."

"Tell me about it." I swallow the lump in my throat. "Sometimes, I feel like he's so close, and other times it's like he's a shadow I can never grab a hold of. I thought I was okay with it at the beginning, but I'm far from okay now, Reina. I feel like I'm on a constant rollercoaster ride with no room to catch my breath. How can I trust him now?"

"Talk it out, Rai." She softens her tone. "It's the only way for you to move forward."

I nod even though I have no freaking clue how I should start that type of 'talk.'

Reina interlinks her hand in my arm. "Come on, spend

some time with Gareth. He came to me crying yesterday when he thought an alien took his auntie."

"Sorry about that."

"Apologize to the little guy, not me. If you let him play with you all day, he'll probably forgive you."

We head to the living room and find Gareth holding a bamboo sword and riding Kyle as if he's a horse. He shouts as he fights the evil monster who is Asher.

My heart clenches at the sight. It's the first time I've seen Kyle so carefree and smiling without calculation.

It's a miracle that he can smile like that after witnessing the monstrous deaths of his parents. It's even more miraculous that he can be so open with a kid.

I don't know why I feel like something's moving in my chest at the view.

"Look at them." Reina's voice is filled with awe. "Gareth doesn't like people so easily, but he's already making Kyle his horse. He watched *Tangled* the other day and the horse is his favorite character, so not anyone can be his horse."

"Kyle has a way of charming people. Seems that not even kids are immune."

Reina smirks, flipping her hair. "Are you telling me that or are you talking to yourself?"

"Shut up." I hit her shoulder with mine and she returns the gesture.

I missed her so much.

⁓

We spend almost the entire day with Reina, Asher, and Gareth. My twin sister won't let me leave, saying she only sees me once in a blue moon and that it's the weekend anyway, so I should rest.

I invite Ruslan and Katia to eat lunch with us, but they

won't leave their guarding spots, not even when I order them to. So I just get them takeout.

Kyle and Asher spend most of the time playing with Gareth or watching TV together. Before I know it, we're all sitting down for a late dinner after Gareth passed out on the couch.

Reina goes to carry him to bed, but Asher gently pushes her aside.

"I can carry him," she argues.

"I know you can, but he's gotten so big, so I'll do it."

She tries to protest, but Asher places a kiss on her forehead, making her go speechless.

My twin sister joins us in the dining room. She went all out and even prepared a Russian soup.

"Since when do you know how to cook?" I ask.

"I took classes. Why?" She turns to Kyle, who's sitting silently by my side. "Is she still a hopeless cook?"

"More or less."

"Hey! I prepared you those pancakes and toast that time."

"*Burnt* pancakes and toast."

"You ate them."

"I had no choice. The non-burnt parts weren't so bad." He takes a sip of the soup, still not meeting my gaze.

Reina stares between us and motions at him. I make a face at her, but that only widens her grin.

Asher joins us after he places Gareth in his room.

"Did he wake up?" Reina asks.

"He didn't even stir. He played too much for his own good." Asher places a hand around Reina's shoulder and leans in to kiss the top of her forehead before he sits down.

I've always loved the way he looks at her like she's the center of his world and everything else is an accessory. Like the world is gray and she's the only one in color.

Lowering my head, I dig into my soup to avoid watching

them like a creep. I startle when my eyes meet Kyle's inquisitive ones. He's been watching me. But why?

He pours himself a glass of wine and finishes half of it in one go.

"Where in the United Kingdom are you from?" Asher asks him. "London?"

"Yes. I lived there for most of my life, but I'm originally from Ireland."

"You don't sound Irish." Reina removes the fish bones and places the clean ones on my plate as if I'm a kid.

"I was raised by an Englishman, thus the accent."

"Asher lived in England for three years." Reina's voice drops with clear sadness. "He went to college there."

Her husband grabs her hand over the table and strokes the back of it as he speaks. "Yeah, that's why I asked. I have a few English friends and they're famous assholes."

"Really?" Kyle finishes his glass of wine and pours another. "Who?"

"Aiden King and Cole Nash."

"The heirs to the King and Nash fortunes."

"You know them?"

"Everyone in England does. Their companies are everywhere like cockroaches." Kyle continues sipping from his wine, or more like gulping it down. "I have a personal acquaintance with Aiden's father, Jonathan King."

"What type of acquaintance?" Reina asks.

"It's not the type to be brought up at family dinners."

"I know what you do, Kyle." She stares between the both of us. "This is a judgment-free zone. I accept my sister and her other half the way they are."

Kyle scoffs at 'the other half' part, and I pinch his thigh under the table. He grabs my hand and gently pushes it away from his pants. My heart thuds as something hard and heavy clinks to the bottom of my stomach.

It's the first time Kyle has rejected my touch. Usually, he would be the one all over me, teasing and making me squirm at Sergei's dining table, and I'd be the one pushing him away.

What happened just now?

"Rai!"

"Huh?" I stare up at Reina, unable to focus. "Did you say something?"

"I was asking if you want a soda."

"I'm good." My gaze trails to Kyle, who's downing his third glass. I lean in to whisper, "You'll get drunk."

"So?"

"You...don't like being drunk." He told me that once, said he rarely allows himself more than a glass because being drunk distorts his thought process.

"Maybe I do." He barely spares me a glance as he pours himself another glass.

By the end of the evening, he's well and truly drunk. Ruslan and Asher have to help me carry him to the back of the car.

I hug Reina, who came out to see us off. "I'm going to put guards on you for the next couple of days, so please don't say no. It'll make me feel at ease."

"And you'll visit more often?"

"I will."

"Fine." Then she whispers, "Remember, talk about it. I almost lost Ash because we didn't sit down and talk, so don't repeat my mistake, Rai."

I rub her back once before I let her go, and get into the back seat. I wave at Reina, and she waves back as Asher spoons her from behind, removing his sweater and wrapping it around her shoulders.

Ruslan stays with them as guard, which reminds me to ask Sergei to send a few more to Reina's side. He always wanted to put guards on her, but I respected her wishes of wanting to live a normal life.

As the car moves, I stare at Kyle, who's passed out beside me. His head is slung back on the leather seat and his lips are slightly parted. The first two buttons of his shirt are open, revealing his taut skin and his lean, muscular build.

Was he always this attractive, or am I just too drunk on him as he is on wine?

I'm mad at him, I am, but I can't resist it as I reach out a tentative hand and palm his cheek. My touch is soft, experimental. I've never actually touched him to my heart's content before. It's always felt as if he's the one who does that and I needn't do anything.

His head tilts until it falls on my shoulder. I suck in a deep breath, but all I manage to inhale into my lungs is his masculine scent mixed with the wine.

He wraps an arm around my waist, and tingles erupt under my skin. I slowly close my eyes, taking in the sensation. Why does it feel so good to be in his hold? It's not even about sex. I just love being in his arms like this.

"Straight home, miss?" Katia asks from the driver's seat.

"Yeah," I say without opening my eyes.

"Since you weren't able to do what you planned for the afternoon, should I clear your schedule for tomorrow?"

"No, not yet."

I think I must fall asleep, because the next time I open my eyes, Katia is calling my name.

Kyle untangles himself from around me, and I try to ignore the loss. I expected that Katia would have to help me carry him upstairs, but he staggers on his own.

"Get some rest," I tell her and follow him.

I try to hold his arm to keep him standing, but he pulls it from mine.

That's the second time he's done that tonight, and I can't control the lash of my tongue. "I'm just trying to help you."

"I don't need your help," he slurs.

"Well, *excuse me* for trying."

I stomp ahead of him toward the room and throw my bag on the bed as soon as I'm inside. My blood is boiling as I remain standing in front of the mattress.

I don't move until I hear the click of the door behind me.

His quiet voice fills the room soon after. "Is having a child with me such a tragedy?"

TWENTY-SIX

Rai

THE AIR RIPPLES WITH A FATAL TYPE OF TENSION, one that suffocates and throttles, one that confiscates not only air but also common sense.

Although a significant distance separates me from Kyle, it's like he's wrapping his fingers around my throat and backing me against the wall.

Is having a child with me such a tragedy?

Why did he say those words with that dead tone? Why does he feel close and far away at the same time? I'm still not over the rejection from when we sat down for dinner or in the car. Strange emotions I've never felt before slam into me all at once and from all directions.

"What are you talking about?" I ask slowly, almost fearfully as I face him.

He pushes off the door and staggers toward me. His voice is sobering up a little, but he's still obviously drunk. "Isn't that why you're getting rid of it?"

"I just..." I trail off when he stops in front of me. He's larger than life, and I still stop and stare whenever he's this close. The smell of alcohol wafts off him in waves that hit me in the nostrils. He's definitely wasted.

He stares down on me with half-droopy, sexy eyes. Their blue, however, appears dark and deep, almost depressed. "You just want to get rid of it?"

"That's not—"

"Fine."

"F-Fine?" How can it be fine?

"Yes, fine. Do as you wish."

"I don't need your permission."

"I'm well aware of that."

God. His meek tone is getting on my last nerve. But instead of shouting and getting in an argument this late, I rein it in. "Let's talk in the morning when you're sober."

"One last time."

"What?"

"Let me have you. One last time." He grabs me by the nape and lowers his lips to mine. At first, his kiss is slow, sensual, but then it intensifies, tongues clashing and his lips devouring mine. It's almost...desperate.

And I share that desperation. He's kissing me after he rejected me—twice. I probably shouldn't be feeling this way since he's drunk, but my emotions seem to be scattered all over the place, and this is the only right thing in my reality.

Kyle lowers the zipper of my dress and slides it down my arms with frantic movements. It pools at my feet, leaving me in only my underwear.

He unclasps my bra with expert deft fingers, and I gasp as they brush against my breasts.

"Fuck, baby. You're so beautiful." He lowers his head to latch onto a nipple and I arch my back, head rolling. The feel of his stubble on my breast creates unbearable friction. My nipples tighten into hard buds as he bites down and sucks on them with a ravenous rhythm.

Beautiful. I smile internally. *He thinks I'm beautiful.*

The rejections from earlier aren't important, after all. They meant nothing.

I hold on to that idea as I try to undo his belt, but I'm not fast enough and my movements are clumsy at best. I was never good with this type of stuff, but I want to be. For him, I want to give back as much as I take.

Kyle tries to take over the task, but I shake my head, my voice too wanton for my own ears. "Let me."

Steadying my hand, I finally finish unbuckling the belt. He kicks the pants and his boxer briefs away. I reach for his buttons, but I barely undo the first two before he rips at his shirt, sending the buttons flying everywhere.

I swallow as his sculpted chest comes into focus. This view will never get old.

Kyle places two fingers under my chin and lifts my head, breathing harshly as his eyes clash with mine. They're raw and intense, and I'm not sure I like what I see there. Behind the lust, there's a sense of sadness that I want to eradicate.

I palm his cheek, my ragged breathing matching his irregular one. "Kyle, I—"

He flattens a finger on my lips and shakes his head once. "Don't ruin it. Not today."

His middle finger glides against my panties, and I shudder before he lowers the cloth down my legs. I willingly step out of them as he slides his middle and ring finger into my pussy, and I briefly close my eyes as I soak him in for a fraction of a second. I've been yearning for his touch since we were in Reina's house. No, it was ever since I woke up this morning and didn't find him beside me.

My legs shake, hardly able to carry me any longer. As if he can feel it, Kyle wraps an arm around my waist, anchoring me in place as he thrusts his fingers inside me and teases my clit. My head drops against his shoulder as tingles erupt all over my skin.

I don't last long—not even a minute—before the orgasm drags me down in its clutches. It doesn't matter that he's drunk; Kyle knows my body more than I ever will, and I guess I got used to that. I got used to how easily he wrenches pleasure and feelings out of me.

I'm still riding the wave when he backs me up, then flips me over and pushes me down. I'm on my knees on the carpet, but before I can react to the positioning, he lowers me further. My breasts brush on the carpet, the soft surface hardening my nipples more.

What…?

I'm lying completely flat on the carpet with my back to him. I stare back at him as he yanks open his drawer. I think he'll bring out a toy, but I should've known better. Kyle might like to torture me with them, but he doesn't like them involved during actual sex. I prefer him to them, anyway.

He retrieves a bottle of lube and a condom, and doesn't bother to close the drawer. Wait. *A condom?* Kyle never used them so I didn't even know he had one.

Besides, what's the use of a condom when he's already gotten me pregnant?

He takes his time removing his shirt, revealing his hard muscles and the tattoos rippling on his abs. I don't dare look away or move. I feel like I'll be missing something crucial if I do.

Kyle throws his shirt away and stalks behind me like a hungry predator about to devour his prey. I follow him with my gaze until he kneels between my parted legs.

He places a hand under my stomach and lifts me up so that I'm slightly bent over on my knees. The position is different from anything we've done before, and that says something considering he's taken me in all positions possible.

Or so I thought…

Kyle parts my ass cheeks, and a cool liquid meets my back hole. It feels soothing against my heated skin. I'm still in the aftermath of my orgasm, so any touch feels like an aphrodisiac. Or maybe it's because Kyle is doing it.

"I'm going to fuck you in the arse then in your pussy, then I'm going to do it all over again."

My thighs clench at his words, but I don't get to ponder them much before he thrusts the liquid lube inside my back hole with his finger.

The sensation is surprisingly pleasurable, tender even. I clench my hand into a fist on the carpet. He adds another finger, and I wince at the intrusion. Pain mixes with pleasure as he pours more of the lube.

But it's not enough. It doesn't feel like enough.

"P-put it in," I moan.

"Put what in, Princess?"

"Your…cock. Just put it in."

"It'll hurt."

"Let it hurt." I want the pain right now and the sense of unbound pleasure that comes with it. Because with Kyle, it doesn't feel like only pain, it's the joining of our bodies and souls in one unified connection.

My husband's fingers leave my ass, and I hear the tearing of the condom packet before something bigger and harder nudges at my entrance. I grab the carpet for balance as he pushes in the first inch.

Holy. Shit.

I think he's going to tear me in half. How the hell did I even take this size in my pussy in the first place?

I'm barely able to catch my breath when he pushes in again.

"Aaaah…" I bite down on my hand. "Mmmm…"

"You know what?" Kyle's fingers dig into my hip, the one he's been lifting me with, and he powers inside in one go. "*Fuuuck.*"

I can almost see stars in my blackened vision. The pain is real. It's even more real than when he takes me roughly from the front. The feeling of being completely filled takes over all my senses. It's like we're joined in a way that will never be the same again.

"Breathe," he grunts from above me. His body covers mine as he opens my mouth with two of his fingers. "Fucking breathe, Rai."

It's then I realize, in my attempt to keep feeling the mixture of sensations going through me, I've been holding my breath. My eyes must be bulging out, tears gathering in them. Using Kyle as an anchor, I suck in deep gulps of air. The oxygen burns my starved lungs and shoots a new rush of life into my system.

"That's it…" He starts moving while his body is still covering mine.

Bursts of pleasure pool at the bottom of my stomach and expand through my whole body. I writhe underneath him even though my trembling knees barely keep me in position. The harsh floor stings so good, adding to the sparkles exploding throughout my entire body.

Kyle grabs me by the back of my nape and thrusts with a force that leaves me breathless. He nearly pulls out, then he rams all the way in again, filling me, stretching me, eliciting a sense of pleasure I've never experienced before.

I have to remind myself to breathe so I don't choke like I always do when it gets to be too much.

He's taking me against the floor without holding anything back, and it's strangely passionate and erotic and…true. I've always felt like he shows his true self when he is close to me, when he has no other way to go but toward me.

I chance a glance at him over my shoulder. He's so big at my back, like a god of sorts. His thrusts are long and deep, and his expression still has that sense of sadness that I want to erase.

Just looking at him drives me over the edge. This orgasm is stronger than any I've had before. It starts in my ass and explodes in my pussy, then all the way throughout my whole body.

My elbows and knees are unable to hold me, so I fall flat on the floor. Kyle holds me upright, a hand under my stomach and the other on my hip as he pounds harder and faster inside me. He's holding himself on his knees, his body rising then falling down with the force of his thrusts.

I think he'll come soon, but he doesn't. He pulls out and flips me on my back, removing the condom and tossing it away. The floor is harsh on my skin, but I don't care about that as my eyes meet his.

We've always had a weird type of connection. The type that's a bit unhinged, a bit sick, but it's also the type that brings peace to chaos. The type I want to sleep cocooned in every night and wake up to every morning.

"One more time." He thrusts into my pussy in one brutal go. Feeling him bare inside me is so freaking good.

My orgasm that hasn't really ended bleeds into another one. *Shit.* I'm so stimulated that only penetration is able to drive me over the edge.

"Kyle...oh...Kyle!"

"One more time." He picks me up so I'm sitting on his lap and drives deeper and harder, sucking and nibbling on my nipples at the same time. He touches me with urgency I've never experienced before as if he can't get close enough or touch me deep enough. Bursts of pleasure explode on every inch of my skin until it gets too hot, too sweaty. Too...much.

Kyle doesn't come inside me. He doesn't come. Period.

He continues to fuck me on and on until I come over and over again. He doesn't soften inside me. If anything, he keeps getting harder and thicker. It's like he's made it his mission to make me orgasm. I come so many times I lose count. I'm sobbing at some point at the amount of stimulation attacking my body from all directions. I'm a sweaty, crying mess, and the sick part is that I don't ever want this to end.

Kyle is touching me. Unlike the rejections from today, he's fucking me like a madman, unable to stay away.

By the time his cum fills my insides, I don't know whether it's a dream or reality. I think I blacked out at some point, so it could be either.

Soft lips brush against my forehead and I moan. "Mmmm."

"I missed you before, and I'll miss you now."

I missed you, too. I try to say those words, but my energy fails me.

Tomorrow. Tomorrow we'll talk and I'll tell him I'm not aborting.

I'll tell him I want us to have the family neither of us had before.

Kyle, the baby, and me.

A smile grazes my lips as I imagine that scene before I drift off to sleep.

TWENTY-SEVEN

Kyle

THE SPLITTING HEADACHE IS THE LEAST OF MY PROBLEMS when I stare at the woman lying on her stomach on the bed. A galaxy of bruises covers her hips, arms, thighs, arse, and even around the snake tattoo on her spine.

Fuck.

I spring awake as memories of last night trickle back in. What the fuck have I done? If it weren't for the steady rise and fall of her back, I would think I'd killed her or something.

Bloody hell.

I shouldn't have touched her when I was drunk. The reason I don't get drunk isn't only because I lose my inhibitions, but also because I can't control myself. There's no stop or even pause button in that state.

Not that I've ever had those buttons when it comes to Rai. Every time I recalled the decision I made, I fucked her more, owned her more, and was nothing short of a madman.

I can't believe I took her on the floor over and over like a fucking animal. She's already too fragile and easily bruises by a simple touch. How could I let my beast side take complete control of me like that?

I reach out a finger to touch a strand of her hair but stop at the last second, my hand clenching into a fist. Do I even have the right to touch her anymore?

"Fuck," I whisper, running a hand through my hair as I spring to my feet.

It's all over now.

I take a quick shower, then change into black trousers and a white shirt. Rai is still fast asleep on her stomach. She probably won't wake up for some time due to exhaustion.

Sitting at her desk, I grab a pen and write until my knuckles hurt. She's always said left-handed people like me have horrible handwriting, and I guess it's true. But instead of writing a generic email or text, I'd rather leave one last personal touch behind.

I place the letter on the pillow, then brush my lips against her forehead, letting them linger there for a second too long.

"Mmmm...Kyle?" she mumbles in her sleep.

If she wakes up now, she'll probably strangle me. I would deserve it, but I can't die before I end it once and for all.

So I slide the covers up to her chin and close the door of our room for the last time.

⌒

If I had wanted to kill Rolan before, it wouldn't have been hard.

He's basically inviting snipers to buildings across from his clubs so they can finish him off.

The reason I haven't done that is because he needed to suffer, and he needed to suffer more than Mom and Dad did.

It wouldn't have been revenge if he didn't face his sins. It wouldn't have been satisfying if I didn't have him writhing in his own blood at my feet, begging me to save him like Ma begged that time.

But the circumstances are different from when I first started.

He got Rai involved.

If those Albanians still had her, she would've lost her life by now. And that's Rolan's final strike. That's the bullet with his name on it.

I might not have been able to prevent my parents' death, but I'll protect Rai even if it's the last thing I do.

If I finish Rolan, the entire war with the Irish will end. Flame said most of the higher-ups on Rolan's side think going against the Russians and the Italians is madness. Now that the Japanese and the Triads are bound to join too, it's a pure suicide mission.

Rolan, being a dictator, killed anyone who was against him in the organization. He's holding them with fear, and as soon as he's gone, peace will return.

Rai will be safe.

I stare through my lenses at the man who's sitting in a lounge area in the midst of the Irish's club. He's older now, in his sixties with completely white hair, but pure evil still lurks in his eyes.

My phone vibrates and I retrieve it without breaking eye contact with him. I can't shoot now, anyway. There are too many people buzzing around him, bringing him reports and whatnot. I need a clear shot at him because a miss would compromise my position.

My lips part when I make out the name flashing on the screen.

Godfather.

It's the first time he's called me in ten years. I thought he wouldn't have my new number, even though I kept his old one.

I swallow as I answer, "Hello?"

"What the fuck are you doing, punk?"

My finger remains still at the trigger. Godfather might be in his forties, but he still sounds as authoritative as when I was five years old and clung to him every step of the way.

"Popping some heads," I joke, because that's the only way I know how to talk to him after all these years.

"Heard you got shot."

"Meh. Shots can't kill me. Not in this lifetime."

"Heard you got married."

"Kind of, but it's...over." My voice lowers before I go back to joking. "Not everyone is made for married life like you, Godfather. Some are just complete bastards who drive their wives to the point of no return."

"Be serious. What type of mess have you gotten yourself into this time?"

"Good old revenge." I pause. "Remember the people I told you killed my parents? I found one of them. I still don't know who the arsehole Russian who betrayed Mum is, but I don't have time for that now, so I will just settle for my fucker uncle."

"Then what? Do you think you'll be relieved or that your parents will come back to life?"

"No, but it will feel fucking fantastic."

"Kyle..."

"And it will keep that wife I drove to the point of no return safe."

"Where are you?"

"In the place where the grand finale will happen."

"Where exactly?"

"Why are you asking?"

"I'm here."

I pause. "Here where?"

"In the States. Come meet me."

"Why...why would you want to meet me after everything that happened? I thought you hated me."

"I hated what you did, but I never hated you, Kyle. You were the son I had before I knew what fatherhood meant, and that didn't change even after I had my own children."

I gulp, then clear my throat. "You're being sappy, Godfather."

"And you're being reckless again. Come meet me. *Now*."

"Hold on, let me finish—"

I cut off when movement sounds from behind me. I spring to my feet, but it's too late. Something fires in my shoulder. At first, I think it's a gunshot, but no blood comes out. The phone clatters to the ground, the screen breaking.

Staggering backward, I fall to my knees and stare up at the fucker who shot me. His bleached hair sticks out in all directions as he blows on his gun, the one with anesthesia in it. "I told you it can be powerful, Kyle."

Fuck.

Peter approaches me until he's staring down at me. "You're not supposed to kill Rolan. That's not what the boss wants yet."

"I-Igor put you up to this?" I croak, barely able to keep my eyes open.

Peter yanks the rifle from my hand as easily as taking candy from a baby. "Boss said I'm to make sure to keep you on track, and that's what I've been doing all along. I'm the one who pushed Rai after she overheard your plan."

This fucker.

I'm going to slice his throat.

No, actually, I'm going to carve his heart out with a blunt knife so it hurts more.

"I went to the length of shutting her up, and what did you do? You've been going against everything we've worked for. You can't do that. That's betrayal to Boss, and I can't allow it. It's time you disappear once and for all. You're not even Russian, so you shouldn't have been a part of the brotherhood in the first place, you filthy Irish."

He swings the rifle and hits me across the head. My body hits the ground with a thud.

The last image that comes to mind is Rai's face and her soft smile.

At least my letter can serve as a goodbye.

It wasn't until I saw you this morning that I realized just how dangerous I am to you. I hurt you, and there are no excuses for it. Last night, I decided to leave, and that's why I didn't stop. I couldn't. Every time I said I would, I remembered that it was the last chance I'd get to have you so close, so I kept going and going until you passed out.

That's why I need to stop.

Years ago, when I became overprotective of Godfather, I ended up hurting him and the woman he loved. So now I'm stopping before I hurt you more than I already have.

I'll kill Rolan and leave. Maybe go back to England. Maybe join a few of my colleagues in the various missions in the Middle East. Who knows? As long as there's adrenaline, I'll be fine.

I have no doubt that you'll do great whether Sergei lives or dies. You have more balls than most of the men in the brotherhood, and it's their loss if they don't see it.

Don't look for me. You won't find me.

Thank you for making me feel like a man, not a shadow, even if you were forced into marrying me.

P.S. Kirill is only threatening you with Reina because he knows you found out Aleksander is a woman. He'll be out for your blood unless you use your recent friendship with her to change his mind.

Live well, Princess.
Kyle Fitzpatrick

TWENTY-NINE

Rai

MY TEARS HAVEN'T DRIED EVER SINCE I FINISHED reading the letter Kyle left me.

When I woke up this morning, groggy and so utterly sore, a smile grazed my lips at the recollections from last night. I couldn't stop grinning like an idiot over how Kyle couldn't hold himself in.

I was looking forward to talking to him today about everything—the baby, the marriage, our future together.

Everything.

I was even willing to divulge my attraction to him seven years ago, that it took so much self-discipline to stop myself from being with him even though I had a major crush on him. That, back then, I kept my bottled up feelings to myself because I was worried *Dedushka* would kick him out if he found out my intentions. I preferred to have him as a guard instead of losing him once and for all. At least that way, I could watch from afar and pretend we were together. That's why his departure hurt more than it should. He disappeared off the face of the earth before I had the chance to express my feelings.

Now he's repeating it.

I'm not fully over the first time, but he did it *again*. The only difference is that he has no plans to come back.

A sob tears from my throat as I hold the letter to my quaking chest. My heart is breaking, shattering, and slowly vanishing. And the worst part is that the only person who can make it better is gone.

Damn him. God damn him.

How dare he leave me with just a letter? How could he?

But you know what? I'm not the same Rai from seven years ago. I'm not the girl who put her pride above everything else and stomped on her heart in the process. This time, I'll find him, and he better be ready for the wrath I'll unleash on his ass.

I try to get ready as fast as possible, even though I'm so sore it hurts to move. The reminder of him inside me, holding me, caressing me, and kissing me brings a new wave of tears.

Shaking my head, I finish putting a dress on and don't bother with makeup. On my way outside, I search the local news articles for anything fishy. There's no mention of Rolan being assassinated, so that means it didn't happen yet.

His death would cause an uproar in the media since he gets involved in many notorious business ventures.

Katia stops in front of me, her eyes holding questions she's not voicing aloud.

"I need to find Kyle. Have you seen him this morning?"

She shakes her head.

"I don't care what you have to do as long as you find him. I'll go ask Granduncle for backup."

I'm marching to his office before she can reply.

Anastasia is waiting near it, her brows drawn together, and she's wearing black slacks and a jacket. It's so rare of her to wear anything but dresses. She smiles upon seeing me, but she must sense something is wrong because she jogs toward me.

"Is everything okay, Rai?"

"It will be."

"Are we going to the company?"

"You go first, Ana. I'll join once I finish my business here."

She swallows, her throat working, and a strange gleam passes in her eyes.

"Is there something you want to say?"

"I…I'm sorry."

"For what?"

"For everything. I love you, okay?"

"Love you, too, Ana."

She wraps her arms around me and then retreats, not allowing me to see her face as she turns around and leaves.

I frown at the weirdness of what just happened and contemplate following her, but my mind is too occupied with everything Kyle to focus on anything else. Once this whole thing is over, I'll talk to her.

My hand is on the doorknob when Vlad's brooding presence stalks down the hall. I assume he's going to Sergei, too, but he breezes straight past me.

God damn it. Being treated as if I don't exist by Vlad, of all people, hurts more than I'd like to admit. I release the doorknob and stride behind him. "Wait."

He halts and spins around, his expression blank. "Do you need anything, Mrs. Sokolov?"

"Yes, I need you to stop treating me like a stranger."

"Should've thought of that before you teamed up with a stranger against your own brotherhood."

"Kyle is not a stranger, Vlad. He's my husband." The truth behind those words hits me to the core.

"In that case." He nods, about to leave.

"I'm pregnant."

That stops him and his eyes narrow. "Another one for show?"

"No. It's real this time."

"Congratulations," he grunts.

"I don't need your half-assed congratulations, Vlad. I need you by my side so I can protect *Dedushka*'s bloodline."

I'm going for a low blow by using his loyalty to my grandfather, but it's the only way to convince his mule personality.

"How about Kyle?"

"Kyle will be there, too. I don't expect you to be best friends, but try?"

He grunts, but says nothing.

"For me?" I soften my tone. "Are you going to leave me alone in the midst of the pack of wolves of the elite group?"

"Of course not."

"Then stop sulking."

"If that fucker Kyle hurts you, I'll happily torture him all over again."

"You might get the chance to do that as soon as I find him," I mutter under my breath.

"What do you mean?"

"He's off to kill Rolan and disappear."

Vlad clicks his tongue. "That idiot always did things without coming back to the inner circle."

"Let me go ask Sergei for backup, then we will sit down and formulate a plan."

"You want me to go with you?"

"Thank you, but I can at least ask Sergei for things on my own."

"I'll be downstairs," he says, and I nod.

After knocking on the office's door, I open it and step inside. I pause when I find an unknown man sitting across from my granduncle.

"Rai. Come in." Sergei motions at me to join him, so I close the door and do just that, bluntly watching the new man.

He appears to be in his mid to late forties. His large frame dwarfs his dark suit. His brown hair is styled back, and he's sitting in a nonchalant position. It's not so threatening as to attract attention, but it's not slack either, like he's ready to jump up any second. It's so similar to...Kyle's.

Tattoos cover the backs of his hands, and they don't appear like the ones I recognize from the Bratva, the Triads, or the Yakuza.

He's watching me as intently as I'm watching him, like we're two predators before a fight over who owns a territory.

"This is Rai." Sergei introduces me.

"So she's the one Kyle married." the stranger observes quietly. British accent. Wait, could he be...

"Are you...Kyle's..."

"Godfather, yes. My official name is Ghost, but you can call me Julian."

"You're the one who told him he's dangerous." My voice rises. "Why would you say something like that to him? Don't you know he lost his parents when he was freaking five? They were murdered in front of his eyes, and he was never able to receive love after that. That's why he becomes overprotective—it's because he doesn't want to lose any more people. He says you raised him and knew him his entire life, so how could you make him believe he's defective?"

"Because he is." Julian remains calm, not a single muscle moving in his face. "He was defective from a young age, and he will never love normally or have fairytale characteristics. He's obsessive, he's driven, and he can become reckless sometimes. It's who he is and it will never change."

"Who told you I want to change him? I accept him the way he is." My lips part at that confession, because it's true. I do accept him the way he is. I even love those darker parts of him, the overprotectiveness, the possessiveness, how he makes me feel like I'm his world. I love everything about him, from his infuriating passive-aggressive attitude to how he provokes me and everything in between.

I love *him*.

I just love him, and that's what has been breaking my heart since I woke up to find a letter in his place.

"No wonder he said he drove you to the point of no return," Julian muses.

My heart picks up speed. "Have you talked to him?"

"Yes, some time ago."

I leave Sergei's side and stand in front of him. "Where is he? What is he doing?"

"Last time I checked, he was trying to kill Rolan."

"He's not dead." I chance a glance at Sergei. "Right?"

"No, he isn't," my granduncle confirms.

"Then…where is he?"

Julian forms a steeple at his chin. "I suspect something went wrong."

"What?" My voice sounds as spooked as I feel.

"When I was talking to him, I believe he was interrupted."

"Interrupted by what?"

"The question is who."

"What happened?"

"That's what I'm here to find out." Julian stares at his watch. "If Rolan has a demand, he would make it about now."

"You think Rolan has him?"

"I'm almost sure. Kyle went there to kill him, and since he's not dead, that means the situation slipped out of control."

I brace myself against the chair, sucking in a deep breath. The idiot. Why did he have to go there? Why did he jeopardize himself like that?

He'll be okay, right? It's Kyle, after all. No one will be able to hurt him.

Sergei's office phone goes off, its ringing echoing in the silence of the space. My head jerks up at the sound.

Granduncle picks it up and puts it on speaker. "Sergei Sokolov."

"Rolan Fitzpatrick. How have ye been, Sergei?" The unmistakable voice with the Irish accent slips through the phone. My fingers dig into the cushion of the chair.

"Good, good."

"Unfortunately, the piece of news I have might ruin yer mood."

"What happened?"

"Sadly, I was attacked by one of your closest men. Your grandniece's husband, I believe. How unfortunate."

"Where is he?" Sergei asks slowly, not losing his cool, which is far different from how I'm barely holding on.

"He's with the lads downstairs. How unfortunate, indeed." He has a provocative way of speaking, slow, but meant to get on your nerves.

"What do you want?" Sergei asks.

"Not much. Just the territories you've been slaughtering my lads over. Hand me those and I'll hand ye yer in-law."

"You think I would ever give up brotherhood territories?"

"Does that mean you'd rather give him up? Unfortunate. Very unfortunate." Rolan pauses. "I'll give ye a day to think about it. After that, I'll send ye his head."

The line goes dead and I stagger against the chair. My stomach churns and I grab it as I slowly sit down.

"Are you okay?" Sergei asks me.

"I'm...not." My voice catches at the end, but I swallow and meet his gaze. "We have to do something."

"I won't give up Bratva's territories, not even for my own daughter. After all, dozens of men died to secure them. The leaders would choose to kill Kyle themselves instead of making the brotherhood appear weak."

I know that. I know it, and yet, my brain is fried. All I keep thinking about is the image of Kyle's head.

Shit.

My stomach lurches again and the need to vomit hits me out of nowhere. I breathe deeply to shoo the sensation away.

I can't fall down now. If I do, I won't be able to protect Kyle and our unborn child.

Sucking in a deep breath, I face Sergei. "Can you call a meeting? I have a plan."

THIRTY

Kyle

"I'M SORRY, SWEETHEART. I'M SO SORRY."

Mam? Where are you?

The place is pitch-black like a cave. It smells rotten too, as if a dead animal is decomposing inside it. My legs get lost in something sticky underneath, but I can't see it.

I can't see anything except for darkness.

The sound of weeping gets louder the more I walk. It's my mother. I'd recognize the sound anywhere, even though it's been thirty years.

"Mam? Where are ye?" I don't know why I'm speaking in a Northern Irish accent, but all of a sudden, it feels as if I'm back to being that small boy. The only difference is that I'm trapped in a grown-up's body. "Mam!"

The only answer is the sound of weeping. It's long and wretched as if her grief is clawing out from the grave.

"Mam, come out. I can protect ye now. No one will hurt ye."

The weeping ceases and a rustle comes from right in front of me. I halt, the sound of the sticky mud under my feet stopping too.

The darkness slowly dissipates like fog in the early morning. A slender woman stands in front of me, tears sliding down her cheeks. Her face is soft, petite, and her nose is straight, like she's from aristocratic origins.

Her hair has a reddish hue and freckles are like specks of dust on her cheeks and nose. My mother used to tell me it's unfair that I look nothing like her and resemble my father instead.

She's wearing the trousers and the jacket from the day when she held me in her arms and attempted to run. Her blue eyes that match mine aren't sad like back then, though. There are laugh lines around them, even as tears continue streaming down her cheeks.

So this is how she looked. I had started to forget her face, and it has turned into a white halo over the years.

"Ye finally found me, baby boy."

"Ma…" I start toward her, wanting to hug her or even watch her closer.

"Don't." She holds up a hand, stopping me in my tracks. "If you come closer, I'll disappear."

"Why would you disappear?"

"You found me but ye didn't find yer father yet, right?"

"Dad is the reason ye're gone, Ma. He's the reason I had to become like this. Have ye forgotten?"

"No, but ye have to find yer father, and if ye can, forgive him."

"I'm not exactly a ghost hunter."

"He's not a wee ghost. He's by yer side, too. I'm sorry, sweetheart. I'm so sorry yer mammy was a such a disgrace."

"What are ye talking about? It wasn't yer fault."

"It was, and ye and Niall paid for it. Now, ye're paying again, and so is yer wife."

"What does Rai have to do with this…?" I trail off when my wife appears beside Mum and places her hand in hers. She's wearing a white nightgown, but bruises cover her porcelain skin, as I left her this morning. Her hair falls to her shoulders in disarray, and mascara streaks down her pale cheeks.

I swallow, forcing myself to look at her. "Rai? What are you doing here?"

She says nothing, her lips thinned in a line, and I hate that I can't listen to her voice even now. What was I thinking? I already left and there's no going back.

But can I have a last touch? Just once more.

I step toward them, wanting to take them both somewhere no one can find them. A large figure appears behind them, and the unmistakable click of a gun ripples in the air.

My legs stick to what's underneath them as Rolan's shadowed face comes into view.

I reach into my waistband for my gun, but my hands find nothing. *Fuck.* I bend over to search at my ankle, but the knife isn't there either.

Fuck. Fuck!

A smirk lifts Rolan's lips as he places the gun to Mum's head then slides it to Rai's. "Choose one, my lad."

"Take me! I'm the one you want, right?"

"Not really."

A shot rings in the air and a patch of blood covers my mother's chest in the same place as it had thirty years ago.

I run toward them, but it's too late.

Rai clutches her middle and falls to her knees, blood gurgling from her lips. A tear slides down and clings to her upper lip as scarlet red explodes from her stomach.

"No," I whisper, then roar, "Noooo!"

I startle awake, my clothes sticking to my body with sweat and my pulse close to beating out of my throat.

For a moment, I think I'm in that dark, rotten place and if

I look down, I'll find my mother's and Rai's bodies lying lifeless at my feet.

"Ye're finally awake, Sleeping Beauty."

My head jerks up, and just like in the nightmare, Rolan is standing in front of me, holding a gun in his hand. The only difference is, we're not in that tunnel anymore. We're in a gray room with a metal door. The only furniture is a table covered in torture devices: nail clippers, whips, screwdrivers, and knives. Nothing I haven't seen over the years.

I'm tied to a chair by thick ropes around my wrists and torso, the thing digging into my skin with how strong the knot is.

A few of Rolan's guards are stationed near the wall. Flame is one of them. *Thank fuck.*

I try not to squint at him or draw attention. He's wearing black trousers and a plain gray T-shirt. His red beard is trimmed and his bland blue eyes are watching me as if I'm a cockroach. He's always been the best at controlling his facial expressions.

"I have to admit," Rolan continues, "I hadn't thought the Russians' sniper would show up at my door like a wee stray kitten."

"Surprise, motherfucker." I grin.

He narrows his eyes. I might not remember my uncle from when we lived under the same roof, but due to later research, I know he doesn't like it when things don't go according to his plan.

"You don't recognize me, do you?" I scoff. "But then again, why would an old man like you recall the good ol' days?"

I keep staring at him. If I'm already caught, might as well face him. Besides, it's my chance to buy Flame time so he can get me out of here.

Rolan places the muzzle of his gun at my cheek, then uses it to make me show him the other side of my face. "I suspected it was ye. I thought ye'd be dead in a hole 'bout now."

"*Obviously*, I'm not dead, Uncle. As I said, surprise, motherfucker."

"Don't call me uncle, ye filthy bastard."

"Why? You don't like thinking about how you murdered your own brother in cold blood?"

"I was never yer fecking uncle. Your whore mother was pregnant with ye before marrying Niall and hid it. But even when I gave my brother all the evidence to get rid of her and ye, he still had a soft spot for that fecking harlot. I had no choice but to do it myself because my brother wasn't fit to lead us. He was too weak and didn't deserve to be boss. I did. So I just took it."

My mouth falls open. Did he just say Niall wasn't my father?

Find yer father, Kyle. He's not a ghost.

Mum's words from the nightmare slam back to me. Could it be a warning about the truth?

"Who is he?" I ask Rolan. "Who's my father?"

He releases a long laugh that echoes in the space around us. "Ah. Isn't this grand? Ye lived with the Russians for years and still didn't recognize yer father? A bastard is a bastard, after all."

"Who the fuck is he?"

"Don't ye worry, my lad. I already called him and gave him evidence that ye're his boy, so if he does want ye, he'll show up. Though, I doubt anyone wants a filthy bastard whose only use is killing from the shadows."

"Was he the one from that night? The one who came when my mother tried to escape?"

"Probably. Yer mother was smart, but not fast enough. My idiot brother promised to protect her and ye, but she knew I'd kill ye both the first chance I got, so she decided to leave. But that didn't turn out grand for her, did it?"

"I'm going to kill you," I mutter through clenched teeth. "I don't care how or when, but it's going to happen."

"Grand threats from a wee boy." He taps my cheek with his gun. "Ye're nothing, Kyle. Ye always were nothing since ye were born. I told the Russians they'd get ye once they give up territories, but here's a secret." He leans in to whisper. "I'll kill ya anyway. This time, I'll make sure ye join yer mother's side." He steps back and motions at his guards. "Take good care of him and make him scream."

"Aye, boss!"

Two guards follow him, leaving me with Flame and two others.

"Guess I should start." Flame appears bored as he heads to the table and retrieves the nail clippers, muttering under his breath. "What a pain in the arse."

I'm actually impressed with his Irish accent; it almost sounds authentic.

He stands in front of me, his eyes gleaming with pure sadism. "Shall we, lad?"

The fucker is so engrossed in his role.

"I don't usually waste time." He taps the nail clippers on his hand. "I know people start with the least painful torture then go up, but I prefer hardcore stuff from the get-go. It's more fun, innit, lads?"

The other two nod like idiots.

I glare up at him, and he hits me in the face with the device. "What are ye looking at, ye little fuck?"

I groan as pain explodes in my temple and hot liquid cascades down my face.

The fucker.

"Blood—yum." He grins, and he's definitely not faking it. The sick fuck does enjoy the sight of blood more than anything. "Let's start with those pretty nails, eh?" He steps behind me and takes my hand in his. I tense, holding my breath. If he hurts my sniper arm, I'm going to bloody murder him.

"Oh wait." He motions at one of the guards. "Pass me a knife, would ya? I want to cut his skin at the same time."

The younger of the two, obviously eager to please, goes to the table, snatches a knife, and comes to our side. His entire attention is on me as he hands the sharp object to Flame.

That's his mistake.

Flame jams the knife in the man's jugular and slices. A bloody fountain splashes on my face and clothes. I close my eyes so it doesn't get inside.

The bastard always goes for the most gruesome methods.

The other guard realizes the situation and yanks out his gun, but he's by no means faster than Flame. My mentor gets his gun out first and shoots him in the forehead, killing him on the spot.

"Ah, pain in the arse." Flame snatches the knife from the man's throat. The victim grabs his neck, choking on his own blood, but to no avail. A few seconds later, he's on the ground, drowning in a pool of crimson.

Flame uses the knife to cut the ropes. I spring to my feet and yank a gun from the bloodied man's hand.

"Now, I got blood all over me." He switches to his bored—and normal—English accent as he wipes his face with the back of his hand.

"Then maybe you shouldn't have slit his fucking throat."

"It's more fun that way."

Crazy fuck.

"Now what?" I head to the entrance. "Is there a clear exit?"

I need to get out of here before the Russians actually decide to save me. That would mean Rai would get involved, and there's no way in hell I'll let her near the bastard Rolan.

"Not really." Flame clicks his gun. "We'll have to get out the old-fashioned way."

"Which is?"

He hits me upside the head. "Kill our way out, punk. Did playing house with the Russians make you lose your skills?"

"Piss off." I narrow my eyes on him. "You were going to clip my nails."

"He said screams." He grins as he types in a code on the door, causing it to open. "You know I like those."

"Fucker."

"By the way, the beep of the door alerts all the other guards. They'll be swarming us any second now. Ready?"

"Always."

"Though, there should be backup coming up."

"Who?"

He rolls his eyes. "Your beloved godfather."

I don't want him involved either, so I'll just get out of here on my own.

We rush in different directions, but unlike what I expected, only two guards come by. We shoot both as we make our way up the stairs. "Where are they?"

"They should be around." He studies our surroundings. "Unless Rolan has them."

"Even better. Take me to him."

"Bloody annoying." He shakes his head, but leads me up the stairs to a lounge area.

I stop short at the scene in front of me.

Rai is here.

With Rolan.

Just like in the scene from my nightmare.

THIRTY-ONE

Rai

I DID IT.

I'm in the Irish's club, which Rolan has a back office in.

It hasn't been an individual effort. Thanks to Julian and his acquaintance with Kyle's insider with the Irish, we were able to figure out the location.

While Sergei was completely against handing over territories, he said he'd turn a blind eye if I took his men and came here.

I had to beg Vlad to help, and it wasn't easy since he doesn't like Kyle. The growly mountain of a man only softened when I mentioned the baby and that I don't want him to grow up fatherless.

Damien agreed to help because, in his words, "It should be fun."

I asked Kirill for his intel help because he has the best

spies. He was the hardest to crack, and only agreed when I gave him an oath in front of Sasha that no one except for the three of us will know of her true gender. Well, Kyle already knows somehow, but I'm not the one who told him.

Igor sent men, too, but Adrian has been MIA today. Even his closest guards couldn't be reached. Something is wrong, and Vlad thinks it has to do with Adrian's wife, Lia.

If—no, *after* I save Kyle, I'll have to check on her and see if everything is fine.

Mikhail insisted on joining, even though no one invited him. It surprised the shit out of me when he showed up with his best guards. Instead of arguing, I left my disagreements with him aside. Those don't matter right now.

Saving Kyle does.

Coming here with all these men with me didn't calm my nerves. Not really, especially since Julian couldn't get ahold of his guy for the last half hour.

Shooting our way inside the closed Irish club wasn't too difficult. The guards were taken by surprise by our large numbers. Damien killed everyone in his path like a bull out to destroy the world.

Julian and Vlad accompany me as I take the stairs two at a time. I dressed for the occasion, putting on leggings and a T-shirt, then completing the outfit with running shoes.

A wave of adrenaline has been holding me prisoner ever since I decided I'd save Kyle even if it was the last thing I do. I feel like I can kill anyone in my path if I have to. I don't care if I'm turning into a monster; they shouldn't have messed with my light.

Because he is. Even with his darkness, he's the light I've held on to ever since *Dedushka*'s death.

By the time we reach Rolan's office, most of his guards are either dead or injured. There will probably be backup soon, but hopefully, we'll be out of here before that happens.

When we barge inside, Rolan is holding a gun in his hand as if he's been waiting for us all along. Vlad and Julian step in front of me, to protect me, I guess, but I don't hide behind them.

I raise my own gun and approach Rolan so we're standing toe to toe. When I speak, my voice is hard, non-negotiable, just like *Dedushka's* when he issued orders. "Where is he?"

He smiles, his upper lip thinning with the movement. "Probably dying. He has my most ruthless lads with him."

I try not to think much about that possibility—the one where Kyle's dying—and repeat, "Where. Is. He? If you don't tell me, I'll blow your brains out."

"That will cause a diplomatic problem, Russian princess. Didn't your grandpa teach you not to shoot leaders no matter what?"

"My grandpa would've shot you in the face if he were alive. If you don't tell me where he is right now, I'm going to kill you."

"Then how will you find him? He's not even here."

Rolan must be bluffing. He couldn't have moved him away from the club this fast. If anyone had left the building, Kirill and Sasha would've told me.

The sound of footsteps can be heard from behind me and my attention falters. It's only a fraction of a second, but Rolan uses it and points the gun at my head. "Drop your weapon."

My breathing shortens as I comply.

He motions at both Vlad and Julian. "Ye too, unless ye're in the mood for her funeral."

Vlad curses under his breath as he and Julian slowly lower their guns to the ground.

Think, Rai. What would Kyle do in this situation?

I slowly close my eyes, contemplating the best option to get rid of Rolan. It would've been easier if it was only me. Now, I have the baby to worry about, so I can't make any rash decisions.

"Stupid little bitch thinks she's all that," Rolan hisses at my ear. "Did ye really believe that a wee thing like ye can kill me?"

I open my eyes slowly, and that's when I see him. At first, I think it's a trick of my imagination because of how much I've been thinking about him all day, but when Julian takes a bit more time to stand up after placing his weapon on the ground, I catch a glimpse of Kyle behind him.

He's soaked in blood, his face, his shirt, and even his hair. *Oh, God—has he been shot?*

Rolan must notice him too because he says, "Ye—"

He's interrupted as a loud shot rings through the air and his weight disappears from my back. I stare behind me to find him lying on his back with a bloody hole in his forehead. His tongue sticks out and his eyes stare at nowhere.

Strong hands grab me by the shoulders and I stare up at Kyle, incredulous.

"Are you okay? I'm sorry. I shouldn't have taken that shot when he was so close to you." He massages my ear, and that's when I realize it's buzzing. "But he saw me and was ready to shoot you so..."

He trails off when I palm his cheeks, wiping the blood with my thumb. "Are you shot? Wounded? Vlad, call Dr. Putin and have Ruslan pick him up—"

Kyle's hand slides from my shoulder to my face. "The blood is not mine. I'm fine."

"Are you sure?" I touch him up the sides and down his chest, feeling him. "Are you not injured anywhere?"

"I'm good as new. Told you bullets can't kill me." He grins, motioning behind him at a red-bearded man who seems to be around the same age as Julian. "Ask Flame or Godfather."

"I told you not to joke about that!" I hit him across the chest, forcing him to release me. "You're not bulletproof, you idiot. And what's with the whole suicide mission? Were you really going to take Rolan on your own?"

"I would've sniped him down just fine if not for that fucking kid. I'm going to kill him."

"So now you're blaming it on a kid?"

"Peter was the one who handed me over."

"That good-for-nothing?"

"He's not good for nothing, after all. He was the one who pushed you down the stairs, and I'm going to find him and push him into a grave."

Oh. So Peter was the perpetrator. I knew his voice sounded familiar back then. I shake my head, not wanting to focus on that.

"Don't change the subject," I scold. "This is about how you went on this mission without telling anyone."

"It's what I do."

"I can't believe you. I *really* can't believe you. You will never change, will you? You'll just continue to do whatever you please and to hell with what everyone else thinks or feels." My voice breaks at the end and I hate the vulnerability in it.

God damn him.

"Hey, Princess…" He tries to catch me by the arm, but I pull away and stride to the exit.

"Let's go home, Vlad."

The latter glares at Kyle as if he wants to kill him on my behalf, then follows after me.

"You're leaving?" Vlad asks once it's just the two of us.

"What does it look like I'm doing?" I breathe harshly, then whisper, "Is he following?"

"No."

"Really?" I snap.

Vlad grunts. "If you wanted him to follow you, then maybe you shouldn't have, I don't know, rejected him?"

"Screw him."

If he doesn't know how to take a hint, I'm not going to do his job for him.

But he will eventually follow.

Right?

THIRTY-TWO

Kyle

"**F**UCK!" I kick Rolan's lifeless body. Even the arse-hole's death doesn't feel as victorious as I thought it would.

Rai disappeared down the hall with that fucker Vladimir. He'll have even more of an opening to be beside her now that I'm not there, which has been his purpose all along.

Motherfucker.

"She has you by the balls. I'm disappointed." Flame leans against the doorframe and places a cigarette in his mouth, but instead of lighting it, he keeps flipping his lighter on and off. His *Beware of Fire Hazard* tattoo peeks out from underneath his sleeve with the movement.

"Shut the fuck up, Flame. He almost clipped my nails from my sniper hand, Godfather!"

"It didn't happen." Flame pauses flipping his lighter.

I narrow my eyes. "You wanted to do it."

"But I didn't. And stop moaning to Ghost like a little kid."

"I'm going to—"

"Enough." Godfather sighs, staring down at me. "Do you have the time to bicker with Flame right now? Shouldn't you go after your wife?"

My throat bobs up and down with a swallow. "You saw how mad she got. Besides, I've already let her go."

"Have you?"

"Yes, I have. Aren't you the one who told me I'm dangerous to those I care about?"

"She didn't seem to mind your craziness."

I stare at him, unsure. "Really?"

"She was more worried about saving you, and did everything in her might to have as much manpower as possible. She was trembling when she found out you were taken by Rolan."

That means...she cares, right?

Hope mounts and explodes in my chest with a force that leaves me breathless for a second. She would probably kick me in the balls if I chased her, though. But would it be worth it? *Fuck yes.*

Godfather slaps me upside the head, and I groan. "Ow. What was that for?"

"You're married, already. Stop making people worry about you."

"You..." I scratch the back of my head. "You don't have to worry. I've changed."

Flame scoffs from the background. "Changed, my arse."

"Piss off, Flame. Your job here is done."

"I think I'll stick around for some time. Take me with you to the Russians. Heard there's much more action there."

"Over my dead body."

"That won't be a problem, punk." He points his lighter at me, then flips it. "I made you."

"*Made* me?"

"Yes, I did."

"Fuck you." I sigh, then focus back on Godfather. "Anyway, I'm a grown-up."

"Then act like it." He flicks my forehead. "And come visit. Elle asks about you."

"She does?" I whisper my bemusement. "After everything that's happened?"

"Not everyone is hardened like us, Kyle. She doesn't hold a grudge against you—for reasons unknown."

"The little punk always made people forgive him fast," Flame says.

"It's because of the charming face you'll never have, Flame. Stop being jealous." My mother said I get it from my father, but, apparently, that's not Niall and I'm not a Fitzpatrick.

If my father is Russian and has been around long enough to have me, then he should be in his late fifties or early sixties…

The sound of footsteps cut into my thoughts as guards barge inside. Flame straightens.

"They're Russians," I say, squinting to recognize whose men they are. The showoff Mikhail. He always has his guards storm in before his majesty comes along.

No idea why he came here in the first place. *Wait a fucking second…*

I already called him and gave him evidence that ye're his boy, so if he does want ye, he'll show up.

Rolan's words roll in my head with crystal clarity.

My mouth hangs open as Mikhail rushes inside, holding a gun. He's old, around his late fifties or early sixties, and yet, he's still in shape, aside from the panting.

"Where is he…?" He trails off when his eyes meet mine.

I see it then, the thing I was too blind to see over the years—the resemblance. Though his hair is sprinkled with white strands, it's the same color as mine. His angular jaw and the shape of his eyes…they're the exact fucking same as mine.

How the hell have I not noticed that before? Well, I never had a reason to believe Niall wasn't my biological father, but still.

Mikhail studies Rolan's body, and once he makes sure he's dead, he approaches me slowly, expression softening. His guards remain behind, their guns tucked in front of them.

"You okay?" he asks, his accent thicker than usual.

"Why would you care?" I draw in a breath, then release it through my nose. I have no time for this. I should bribe Ruslan and Katia to give me tips on how to approach Rai without endangering my balls.

"I didn't know." He sheathes his gun under his jacket.

"You didn't know about what?"

"You. Amy didn't tell me."

I throw my hands up dismissively. "Well, surprise."

He watches me for a second too long without saying anything, as if he's seeing me for the first time.

Is this awkward, or what?

"You were there that night," I say. "The night she died."

"Yes."

"Then why didn't you fucking save her? You were supposed to—that's why she called you."

"We were in the middle of an attack, and by the time I got there, she and Niall were dead. There was no trace of you, so I thought you died, too."

"I did, in a way."

"I know. That's why—"

"Save it."

"But—"

"This changes nothing, old man. The only father figure I have ever had is right here." I point at Godfather. "He's the one who taught me how to survive, even if it meant killing to do that."

I expect Mikhail to show hostility, because he has that petty personality and tends to act up whenever things don't go his way, but he stares at Godfather and says, "Thank you."

"You don't need to thank me. He grew up into a reckless bastard."

"Hey!"

Godfather wraps an arm around my shoulders. "When he was young, he was weak and always felt sick. The other kids ganged up on him."

Mikhail stares at me with an expression I'm seeing on his face for the first time.

Guilt.

Isn't that fucking ironic?

"Too much information, Godfather," I mutter.

He ignores me and continues speaking to Mikhail. "But even though they were way older than him, he kicked, clawed, and scratched them. Who knew that the little boy would grow up to be one of the best we have?"

I clear my throat at the note of pride in his voice. I never thought Godfather would ever speak about me like that after all the shit that went down ten years ago.

"I'm sorry I wasn't there," Mikhail's voice holds a genuinely regretful note. "If I knew, this wouldn't have happened."

"Save your breath, old man. I don't give two fucks about you or what you could've done."

"I do." He pauses. "I know we didn't start off on the right foot, but I'm asking for a chance."

"A chance for what?"

"To be your father."

I scoff. "Don't you have two sons already? Why would you want to add another?"

"Because you're my eldest. My heir."

"Like hell, I am. In case you haven't noticed, I have no interest in the Bratva."

"But you have an interest in Rai, yes?"

"Bringing her into this discussion won't help you. In fact, it takes away brownie points."

"If you're strong enough, you can help her."

"I thought you hated her."

"I did, but only because she kept ruining my business. If you give me a chance, I will stop antagonizing her."

"You'll stop antagonizing her even if I don't give you a chance." I tower over him. "Mess with her and you're messing with me." I stroll past him. "I'm off, Godfather. I'll be in touch."

"Does this mean you agree?" Mikhail calls after me.

"Depends on your behavior," I shoot back without turning around.

His guards step aside to make way for me, and I can sense how annoying this treatment will get in the long run.

Oh well, we'll wait and see.

Right now, it's time I get my wife back.

THIRTY-THREE

Rai

H E DIDN'T FOLLOW.

He really didn't follow.

I stand on the balcony for several minutes in case he shows up, but there's no trace of him.

None at all. No call. No text.

I stare at the letter he left me that I tucked in my bag. Is that the last I'll see of him? Really?

I ought to kick his ass for everything he made me go through. I gave him all the reasons to come back and at least talk to me. I went to him. I didn't remove the wedding ring. I didn't tell him he was an idiot for thinking that leaving is the solution.

I did it all, but he didn't even follow.

Fuck him.

I'm about to go take a shower when commotion comes from outside my room.

My heartbeat skyrockets and I nearly trip over my feet as I swing the door open.

It's not Kyle's face that greets me. Instead, it's Ruslan and Katia arguing with Lia, telling her she can't go inside.

"What's going on?" I try to hide the disappointment in my tone.

"You said not to disturb you, miss," Ruslan says, "but Mrs. Volkov insists on seeing you."

"It's okay." I smile at them, then her. "Come in, Lia."

She follows behind me and closes the door. Her face is pale, lips dry. Her dress's buttons are done up wrong, as if she was in a hurry to put clothes on.

"Sit down." I motion at the lounge area.

She shakes her head frantically, catching her breath.

"Is everything okay, Lia?" Maybe there is a reason behind her husband's absence. "Is Adrian okay?"

"Of course he is—when has he not been?" she snaps, but it's not entirely in anger. There's something else underneath, but I can't put my finger on it. Hatred? A grudge?

"Okay. Can you tell me why you came here?" It's weird, and knowing Adrian's strict, secretive nature, he wouldn't let her roam around unescorted.

Her huge eyes stare at me, tears clinging to her lids. *Woah—what's going on?*

"The other time, you said you'd help me, Rai."

"I would."

"Promise?"

"Yes, of course. Just tell me what's going on."

"P-please...p-please help me escape Adrian." She takes my hands in her trembling, sweaty ones. "If you don't, I will die."

Well, shit.

After I have Katia and Ruslan send Lia to one of our safe houses—that Adrian doesn't know about—I go to take a shower.

I don't know what I will do, but she was on the verge of a breakdown and desperately needed to get away from Adrian. If he did anything to her, I'll murder him.

Standing under the stream, I place a palm on my stomach. "If you're a boy, don't you dare mistreat women. If you're a girl, don't you dare let men mistreat you just because you don't have balls."

I shake my head. I can't believe I'm talking to a fetus, but I remember Reina saying Gareth used to move in her stomach whenever she or Asher talked to him.

My chest tightens at the thought of my child not having a complete family like Gareth. Whatever happens, I'm going to take care of this child. I've been feeling these small bursts of excitement since I had that heart-to-heart with Reina.

I want to be like Mom. I want to protect my children with my life.

After wrapping my torso in a towel, I step outside the bathroom, drying my hair with a smaller towel.

My feet come to a halt of their own volition when I spot the man standing in the middle of our bedroom.

Kyle.

He followed me.

The thought causes my lips to tremble before I set them in a line.

He must've had a shower because all the blood from earlier is gone. He's wearing a clean white shirt that molds to his taut muscles. His hair is slightly damp, some strands falling on his forehead.

He's really here.

For a second, we stare at each other silently, as if we're both processing the reality.

"Can you hear me out?" he asks in a quiet voice.

"About what? Didn't you already leave a letter and say goodbye?"

He blows out a long breath. "That was a mistake."

"A mistake?"

"No. I meant what I said, except for one thing."

"What?" My voice is barely audible.

"The part about how leaving you is the right choice."

"It isn't?"

"It fucking isn't. I know it should be, but I can't bring myself to part from you." He smiles a little. "It's ironic considering I ripped my heart out when I left the room this morning."

"Why did you, Kyle?"

"I told you, I'm dangerous for you."

"I get to decide that."

"I hurt you." He motions at the bruises at my shoulders.

"Do you think I would've let you touch me if you hurt me?" My voice lowers. "I came more times than I could count, if you didn't notice. Besides, I never asked you to stop. I would've if it got to be too much."

"Still...I was too rough."

"I love it rough."

His eyes gleam. He likes that more than he will ever admit, and maybe I'm the same.

"Anything else you'd like to say?" I probe.

"Yeah...I'll take you to the clinic. I'll be there for you."

"I only need a doctor, not the clinic."

His brows furrow. "Why? Is something wrong?"

"No. The doctor at the hospital said I need an OB-GYN."

Realization dawns on him and he remains silent before he whispers, "You're..."

"Keeping it," I finish for him.

"Why?"

"Because I want to."

"I thought you didn't want children."

"That was before, when my insecurities were getting the better of me."

"And now?"

"Now, I'm confident enough to do it. I want to be a good mother like Mom and Reina. Don't get me wrong, though— switching my pills was a dick move that I'll hold over your head for the rest of your life."

He remains silent for a beat before he shoves a hand in his pocket.

I watch him and his silence before I blurt, "Aren't you going to say anything?"

"I want to ask something, but I'm not sure if I want to hear the answer."

"You won't know unless you ask." And he needs to get closer because the distance between us is getting on my nerves.

"Do I have a place in the child's future?"

"Why wouldn't you? You're the father."

"How about *your* future?"

"What do you think?"

His intense blue eyes bore into mine before he sighs. "I don't know. All I know is that I realize I fucked up, and I'm ready to do whatever it takes to make it up to you."

"Whatever it takes?"

"Anything, Princess."

"Then don't ever leave me. *Ever*. I mean it, Kyle. If you dare leave me again, I'll unleash my wrath on you."

A small smile tugs on his lips as he stalks toward me, his long legs eating up the distance in no time. He stops right in front of me until my space is filled with his scent. "Does this mean you'll have me back?"

I grab him by the collar of his shirt and rise up on tiptoes to seal my lips to his. My head feels light, even though it barely lasts a couple of seconds.

When I lower back down, it's like I've been levitating and I'm finally hitting the ground.

"I love you, Kyle. I've been in love with you for as long as I've known you, but I never had the courage to admit it to you or to myself."

"Fuck, Princess," he says breathily. "I think I've loved you ever since the first time I met you."

"You have?"

He nods. "But I was a coward."

"We both were." I stroke the collar of his shirt that's still bunched in my hand. "I think we should make it up to each other."

"I think so, too."

"Are you going to kiss me now, husband?"

"Oh, I'll be doing more than kissing you, wife."

He picks me up in his arms and I squeal, but the sound is devoured by his lips on mine.

EPILOGUE 1

Rai

One year later

I STAND IN FRONT OF MY WALK-IN, PICKING A NIGHTGOWN—though I probably won't be needing it tonight.

Not that I do on most nights.

My hand barely touches one before a warm body glues to mine from behind. I briefly close my eyes, breathing in his clean scent mixed with his special masculine odor. It clings to me like a second skin.

I love smelling him on me. I feel like I have him with me at all times even when we're apart.

Turning around, I don't bother to hide my nakedness—I'm completely free with Kyle. Besides, I love the way his eyes darken to the furious blue color of a stormy sky.

I'm the only one who's able to put that look on his face. The only one who gets under his skin as much as he gets under mine.

"You're back early. Mikhail isn't giving you a hard time, is he?"

"As if he can. I'm making him profit. Also, I'm the one who's giving him a hard time, not the other way around."

I chuckle, almost imagining that. Ever since Kyle found out Mikhail is his father, he's been slowly taking care of his brigade and teaching his younger, reckless half-brothers and half-sisters some sense. I guess the behavioral issue runs in their blood, but Kyle is old enough to not let it guide him anymore.

I wouldn't say my relationship with Mikhail is rainbows and roses. I still don't approve of his ways and he still thinks I meddle too much for my own good. However, we tolerate each other for Kyle's sake.

"And why are we talking about my father when I'm about to devour you?" He lowers his lips to my neck, sucking on the skin and eliciting a moan from me.

"You are?"

"Fuck right, I am." He speaks against my skin as he fiddles with his belt. "Quick before the devil's minion wakes up."

I laugh, but the sound turns into a squeal when he carries me, both of his big hands resting beneath my thighs. My legs loop around his waist as he powers inside me. He doesn't even bother to back me against the wall. Kyle holds my entire weight against him as he rams into me. The position doesn't diminish his strength; if anything, it makes him go deeper.

I hold on to his shoulders with all my might, moaning. "Oh, K-Kyle…there…there…"

"Shh, you'll wake him up." He smiles against my lips even though he thrusts exactly where I need him.

It's crazy how he keeps learning my body like it's his masterpiece and he can't stop. He still brings me to heights of pleasure I never thought would be possible.

People say we'll fall into a routine soon and that things

will become normal, but they still haven't. We had more sex when I was pregnant than ever before—I blame the hormones for that. Even after I gave birth, Kyle wouldn't stop touching me and bringing me to orgasm. As soon as the doctor said I could have sex again, I barged into Kyle's office and climbed him. I could probably blame the postnatal hormones for that too.

But this? The way I come undone around him in no time? I can only blame my stupid body and heart, which are easily stimulated by his presence.

Kyle empties himself inside me at the same time as I shatter to pieces, my nails digging into his shirt.

Panting, I rest my head on his shoulder, catching my breath. Kyle doesn't seem to be tired of holding my weight since he remains in the same position.

His lips brush against my temple as he strokes my hair away from my face. God, I love the gentle way he touches me as much as the rough and unapologetic ways he fucks me.

This might have become an everyday occurrence, but I don't take anything for granted. We suffered a lot to get where we are and every day is a war zone in our world, but Kyle and I wouldn't have it any other way.

Sergei is still holding on, and he's trying a new treatment that may cure his cancer, so that hasn't changed.

Many other things have, though.

The most important of all is Anastasia. A few days after Kyle and I got back together, we woke up to find her gone. The only thing she left behind was a note which said she stole the money, that she's sorry, and we shouldn't look for her.

Of course, we searched for her, but it's like she was sucked into a different dimension. She left absolutely no trace behind.

Her strange behavior before her disappearance made more sense.

No one would've thought the sweet innocent Anastasia

would do something like that, but I think we all ignored how smart she is, ignored the possibility that the naïve façade could be just that—a façade.

After an internal investigation in V Corp, I figured out how she discreetly hacked into the system. During her internship, she embezzled small amounts every month, then took them and left.

Sergei, who was ready to have Kyle snipe down the thief, told me we needed to cover up for her after we found her note. Because if anyone else from the brotherhood knew she stole, she'd be found and killed. There's no mercy for thieves.

Peter, the young guard who handed Kyle to Rolan, disappeared, too. Igor thinks he went back to Russia, but he can't tell for sure. Kyle is still insistent on finding and murdering him, though, not only for handing him to Rolan that day, but for pushing me down the stairs.

The war with the Irish isn't completely over, but their new leader isn't as aggressive toward us as Rolan was.

Damien and Kirill still get on my nerves, but neither of them comments on my presence at the table anymore. Considering the net profit I bring to V Corp, no one can question my worth.

I've even started to openly meet with Reina, Asher, and Gareth now. If Kirill found out, the others would've soon followed, and I wasn't going to hide my twin sister as if she was a dirty secret.

Well, I had to bug them about security, but Reina said it's worth it if she gets to see regularly. Then she arranged 'double dates' for us. We attempted to dress at each other to misguide our husbands, but they figured us out in an instant. When I asked Kyle how he knew, he said it's the look in my eyes. No one, not even my identical twin sister, could emulate it.

Stroking Kyle's hair, I push back to stare at his face. "Do you know that I love you?"

He grins. "Not really. Can you repeat it?"

I brush soft kisses on his cheek, eyelids, and nose, ending with his lips. "I love you more than anything."

While I show my stern business face to the world, I get to be entirely free in Kyle's presence. This feeling is my aphrodisiac.

I'm about to deepen the kiss and go for round two when a crying sound from the adjoining room interrupts me.

Kyle groans as I climb down his body. "That cockblocker."

"Stop it." I laugh, put on the first robe I find, and quicken my pace to the crib in which our baby boy is lying.

I pick him up and he immediately quiets. Nikolai is two months old and has the most beautiful blue eyes I've ever seen. Reina says it's a mixture of mine and Kyle's. His hair is the same shade as his father's, and his skin is so soft I would kiss him all day if I could.

My pregnancy with him was so smooth I almost didn't feel the time passing me by. He was such a docile baby who only kicked when I was awake or when Kyle was holding me. It was like he felt us both and wanted to make his presence known. The easiness of the pregnancy might have also been caused by how Kyle was caring for me every second of every day. He barely left my side and made me feel like I was the most precious thing on earth.

He still does.

"Were you scared because you were alone, baby?" I smile at him and he smiles back. "Kyle! Did you see that? His first smile."

"He's just taunting me." Kyle wraps his arms around my waist from behind and lets Nikolai grab his finger. "The first rule in the father-son manual says that you don't cockblock your dad, Nikolai."

"You're so awful." I laugh as I lean my head back against his chest. "He's just a baby. Besides, you were the one behind the idea of having him, remember?"

"And now I'm paying the price."

"It's worth it, though. We have our family."

He kisses the top of my head, and I melt in his embrace. "We do. I'll protect you both with my life."

"So will I."

EPILOGUE 2

Kyle

Three years later

I F SOMEONE HAD TOLD ME I WOULD EVER BE SITTING IN a toddler's bed, telling them bedtime stories, I would've shot them.

Me, with toddlers?

Me, telling stories?

I don't know what I was thinking when I figured impregnating Rai was the best idea. But that's the thing—I wasn't thinking.

I didn't count on the tiny humans who would invade our lives and demand all our attention—and more.

As if Nikolai's cockblocking activities weren't enough, I somehow ended up knocking up Rai again, even though I didn't mess with her pills that time. She was the one who went on without birth control and ended up pregnant.

She gave birth to not only one baby, but two. Yes, that's

correct. We have identical twin girls, Mia and Maya, who are almost two years old now and have their mum and aunt's spiky natures.

Rai and Reina keep saying they remind them of themselves, especially since they're both blondes like them.

The twins settle on either side of me, and Nikolai is in the middle, as I sit down to tell them a bedtime story. I picked one from the countless children's books on the shelf, but Nikolai pushes it away. "We already know that one, Daddy. Something new."

"Something new!" Mia agrees.

"New! New, Daddy!" Maya pulls on my sleeves.

These little shits are my kids, but they're demanding as fuck. Rai says they take after me. Ha. *Me?* They give me a run for my money. Even Godfather can testify in my favor.

"Fine, fine." I close the book. "So, once upon a time, there was a monster."

The kids' eyes bug out at that. They love stories about monsters more than those about princes.

"The monster didn't know what to do."

"Why?" Maya asks. "Was he hurt, Daddy?"

"I guess you can say that. He was hurt badly."

"Poor monster." Mia pouts. "Can someone come and kiss it better?"

"No!" Nikolai protests. "He's a monster. No one kisses him."

"That's right," I continue. "He was all alone and with nowhere to go. He felt empty and with no purpose and always thought his existence didn't matter. To make it worse, other monsters wanted to kill him."

"Oh," Maya and Mia say at the same time, their little chins trembling.

"And?" Nikolai's eyes are as huge as saucers.

"He was saved by a strong princess."

"Really?" Maya's expression lights up.

"Yeah, my little pumpkin."

"Is the princess very beautiful?" Nikolai asks.

"The most beautiful princess to ever exist."

"Like Mommy?" Mia stares up at me.

"Just like your mommy."

"And then what?" her sister asks.

"Yeah, then what, Daddy?" Nikolai follows.

"Then, she took him to her castle and healed his wounds. After that, they gave birth to three beautiful monsters who looked just like you."

The twins giggle, and I tickle them. Nikolai tries to escape, but I bring him in, too, until the three of them are squealing and gasping.

After expending so much energy, it doesn't take them long to fall asleep. I carry Nikolai to his bed, but don't bother with the twins. They always end up sleeping next to each other, anyway.

"Good night, my little monsters." I hit the light switch, and their room fills with images of dim stars.

We eventually moved out of the main Bratva house soon after Nikolai was born. I demolished the small cottage by the lake and built a house that's worthy of Rai and our family.

Sergei's cancer is in remission, and he's still reigning over the brotherhood.

Mikhail has been obviously favoring me over his other sons—my half-brothers—who need sense beaten into their psychotic heads. But, well, it's a marathon, not a sprint.

I never thought our lives would be full of unicorns, and honestly, neither Rai nor I could adapt to that sort of a boring existence. She lives for the excitement as much as I do, and we wouldn't have it any other way.

As soon as I close the door, slender arms wrap around my waist. I smile as I turn around to face my beautiful wife.

Her lips meet mine, and I kiss her with a hunger that hits me in my bones. It doesn't matter how long we've been together; there'll never be a day when I'll get enough of this woman.

"Were you telling them our story just now?" she whispers against my lips, running her fingers over my chest.

"Maybe."

"You're not a monster, Kyle."

"I was once. I still am sometimes." I bite her lower lip, sucking on it before I release it. "Do you want to see my monster side tonight?"

"You know I wouldn't say no to that."

"Fuck, baby. I'm going to devour you."

"Is that a promise?"

"Say the magic words."

She wraps her arms around me, sighing. "I love you, Kyle."

"And I love you, Rai."

Then I'm carrying her into our bedroom as she laughs, her happiness ringing in the air around us.

Our happiness.

THE END

Curious about the mysterious Adrian who appeared in this duet? You can read his story, a forced marriage mafia romance, in *Vow of Deception*.

You can read Rai's twin sister's story, Reina, and Asher's in *All The Lies*.

WHAT'S NEXT?

Thank you so much for reading *Throne of Vengeance*! If you
liked it, please leave a review.
Your support means the world to me.

If you're thirsty for more discussions with other readers of the
series, you can join the Facebook group, Rina's Spoilers Room.

Next up is the twisted forced marriage saga, Adrian's story,
Vow of Deception.

ALSO BY RINA KENT

For more titles by the author and an
explicit reading order, please visit:
www.rinakent.com/books

ABOUT THE AUTHOR

Rina Kent is a *USA Today*, international, and #1 Amazon bestselling author of everything enemies to lovers romance.

She's known to write unapologetic anti-heroes and villains because she often fell in love with men no one roots for. Her books are sprinkled with a touch of darkness, a pinch of angst, and an unhealthy dose of intensity.

She spends her private days in London laughing like an evil mastermind about adding mayhem to her expanding universe. When she's not writing, Rina travels, hikes, and spoils cats in a pure Cat Lady fashion.

Find Rina Below:

Website: www.rinakent.com

Newsletter: www.subscribepage.com/rinakent

BookBub: www.bookbub.com/profile/rina-kent

Amazon: www.amazon.com/Rina-Kent/e/B07MM54G22

Goodreads: www.goodreads.com/author/show/18697906.
Rina_Kent

Instagram: www.instagram.com/author_rina

Facebook: www.facebook.com/rinaakent

Reader Group: www.facebook.com/groups/rinakent.club

Pinterest: www.pinterest.co.uk/AuthorRina/boards

Tiktok: www.tiktok.com/@rina.kent

Twitter: twitter.com/AuthorRina